NINA BAWDEN

was born in London in 1925 and evacuated to South Wales during the war. She was educated at Ilford County High School for Girls and at Somerville College, Oxford.

Her first novel, *Who Calls the Tune*, appeared in 1953. Since then she has published nineteen other adult novels including: *Tortoise by Candlelight* (1963); *A Little Love, A Little Learning* (1965); *A Woman of My Age* (1967); *The Grain of Truth* (1968); *The Birds on the Trees* (1970); *Afternoon of a Good Woman*, winner of the Yorkshire Post Novel of the Year Award for 1976; *Walking Naked* (1981); *The Ice House* (1983) and *Circles of Deceit*, which was shortlisted for the Booker Prize in 1988 and filmed by the BBC. Her most recent novel is *Family Money* (1991).

Nina Bawden is also an acclaimed author of sixteen children's books. Many of these have been televised or filmed; all have been widely translated. Amongst them are: *Carrie's War* (1973); *The Peppermint Pig*, the recipient of the 1975 Guardian Award for Children's Fiction; *The Finding* (1985), *Keeping Henry* (1988) and *The Outside Child* (1989).

For ten years Nina Bawden served as a magistrate, both in her local court and in the Crown Court. She has also sat on the councils of various literary bodies, including the Royal Society of Literature – of which she is a Fellow – PEN, and the Society of Authors, and is the President of the Society of Women Writers and Journalists. In addition she has lectured at conferences and universities, on Arts Council tours and in schools.

Nina Bawden has been married twice and has one son, one daughter and two stepdaughters. She lives in London and in Greece.

Virago publish eight of Nina Bawden's works of fiction. *Familiar Passions* and *George Beneath a Paper Moon* are forthcoming.

VIRAGO
MODERN
CLASSIC

NUMBER

316

Critical Acclaim for Nina Bawden

'An exceptional picture of disorganised family life, in which both adult and childish preoccupations are portrayed convincingly . . . Imaginative, tender, with a welcome undercurrent of toughness' – *Observer*

'As a foray into the eerie moonscape of youth, it is continually fascinating and on target' – *New York Times Book Review*

'Emmie transmits her furious energy to the whole book to give it more than a touch of Carson McCullers' – *Sunday Times*

'An intelligent, artful, superior novel' – *New York Times*

'*Tortoise by Candlelight* in actual quality of writing suggests comparison with Colette, though Miss Bawden has perhaps a wider range' – *Margaret Kennedy*

'This is by far Miss Bawden's best book . . . beautifully observed' – *Daily Telegraph*

'Nina Bawden is a past mistress at conveying the raw, unformed impressions of a child's mind. She is also a delicate, thoughtful writer, quite without sentimentality' – *Books and Bookmen*

'Like enemy patrols that pass in the fog of no-man's land, foreign language, maturity and childhood baffle and intrigue each other in *Tortoise by Candlelight*' – *Guardian*

'A captivating story, with many truly moving moments, this novel should be read by all who think they understand children' – *Liverpool Daily Post*

Nina Bawden

TORTOISE
BY
CANDLELIGHT

Published by VIRAGO PRESS Limited 1989
20–23 Mandela Street, Camden Town, London NW1 0HQ

Reprinted 1991, 1993

First published in Great Britain by Longmans Green & Co. 1963
Copyright © Nina Bawden 1963

A CIP catalogue record for this book is available from the British Library

Printed and bound in Great Britain by
Cox & Wyman Ltd, Reading, Berkshire

for
PETER and ROBIN
in memory of
HENRY

1

THE gravel pits circled the town, turning it at night into a suburban Venice, glimmering over a waste of water. Darkness hid the scars: the gaunt, naked machinery, the illegal caravan site, the municipal rubbish tip, the new bungalow foundations. From the evening trains, roaring across the embankment between the small, shabby stations, the commuters looked down, briefly, at a different world: the dead, grey lakes, the living river, the long curve of Lombardy poplars, silver-lined.

The poplars were darkening as Emmie ran home. The light on their rustling tips was always the last to shiver and die. Emmie skirted the filled-in pit, ducked under the loose wire by the notice that said Danger and ran across the tough, tussocky field, cutting out the bend of the river. She came on to the tow-path where the houseboats, rocking a little, were lit: River View, Home is the Sailor, Water's Edge. Emmie ran past them on spiky legs, clutching something to her skinny chest. As the path swung close to the road the car lights caught her face and made her eyes flash like headlamps in answer. Once past the shelter of the trees, her dark, flannelly skirt and her dark hair streamed out; she lifted her face to the wind and looked like a young, fierce, bespectacled avenging angel.

The tow-path ran along the back of two houses. The black water sucked and slapped in the boathouse as she thrust open the second gate. Light streamed from the kitchen. Emmie stopped by the holly tree and cautiously parted the branches.

The robin sat on the nest warming her cuckoo but

Emmie was not interested in the black, toad-like change-ling. She bent to examine a small, still object lying on a leaf a few inches below the nest. When she touched it with her finger, it twitched a little. She let the branch go, squelched up the gritty path, paused once more, by the rabbit hutches, and flung open the back door. An elderly retriever rose stiffly and sniffed at her skirt in welcome.

The kitchen was large; a large, deal table stood plumb centre with an open sewing machine at one end and supper for three, egg-cups and plates, laid on a plastic cloth at the other. There was an American organ against the far wall and a blue flag hanging from the picture rail above it. The flag had a message worked on it in yellowing silk: BEHOLD, THE LORD IS WITH THEE. The room was lit by one light hanging low; the high, sagging ceilings lurked in darkness. The light shade was fringed, the fringe swayed in the draught as Emmie opened the door and its shadow danced on the dark wall.

Her brother, Oliver, sat on the rug in front of the wood fire and boxed with Mo. Oliver boxed one-handed, the red squirrel fought with all four feet, kicking with his hind-quarters, clinging to Oliver's thumb with his front paws, with his strong, stumpy thumbs and long toes. He chattered and nipped with his teeth.

'We've had four rounds,' Oliver said. 'I'm winning.'

The squirrel was eight months old, Oliver eight years. He was small for his age and fair, with hair like soft, white cotton. A pale fringe of thick lashes hid his eyes. He was gentle and obstinate and untrustworthy. His smile was sweet.

'You haven't cleaned the rabbits,' Emmie accused him.

His smile remained sweet. He simply looked down and away. The light glinted on his lashes, on his beautiful, bent head and Emmie watched him, raging. She loved him as she loved all her family – deeply, from the soul and with a fierce intolerance.

'*And* I didn't say you could play with Mo,' she said. He hummed insolently under his breath. Emmie put her big leather notebook on the table and dived at him. Her weight bore him down. He rolled over on his back like a puppy, smiling up at her as she pinned him to the rug and sat on his stomach. Nervous as a Victorian miss, Mo ran up the dresser like a flicker from the firelight and perched on the top shelf, chattering his alarm.

'I've been sick,' Oliver said plaintively.

Their grandmother, Mrs Bean, came in from the scullery. 'Brought up his dinner,' she said. 'Get off him.'

She was very tall and so thin that her body moved like unfleshed bone beneath her loose jumper suit of hand-woven wool. She wore long, dangling rows of beads, coral and amber, not as decoration but from habit: she had worn them since she was a young girl. Her grey hair was hidden beneath a man's fishing hat of blue and green tweed. She had once been a fine, big woman, a singer; now where Emmie was flat, in the chest, she was almost concave. She was deaf, going blind, but her voice was still deep and rich as a good bell.

Emmie stood up reluctantly. She said, glaring at Oliver, 'Didn't he go back to school this afternoon?'

'Miss Carter sent me home,' Oliver said. He watched Emmie slyly and when his grandmother sat down, slid on to her bony lap.

'He should've gone back. You know he can be sick when he likes.'

'He's got a nervous stomach,' Mrs Bean said, half apologetically.

'Only when it's something he doesn't want to do. Or when he's done something he shouldn't.'

9

Emmie chewed at her lower lip. There was a tingling feeling all over her body like a thousand tiny electric shocks under her skin. She knew what Oliver was likely to have done. The look she shot at him said – just wait till I get you alone. Oliver stared back at her triumphantly: he was safe for the moment and didn't look beyond it. Then her threatening expression defeated him. His lashes came down like a muslin veil and hid his eyes.

'It's bad for him to get away with things.' Emmie's voice was loud, her indignation flew like arrows. She had a sense of immense responsibility for others. It didn't worry her: she was too young to feel burdened, too young to doubt her own strength or be frightened of failure. She was fourteen and not frightened of anything very much except water and drowning; the things that drain the spirit out of people, illness and pain and hope deferred, had not touched her yet. Her youth gave her a false air of certitude and strength. 'You know what he's like,' she said inflexibly.

Oliver wriggled on Mrs Bean's lap, he was too heavy for her, but she rocked him gently. Beneath Emmie's stern gaze they became a useless old woman and a child who couldn't be trusted. Perhaps that wasn't so far from the mark either, Mrs Bean thought, and sighed. All her life she had been a tough, nerveless woman, so healthy that she had never noticed her body any more than you notice an efficient and enduring piece of machinery. Her husband and two of her sons were dead but if she had ever thought of death for herself it was with her head, as young people do, not with her stomach. Until she was seventy she had avoided most of the physical inconveniences of being alive. Now, suddenly, old age had struck at her with its long cavalcade of indignities; her eyesight, her hearing, even her endurance had begun to desert her, creeping away one by one like rats leaving a doomed city. She wasn't finished yet but she felt like a shell, a framework; everything was still there, but reduced to the thinnest lines.

She said, 'I expect I should have sent him back. But you can't always do the exact, right thing, Emmie. You can only do the best you can. And trust in the Lord. He guides His children.'

Normally Emmie was indulgent towards her grand-mother's piety, treating it rather like a child's belief in Father Christmas. But in this situation it seemed unhelp-ful. 'He doesn't keep much of an eye on Oliver,' she said crossly.

'Now, Emmie . . .' Mrs Bean's voice was more placating than reproachful. Above Oliver's cottony head her face looked like a skull, a beautiful, pale, strong skull.

Emmie looked at her. She said, suddenly scared, 'You all right, Gran?'

Oliver heard the change in her voice and knew her attention was diverted. Thankfully, he slid off the old woman's lap and went to the dresser to get his scissors and the remains of the morning newspaper. He had already cut out all the people in the photographs. He laid them out on the rug and began to snip their heads off, one by one.

Mrs Bean said, 'A bit tired. I'll live.'

Emmie shifted from one damp foot to the other. The exhaustion in her grandmother's face terrified her and at the same time roused up all her bursting love, so that she felt as if her throat was swelling up. She wanted to wrap her grandmother's head in her thin, strong arms and hold it close for hours. She said in a choking voice, 'Shall I make you a cup of tea, then?'

Mrs Bean saw the expression on her face and heaved herself up out of her chair. 'Heavens child, I'm all right.

You'd better change your socks. You're slimed up to the knees.'

'I went in a puddle near the pits. There's a pair of grebes nesting.'

The tightness left Emmie's throat and she breathed out slowly, with relief. There was nothing wrong, after all. Gran wasn't ill, only old, and she had been old for years. 'What's for supper?' she said.

'Eggs. But get yourself dried off first. Then you can come and make the cocoa. Alice has had hers. She wants to get out.'

'Not again?' Emmie said with disgust. 'She'd better go before Dad comes in, then. You know what he'll say.'

'That's not your business, Emmie.'

'He'll be back early. He said he'd help me with my Latin.'

'You know better than to count on that,' Mrs Bean said shortly, and went into the scullery.

Oliver looked up from his murderous ritual on the rug. 'He never comes back when he says. He forgets and goes to a pub.'

'Oh shut up,' Emmie said. 'He has to go to pubs because all journalists go to pubs. It's where you pick up contacts. I expect if he's late it's because he's met someone important who wants him to write something.'

She thought that she did not really believe this and felt, suddenly, sad and ashamed as if she had done something wrong. Frowning with a kind of embarrassment, she picked up her notebook from the table and held up her wrist for the squirrel who jumped off the dresser and ran up her arm to sit on her shoulder and bite her ear.

'He's got fleas,' Oliver said. 'I wish I could catch a flea and train it. Do you think I could catch one of Mo's fleas, Emmie?'

Emmie ignored him and left the kitchen, chirruping to Mo. It was dark in the hall and there was a cold, sweet, dusty smell which Emmie did not notice any more than she noticed that the house was dark and Victorian and dilapidated. She knew it needed painting but her father had said it was not worth painting a rented house, certainly not one that was due to be pulled down in two years when the gravel pits expanded into the field beside it.

The thought of the house being pulled down hurt Emmie like the thought of someone dying. The house was beautiful and familiar to her and she loved it uncritically; the big, shabby kitchen, the solid oak staircase with the slippery, carved banister rail, the lovely, red glass above the front door. She even liked the two large rooms at the front which the laurel bushes, pressing against the church-like windows, turned into mysterious, green caves. These were not rooms for living in; Emmie went into them when she wanted to be alone or, sometimes, to look at the birds. The walls were covered with photographs of living birds; on the tables, on the roll top desk, on the bookcases – on every available piece of massive furniture there were glass cases of dead, stuffed birds. They had belonged to her grandfather, the ornithologist; the photographs had been taken by his daughter, the children's mother, the author of *Now Calls the Kittiwake, Little Eagle of the Fastness,* and *Fly, Lovely Ghost – the story of a mute swan.* Over the unused grate with its dusty fan of red crêpe paper, there was an enlarged snapshot of her with the tame swan they had had one year. For a little while it had hung in the girls' room but Emmie had put it back in its proper place after Alice had taken it to bed with her and cried over it, late one night.

*

13

When Emmie went into their bedroom at the top of the house, Alice was standing in front of the cheval mirror. She was only two years older than Emmie, but it could easily have been ten. She was fair, a warm, creamy girl, plump and soft-eyed like a romantic eighteenth-century portrait of a flower girl. Just now, she was wearing a pair of black nylon tights and nothing else. She had a roll of sticking plaster and a pair of scissors in her hand.

Emmie plumped down on the edge of the double bed and Mo jumped from her shoulder to run, squeaking, backwards and forwards under the eiderdown.

'His back itches,' Emmie said fondly. She pulled off her soaking socks. Underneath her legs were grey and slimy.

'You smell like a sewer,' Alice said.

Emmie wrinkled her nose. 'The fledgling's out of the nest. That's the last one.'

'Did you put it back?'

'What's the use? It'ud only be pushed out again. It was still alive, though. I touched it.'

Alice gazed at her reflection. 'How awful.' Her eyes filled with tears: she wept easily, at any conventionally sentimental situation. 'The mother bird must be so upset,' she said, admiring her sad face in the glass.

'Not her.' Emmie wiped the mud off the soles of her feet with the wet socks.

Alice said reproachfully, 'How would *you* feel if the baby you loved was pushed out of the nest?'

'Birds don't love,' Emmie said. 'They only feed their babies because they gape. That's why the insides of their mouths are such a nice colour. Cuckoos' mouths are awfully pretty – a lovely, bright yellow.'

Alice wasn't listening. She seldom listened to answers that were more than two sentences long. She was leaning forward, holding her bare left breast in one hand. With the other, she stuck a piece of sticking plaster on one side of the breast, passed it underneath and drew it carefully upwards on the other side so that the breast jutted out like a milky cone, pink-tipped.

'What on earth are you doing?' Emmie said.

Alice mumbled as if she had pins in her mouth. 'My bra's no good. It pokes. The poke shows under my sweater.'

Emmie gasped. 'You can't go out with nothing on underneath.'

'Who's to know?'

Emmie opened her mouth and shut it again. She watched Alice: the tongue curling between pink lips, the light from the hanging bulb above her shifting on the smooth skin. Like silk, thought Emmie, but it wasn't. It wasn't like anything except young, washed skin, gleaming like pearl. But pearl's too hard, she thought. She took off her glasses, frowning and rubbing the bridge of her nose where it itched. Her eyes were cobalt blue. They had a stern, watchful expression as if she were constantly on guard, like a woman with small children.

'You're going out with Dickie,' she said.

Alice nodded. She had finished strapping up the other breast and surveyed her outrageously deformed image in the glass. It seemed to satisfy her; she wriggled into a tight, short skirt, pulled on a white cotton sweater and turned sideways to look at her profile.

'You look disgusting,' Emmie said. 'What d'you think Gran will say?'

'She won't see.'

'She's not as blind as *that*,' Emmie said contemptuously.

Alice hesitated. The three-quarter view was startling. 'I'll put on my leather thing,' she said. She took a grubby green coat off the hook behind the door and slipped her arms into it, blushing a little.

'You'll have to keep it on all the time, you'll be indecent otherwise. And it's too hot.' Emmie put back her glasses and gave them a little push. They were too big across the bridge of her nose. 'What if Dad finds out where you've gone? He'll raise hell.'

Alice gave her a cold look. 'He won't know unless you tell him, will he?'

'Why should I always have to tell lies for you?'

'You always have. Why should you get squeamish now?' Alice's expression became dreamy. 'Anyway, he'd like Dickie once he really got to know him.'

'Fat chance of that! You know why he doesn't like Dickie.'

Alice went fiery red. 'It's not *fair*,' she said passionately. 'Dickie's not a bit like his father. He's been to technical school and he's got ambitions – he's not going to stay at the gravel pits all his life. It's just good money at the moment and he's got a responsible job being a pontoon man.' She added bitterly, 'The trouble is, Dad wouldn't know what a responsible job *was*.'

Emmie sighed but did not contradict her. There was no point. Alice was fond of Dad but she did not respect him. She listens to Gran too much, Emmie thought – Mrs Bean did not think much of men. Emmie would have laid down her life for her grandmother who was the warm centre of her world, its heart and stability, but she knew she was sometimes wrong, that she *was* wrong about Dad. She didn't understand him. Creative people were always misunderstood, Dad said. One day he would show them all, Emmie was sure of it, though sometimes she wished he would hurry up and do it soon.

She sat, hugging her thin arms round her thin knees and

watched Alice brushing her hair. She said, 'What about your homework? You shouldn't go out if you haven't done your homework.' She knew it was no good: Alice would do what she wanted as she always did, managing to be both stubborn and light-hearted at one and the same time. She was a calm, sensual, slow-moving girl who avoided difficult situations and got other people to do things for her. Her teachers said she was lazy but Emmie knew that she simply saved her energy for the things she thought important: eating, sleeping, dreaming about being a nurse. Emmie said, 'You'll never pass the hospital exam if you don't work.'

'I'll pass,' Alice said. 'D'you think I'd go out if I thought it'ud make any difference to *that*?' She lifted her hair back over her collar and took a last look in the glass. The down glinted on her short, very pretty upper lip. She wore no make-up and the light washed over her skin like oil.

Emmie swallowed. Alice was so beautiful that she wanted to cry. 'I don't see why you have to go out.'

Alice gave her a kindly glance. 'You will one day.'

'It spoils everything,' Emmie said. She sat, hunched and miserable. Dickie was new, Alice going out in the evening was new. Emmie was not used to it yet, she thought she would never get used to it. She wished she could keep all her family safe inside the house, isolated from the indifferent world. 'I wish we all lived on a desert island,' she said.

Alice leaned across the bulky chest of drawers that stood in front of the sash window and drew back the curtains. She could only see her own reflection. 'There's new people coming next door,' she said as she hoisted herself up on to the chest. 'Dr Rapier's going to Corsica for six months. Mrs Hellyer told Gran.'

'Bad luck,' Emmie said. Ever since Alice had had her

tonsils out she had been mad about doctors, about nurses, about anything to do with the medical profession. She loved the smell of hospitals, sniffing the air with excitement whenever she went into one, like an animal returning home. For pleasure, she read back numbers of *The Lancet* begged from the Rapiers next door.

'There's some other people coming,' Alice said. 'Friends from Africa.' She cupped her hand against the glass and looked down into the road. 'There's Dickie.' Eyes alight, she tumbled down and made for the door.

'Where's Oliver's satchel?' Emmie said.

Alice groaned. 'Under the bed. You'd better put it back on his hook before he notices. He took a pencil case this morning and two fountain pens.'

'Oh *no*,' Emmie said on a wailing note. 'Why didn't you say before?'

'Because I was in a hurry, because I forgot, because – oh does it matter?'

'Because you want to go out on Dickie's bike. *We* can all go to pot just because you want to go out on Dickie's bike.'

Alice sighed heavily. 'As if I cared about an old bike.'

Emmie said, 'You needn't sigh at me like that. I'm not crazy. I just said it was the bike to be polite. I know what's wrong with you. I've read about it.' She stood up with a superior smile. 'You've got to the age when girls become aware of the deep, secret urging of their body.'

Alice drew a deep breath. Then she shouted, 'Oh – will you leave me alone, will you please leave me *alone*?' The tears came into her eyes and she rushed out. The front door banged hollowly, a few minutes later there was the sound of a car slowing, then the motor bike started up. Emmie sat on the bed, glowering at her dirty feet. She scuffed them on the wool rug to take off the dried mud and padded across the cold linoleum to get her white plimsolls. She stood with them in her hand, thinking. There were a lot of things she had to do – homework, cleaning the rabbits, feeding the hens and the Muscovy ducks – but she couldn't start on anything until she had worked out the two things on her mind. The first thing was to decide what to tell her father if he came home and asked where Alice was. The second was to decide what to do about Oliver. This was the more difficult. She put the plimsolls on and tied the scraggy laces slowly.

Mo watched her from the chest of drawers. He could dart round the room, quick and light as a bird, or he could sit still for a long time, nose quivering, paws folded like an old man settling for a good nap after dinner. Just to look at him, whatever he did, made Emmie feel happy and comfortable; when she was bothered about something she liked to hold his soft, throbbing body in her hand and let her mind go lazy and blank to everything except her love for him which was quite different from the love she felt for her family, more tender, less demanding.

She pursed her lips and made a gentle noise at him before she bent to get Robert's satchel from under the bed. She emptied out his loot, the pencil case, the pens, and put them in the hiding place in the bottom of the big, old-fashioned wardrobe under a pile of old, outgrown shoes. There was something there already, a Parker fountain pen wrapped in a scrap of newspaper. She put the pen with the others and smoothed the paper out on her knee. It was the picture of her mother with the swan, reproduced in the *Surrey Clarion*. Underneath it said, *Our local celebrity, the famous naturalist Clemence Bean who plans a trip to Kenya to study the East African Flamingo.*

Emmie looked at the picture for a minute, then crumpled it in her hand and threw it to the back of the wardrobe. She shut the door, locked it, and put the key under the linoleum next to the wall at the side of the bed.

Downstairs in the kitchen, Mrs Bean was playing the organ and Oliver was singing. His voice rose, high and sweet and pure in a martial hymn. It was one of his favourite occupations; another was having Emmie read aloud to him from the *Murders in the Rue Morgue*. Emmie picked up Mo and stroked him under his chin. He lay back on her forearm in rapturous enjoyment. She went on tickling him and thought about Oliver. She wished there was some way in which you could find out what was the right thing to do—some good place like a library where you could go and look up the right answer to everything, set out clear and plain. But although this was something she thought of a great deal she knew, in her heart, that there was no such place.

2

THE car slowed and turned across the road. The headlights, undipped, caught Alice in their white glare as she sat on the pillion of the motor bike, one foot still on the ground. Her skirt was rucked up over her thighs and the treacherous wind blew the leather coat out behind her.

The taxi driver whistled appreciatively and Nick Sargent said, 'When I left England, girls were dressed rather differently. They were wearing something called the New Look – skirts down to their ankles.'

The taxi stopped outside the house; the driver glanced over his shoulder at his passenger. 'You've been away a long time, then?'

'Fifteen years.'

'It must be nice to be home.'

'Home?' Nick said. 'Yes – yes, I suppose so.'

He got out of the cab and felt in his pocket for change.

The driver said, 'Dr Rapier's gone away, hasn't he? My wife was telling me. She said he was taking a long holiday.'

'Six months.'

'Well – he deserves it.' The driver humped the suitcases out of the boot and set them down in the pillared porch. 'He's a very nice doctor. The specialist at our hospital here, you know. He was very good to the wife when she was bad last year. Took no end of trouble. He's got a very fine reputation round here.'

'I'll tell him when I write,' Nick said.

'Friend of yours, is he?'

'We were at school together.'

The driver looked at Nick, then at the house. It was the same age as the Beans' house next door but presented a quite different aspect: neat, solid, freshly painted. The driver said, thoughtfully expansive, 'Funny sort of place for Dr Rapier to live in, I always thought. Not that it isn't a nice old house but it's a funny position, stuck out here. Nothing but pits and water.'

'I daresay he likes it,' Nick said dryly. He thought of the letter Joe had written, offering him the house. *There's a road – a rather hideous main road, in fact – but except for that, you might be living on an island. Just the two houses and two or three boats on the river. Some of the pits are filled in and the local people sail on them but others are still being worked. You can see the pit machinery from the front windows. Fascinating – especially the grabs. They're like some kind of prehistoric monsters, reptilian and menacing. Sometimes the whole place looks like a landscape on the moon. Jean says I have a nasty, macabre taste. She also says to tell Marjorie that the nearest main line station is twenty minutes away and that we get a lot of fog with all that water . . . All the same, if you want peace, this isn't a bad place. As isolated as anything could be, so near to London. Though I can't imagine Marjorie wanting peace . . .*

Joe had said something like that again today. Nick had been spending his first week in England with his father-in-law in Birmingham and had cut his visit short in order to come to London and lunch with the Rapiers before they caught the boat train. Jean said she hoped the house wouldn't be too much for Marjorie. 'There's a woman comes in, but it won't seem much, after a houseful of servants.' Nick smiled at her – nice, anxious Jean – and said, 'She's looking forward to it. She feels she needs occupation.' Then Joe had laughed suddenly, 'That doesn't sound much like Marjorie, longing to sink herself in domesticity just to find something to do,' and Nick had smiled back at him self-consciously, realizing with a dull ache of pain that Joe was remembering a quite different person from the woman who had clung to him only a few hours before sobbing that she couldn't, couldn't bear to meet anyone, not even the Rapiers, that Nick must go, *of course* he must go, and give them her dear, dear love, but he must promise, *swear* not to talk about her because she couldn't bear it . . .

If he made an effort, Nick could remember the old Marjorie too, though nowadays he had to try very hard indeed and even then the image that came to him was rather meaningless and fixed, like a smile in an old photograph. It had been somehow easier with Joe sitting there, talking of her as if she hadn't changed at all, as if she was still the capable, energetic girl Nick had married, gay and fighting fit as a smart little bull terrier and as ready to tackle anything, anywhere; the girl who had come out to Africa and gone everywhere with him, into villages riddled with smallpox and leprosy; the girl who had despised the other European women for their gossiping and their boredom and their eternal grumbling about servants; the girl who had never once wanted to go back to England on leave because she loved Africa as much as he did. Or had pretended that she did . . .

The taximan said, 'You staying here alone, sir? Or are you expecting the family?'

'Only my wife,' Nick said. 'How much do I owe you?'

He watched the car drive off, fumbled for a few minutes with the strange latchkey and let himself into the house. The door closed behind him with a comfortable, solid sound. The narrow hall was light as white paint and polished floors could make it; on a low table there was a great bunch of daffodils in a Copenhagen vase. There were more daffodils in the drawing-room; the house was filled with their dry, polleny smell. Nick put a match to the wood fire in the grate and carried his suitcases upstairs. Most of his things were in store and he had little to unpack except his clothes and a few books. They were mostly on tribal customs – his favourite reading – but among them was Hemingway's *Green Hills of Africa*. He put this book on his bedside table and thought, as he always did, that Hemingway must have been blind. African hills were blue.

After he had hung his suits in the empty wardrobe and arranged his books on a shelf, he wandered through the strange house, a little lost but innocently curious, opening doors, cupboards, lifting the lids of cigarette boxes. On the kitchen table Jean had left an envelope with a note scrawled on it. *Here is the car key, Nick dear. Joe says that the gear sometimes jumps out of second. Hope you can find something in the store cupboard.*

He smiled, sentimentally touched by the evidence of their thoughtful affection: the flowers, the whisky set out in the drawing-room, the well-stocked refrigerator. He was not hungry but felt, absurdly, that it would be ungrateful not to eat, so he poked about in the shining kitchen and made himself a scratch supper. He was drinking coffee, a difficult monograph on the inheritance laws of the Gusii propped against a pot of marmalade, when the door bell rang, a long, threatening peal as if someone had leaned against it.

For a moment he stayed in his chair, stiff, listening, ridiculously nervous. The bell shrilled again. He got up and went slowly to the door. A man stood there, tall, rather bulky; Nick switched on the porch light and saw a pink, pouchy face, a straight heavy nose beneath which drooped a sad, orange-coloured moustache. The man said, 'Oh. Have the Rapiers gone?'

'Yes,' Nick said. 'They left this morning.'

'Ah well. Missed the 'bus again.' He grinned, a man cheerfully resigned to his own ineptitude. 'Don't suppose it'll make any difference to them. I just dropped in to say goodbye, wish them luck, lots of sun and the old vino – that sort of thing.' He paused and looked at Nick with a slightly puzzled air as if he knew there was something that needed explaining though he couldn't, for the moment, remember what it was. Then he grinned again. 'I live next door. The name's Bean. Martin Bean. You're Sargent, aren't you? Joe Rapier told me you were coming.' He peered past Nick into the hall. 'Settling in all right?'

'So far.' They shook hands. Nick said, rather unwillingly – it was a long time since he had spent an evening alone and he had looked forward to it – 'Won't you come in?'

'Well . . . that's very civil.'

He came in with alacrity, stamping his feet energetically on the door-mat like a well-trained schoolboy. He followed Nick into the drawing-room, blinking mild, pale eyes at the light. He had very large red hands, like ham-bones that protruded a long way out of the sleeves of his tweed jacket. His moustache had a shabby, loosely-tethered air as if he had borrowed it from a cheap theatrical costumier's. Nick thought: a military gentleman manqué, slightly drunk. 'Whisky?' he said.

'Well . . . if you insist.' He laughed. 'Or even if you don't. Might as well celebrate, don't you think? Good neighbours – that sort of thing? We must get together, borrow each other's lawn mowers. Just a splash of soda, old man. That's fine.' In spite of his bumbling inanities, the blue eyes were shrewdly intelligent. He lifted his glass, regarding the amber liquid with thoughtful pleasure, and toasted Nick. 'Here's to a good leave. You are on leave, aren't you?'

'I've come back for good,' Nick said.

'Retired? You look young for that.'

'Forty.'

25

'That *is* young. Not a bad age to make a fresh start, though. New life, that sort of thing. You got something lined up?'

'Not yet . . .' Nick was half-prepared to resent this questioning, but the big man's curiosity was simple and inoffensive as a child's.

He said encouragingly, 'You'll find something soon enough. Still, it's a worry, I imagine. Pensions don't go very far nowadays.'

'No,' Nick hesitated. He hated admitting that he did not need money. On the other hand, the kindly concern on Bean's face embarrassed him : he had no right to it. When he had married Marjorie, he had opted out of the freemasonry of poorer men. He said, 'Of course I'll have to look for a job eventually. For the moment – well, I've got my gratuity and, anyway, I can't summon up much enthusiasm. I don't want a new life. I had a good life in Africa. I feel that anything I do now can only be secondary – a kind of using up the fag ends.'

He was surprised that he had said this to a stranger and somewhat ashamed. Self-pity was something he disliked in other people and loathed in himself, particularly now. He thought angrily : I can only afford to be sorry for myself because I have a rich wife and a father-in-law who will give me a job, any time . . .

'Hard luck. That's *very* hard luck to feel like that.' Martin Bean blew out, a mournful exhalation. The ends of his moustache quivered. He held out his empty glass and Nick refilled it generously, feeling uncomfortable. Bean said, 'I don't understand, though. I mean, I know the colonies have been folding up career-wise for a long time – but you're from Kenya, aren't you? I thought that was a going concern for a year or so, though not much longer, I daresay . . .'

'My wife got ill,' Nick said. He added, because the best thing was to make the point and get it over with. 'She's come back to England for a complete rest – needs to get away from people, that sort of thing.'

'She's come to the right place, then. No one much here. Only me and the kids next door. And my mother. And *she* only really talks to God.' He laughed suddenly, in excellent, sweating good humour and drained his glass. 'D'you know what she's doing now? *Playing the harmonium.* He lifted his chin and crooned, '*A few more years shall Roll, A Few more seasons come, And we shall* Be *with those that* ARE, *Asleep within the Tomb.*

He sat down so suddenly on the sofa that his knees rose in the air. He restored his balance and held out his empty glass to Nick, smiling. His smile was delicately reassuring and all-embracing and drunkenly innocent – the smile of a man sufficiently full of whisky to take the whole world on trust.

Nick smiled. He said. 'There are some houseboats, aren't there – at the bottom of the garden?'

'That won't trouble your good lady. No one much there – not socially, you might say. There's a little insurance man in one – an ex-gaol bird in another. Colourful, I suppose, but not a nice neighbour really, particularly if you have children.' He frowned, contemplating his glass. 'The wife works for us as a matter of fact. Of course, the kids don't know her old man's been in jug – doesn't do to tell them too much about that sort of thing. Not suitable. Kids are very . . . ' He yawned suddenly, hugely, showing a great, red cavern of a mouth, blackened teeth. '. . . very moral-minded, you know. Very easy to shock. You have to keep things from them. You got any children?'

'No.'

'Lucky man.' He yawned again, then shook his head

27

ponderously. Nick thought suddenly: he's like a great bear, heavy and slow – I wonder if he walks with his toes turned in. Bean said, 'One minute there they are, easy to manage as puppies, the next they're off with any Tom, Dick or Harry, lying like troopers, secretive as cats. Take my eldest girl, Alice.' He stared at Nick challengingly. 'She's sixteen. I tell you I just look at her sometimes and think: My God, I'm responsible.' He sighed deeply: he had made the drunk's quick change from jolly benevolence to maudlin solemnity. 'Sometimes I wake up in the night in a cold sweat. Terribly difficult business – girls growing up without a mother's influence . . .'

'It must be,' Nick said, a little confused. Jean Rapier had said something about Martin Bean's wife. What was it? He couldn't remember. 'Have another whisky?' he said, and looked with surprise at the bottle. Had it been full?

Bean went on, his voice thickening slightly. 'Alice is growing up – changing all the time. You can't talk to her, any more. She's my wife's child actually, not mine, though I've never felt the difference before. When we married, she was a warm, loving little thing, she always called me Daddy.'

Tears stood in his pale eyes. Nick was embarrassed by his sad, ridiculous earnestness. He said quickly, 'All girls get to a difficult age, don't they?'

He hadn't meant to sound unfriendly but there was a certain stiffness in his tone: he thought that, tomorrow, they would both be embarrassed by this conversation. Bean glanced at him, finished his drink and carefully set down his glass on the extreme edge of a small table. 'I suppose so.' He stood up, not quite steady but with a fair amount of dignity. 'Well – I must be getting back. Nice to have met you.' He shot out his hand and gripped Nick's.

Bean said solemnly, 'This has done me good – really – you can't imagine.'

Without a glass in his hand he looked lost; large and shambling and pathetic. As he followed him to the front door, Nick noticed that he did turn his toes in, very slightly. On the doorstep, they shook hands again. The air was soft and warm and damp. A full moon rode high in a windy sky. An owl hooted.

'You'll find this a change from Africa,' Martin Bean said.

'Yes.'

Nick watched the heavy man fumble with the gate, then turn with a last, grave salute when he had succeeded in opening it. Nick called 'Good night', but he wasn't really thinking of him. He was thinking of his bungalow at Embu where he had lived for the last two years, his last posting as District Commissioner. His bungalow had been built on a ridge, facing Mount Kenya. You could see the white peaks most mornings, when the clouds cleared briefly, and sometimes in the evening. Nick had thought it the most beautiful place in the world.

*

Cross-legged on her bed, Emmie was writing in her Diary. It was a heavy, brown leather book with a brass clasp and lined, yellow paper, that had belonged to Mrs Bean's mother. The early pages were filled with dark, sloping writing, with recipes for Pig's Fry, Melts, Devil's Food Cake.

Emmie wrote: *This morning, I saw the Great Crested Grebes. They were . . .* She stopped, chewing the end of her ball point pen. There had been four birds. The two males had swum towards each other, their long necks outstretched, their ruffs raised, their bodies almost submerged. They had looked less like birds than fish – sword-fish, Emmie

29

thought. And the two females, watching, looked like women in a ringside seat at a boxing match, curious, bright-eyed, craning their elegant necks for a better view. The male birds stood on the surface of the lake, beating their wings and crying Kuk-Kuk-Kuk in their loud, harsh voices, stabbing with their sharp beaks. Emmie wrote: *It wasn't a real fight, only showing off. It lasted about ten minutes. Then one of the birds dived and swam back to his mate, face to face with her and bowing. It was like a dance. They both bowed and stretched their necks out, flat on the water.*

Emmie sighed. What she had written did not satisfy her. It was true, but somehow what she had seen was different. She turned the pages of the book and stroked the stiff, thick, musty-smelling paper, sitting erect and tense for a minute. Then she wrote: *Alice has gone out with Dickie Hellyer. Dickie is a pontoon man at the pits. It is a very responsible job because he has to watch the engines and lift the pipe so it doesn't get blocked. You can hear the gravel slithering in the pipe and the pontoon shakes all the time with the engine. Dickie lives in the houseboat at the bottom of our garden. His father has been in prison because he robbed a post office van and he came out just before Christmas. Mrs Hellyer says he got time off for good behaviour so he can't be a very bad man. Sometimes he gets very angry, though, and knocks Mrs Hellyer about. The other day he gave Mrs Hellyer a black eye. Mrs Hellyer says she started that one and she's going to finish it.*

As she wrote, her forehead became damp with excitement. She had listened from the tow-path after dark, her heart hammering in her throat; fascinated, unable to move, yet terrified that they would come roaring out of the boat and catch her. Though she had not felt she was doing anything wrong. There was nothing private about the Hellyers' life – it was an open book, a splendid, endless, serial story. In fact, to Emmie, listening to the weekly instalment every Saturday morning when Mrs Hellyer came to clean, it was twenty times better than a serial. Emmie preferred fact to fiction and Mrs Hellyer's life had the untidy, hustling roar of reality. In comparison, Emmie felt that her own life lacked incident.

Mrs Hellyer had a fight with her husband because she found out that he was keeping another woman in a caravan in Turpin's Fields. She met the woman outside Woolworth's and pulled her off her bicycle. They had a rare old fight until the policeman came along to stop it. Mrs Hellyer says, never mind, she'll finish her one day, the little Irish cat. Though she is fat and has asthma, Mrs Hellyer is terrible when she is roused. She told her husband what she had done and he gave her a black eye. But Mrs Hellyer didn't care. She says he can't kill her, he hasn't the spunk. Mrs Hellyer has a lot of spunk. She is a very brave woman and knows a lot about life. Life is quite different from books. It is more exciting. A lot of dreadful things have happened to Mrs Hellyer's family. One of her children was burned to death and her sister's husband went to prison because he tried to do his wife in with a chopper and Mr Hellyer has been in prison too. Mrs Hellyer doesn't hold it against him, though. She says we all make mistakes. I think she is really very fond of her husband. She says she has always tried to be a good wife. I think she must be very kind to him because she says she never refuses her husband.

Emmie frowned at this last sentence. She wasn't sure that she quite understood what Mrs Hellyer had meant.

She heard the front door slam. She flew to the chest to put her Diary away and got back into bed, closing her eyes. She listened to her father's tread on the stairs, the creak of the door as he opened it and his heavy breathing as he stood beside the bed. He whispered, 'Emmie,' and then spoke in his ordinary voice. 'You're foxing.'

His large face hung above her, shutting out the light. He smelt of whisky and tobacco. 'Where's Alice?' he said.

Emmie yawned and rubbed at her eyes. 'I told you, she went to the youth club.'

'D'you know what time it is? Ten-thirty. The club closes at half past nine.'

'I expect she's gone to the coffee bar,' Emmie said hopefully.

Martin scowled. 'She should come straight home. Staying out till all hours.'

Emmie sat up. 'Alice is all right, Dad. She's not a *child*. She's nearly grown-up.'

She spoke in an infuriatingly calm, authoritative voice that gave the impression she knew much more than she did. Martin looked at her, at the dark eyes squinting slightly without the corrective spectacles, in her small, pale face and felt worried and helpless. He was sometimes a little afraid of his children, a fear that sprung partly from guilt: he guessed they were neglected but did not know what to do about it.

He said angrily, 'It's not good enough by half. Alice should be home at a proper time, not staying out till all hours.' His face grew red. 'I've been too soft, that's the trouble. And not just with her. You're all getting out of hand. Look at Oliver. I hear he didn't go to school this afternoon.'

'He was sick.'

'Just an excuse. Time he stopped going to a girls' school, anyway. He's too old – nearly nine.'

'*No*,' Emmie said, but her voice was nervous. She was unsure how far her father's authority stretched. 'Gran says . . .'

'I don't want to hear what your grandmother says.' He looked at her coldly. 'Let me tell you something, *I* make the decisions in this house. Not your grandmother.'

Emmie said quickly, 'Oliver's young for his age. He's

better where I can keep an eye on him.' Her face was hard with anxiety and Martin was uneasy suddenly: surely no child should look like that?

He muttered, 'Apron strings – they're the worst thing out for a boy,' and then thought that this sounded foolish. Whose apron strings after all? Emmie's? 'You fuss him like an old hen. Too much mothering's a bad thing.'

'He's hardly had too much mothering.'

A muscle twitched in his cheek. 'That's enough,' he shouted.

Emmie's expression did not change. There was a certain way she held her head when she was determined about something. She held it that way now. She said, 'I'm sorry, Dad. But I won't fuss him if you let him stay. Just keep an eye on him. I'll tell you when he's ready to go to a different school.'

Her calmness defeated him. He had not been serious anyway. 'All right,' he said grudgingly. 'I daresay you know as well as anyone.'

He thought she looked thin for her age, and tired. Maybe she had been staying up too late. He didn't know what time girls of her age ought to go to bed. He said, 'You're not getting enough sleep, Em.'

'I don't like sleeping. I'm not like Alice. Sleeping's a waste of time.'

He said, 'Children need sleep. Get your head down now.' He hesitated. 'Give your old Dad a kiss.'

She lifted her face submissively. It was not inviting. He said wistfully, 'You all right, Em? Anything you want?'

'No thank you, Dad.'

'Ask me if you want anything, won't you?' He touched her head lightly, smoothing the soft, dark hair. 'Do you remember the time I went to Hong Kong? I brought back a lot of stuff.'

Her eyes watched him. They were very blank. A queer thought struck him. He said, 'You're not scared of me, are you?'

There was a tiny pause before she shook her head. He bent and kissed her. 'Go to sleep, then,' he said.

*

Emmie's skin pricked where his beard had rubbed her. She heard the door close downstairs and counted to a hundred before she got out of bed and went to the bathroom. She climbed on the lavatory seat and opened the window. A wooden wedge dangled on a piece of string from a nail in the sill. Outside the window there was a sloping roof and a lean-to shed where the rabbits were kept in winter. Alice could climb on to the roof if Dickie helped her. Emmie placed the wedge carefully and closed the window on top of it. The wedge wasn't visible from inside unless you were specially looking for it. She pulled the chain in case her father had heard her come into the bathroom and went out òn to the landing.

The house was silent, except for the faint *ting* as the typewriter reached the end of the line. For some reason, Emmie felt restless. She crept downstairs into one of the dark rooms where the birds were kept. There was a glass window in the wall through which you could look into the conservatory where her father had made himself a study of sorts, among the geraniums and the packing cases and the specially constructed cages that had housed his wife's specimens at one time or another. Emmie looked at him through the window. He was typing away fast, a cigarette stuck to his lower lip. He never smoked cigarettes unless he was working. A naked bulb dangled from a long piece of flex just above his head and illumined the bald patch that had two or three strands of hair carefully arranged across

34

it. As Emmie watched, he ripped the piece of paper out of the machine, crumpled it up and threw it on the floor. He wound a fresh sheet on to the roller and looked at it. He got up and walked up and down, kicking at the cages in his way. Then he sat down and put his head in his hands.

He was tired, Emmie thought, and then it came to her that he wasn't tired at all. She remembered how he had looked just now when he had asked her if there was anything she wanted. She wished she had thought of something and asked him to get it for her – something easy, like a drink of water or a new pen or something. She thought that she still had one of the things he had brought back from Hong Kong that time, a puzzle box with secret drawers and a pretty pattern of willows and bridges in red and blue and wondered why she hadn't told him about it.

It was partly because he had seemed so different lately. Once, he had always picked her up when he came in and said something to make her laugh. 'It's a fine day for the race.' 'What race?' she used to say, although she had known the answer after the first time. It was part of the fun to pretend she didn't remember, so that he could roar with laughter. 'The human race, Emmie, the human race . . .'

She wondered if she should go in and talk to him about something. Perhaps she could kiss him good night in a friendly way, not as she had done upstairs turning her face to one side so she wouldn't smell his breath. But he was busy writing his book; he would hate to be disturbed. It was important that he should finish his book.

She turned away from the window and met the bead eye of a dead kittiwake in its glass cage. Suddenly, she felt intensely miserable. She went slowly upstairs and into Oliver's room. He stirred as she took the tortoise box off his bed and got into bed with him.

35

'Move over. Just for a little while.' She lay close, curling her legs over his warm, limp body. 'Everything's awful,' she said. 'I wish I were dead.' The statement satisfied her; it filled her with luxuriant sadness.

'You're growing,' Oliver said in hollow, undimensional tones. 'That's what Gran says. That child's growing too fast.' A little later, when Emmie thought he had gone back to sleep, he added, 'Gran isn't so much fun anymore.'

Emmie said in disgust. 'I don't know whether you sound heartless or whether you really are.' She stretched out her legs and a low, steady chuckling rose from somewhere at the bottom of the bed, under the eiderdown. 'And you know you're not supposed to have that hen in bed either.'

He didn't answer. Emmie lay beside him, looking at the car lights on the ceiling. Gran was all right. She got tired sometimes, that was all. One day, perhaps tomorrow, a letter would come to say Gran had been made a Dame of the British Empire. Somebody had remembered her – perhaps the Queen had said, who was that famous singer people used to talk about – and they had decided to make her a Dame. Gran would buy a new dress and go up to the Palace. Or Oliver would get a scholarship at the choir school. He would look beautiful singing the processional, Once in Royal David's City, his face pure and pale above the white surplice, the organ playing softly and everyone weeping because he looked so beautiful. Tears of happiness came into her own eyes as she thought about it. One day all her family would be famous and successful and everyone would know about them and stop talking and look as they went by . . .

*

In the conservatory, Martin Bean read through the fiction

reviews in a weekly magazine. When he had finished, he lit another cigarette and opened the Raymond Chandler he always kept beside his typewriter. He found Chandler very inspirational. Sometimes when he was reading him he began to think he could easily write a marvellous book himself, not simply a best seller but a book the reviewers would get excited about. Now and again, in the middle of a Chandler page, he thought he had got the feel: paragraphs, whole chapters, began to form in his mind. But the moment he began to type, the sentences wouldn't come.

He lit another cigarette from the stub of his old one and drew the smoke deep into his lungs. It made his head feel heavy. He thought of how easily his wife had written her books. It was easy for her, of course, she had a subject. And anyway, the books were terrible – sentimental anthropomorphism. It had always astonished him that she never worried about how terrible they were.

He thought about his wife for a little and then he got up and went into the kitchen to get the gin. There was a little left in the bottle in the bottom of the dresser. When he came back he sat drinking, and wondered if he would ever write a book. The drink made him see things more clearly. A fine, cosmic sadness crept over him. At first, it was a pleasant feeling, full of richness and wisdom. Sitting on his uncomfortable chair in the musty conservatory, he drank gin and enjoyed closer acquaintance with the beautiful sadness of life. Then he began to wonder what would happen to him in the end and the depression started. He gazed at his dim reflection in the black glass opposite him and knew it was going to be a bad attack.

When he was busy or with other people, he was a perennially hopeful man : if he was temporarily discouraged he measured himself against his journalist buddies, against casual acquaintances, against the drunk at the corner of the bar and thought, at least I'm as good as they are. It was when he was alone that the depression seized him. It wasn't a tangible thing but a sort of composite fear of age and failure and death that crept over him like a chilly fog: he saw his life as shapeless and useless and guessed it would hold nothing but disaster.

3

Mo slept at night in his nest on top of the wardrobe. He had a cage in the corner of the conservatory that he never inhabited from choice and only occasionally by persuasion, if the house was shut for the day. Mostly he came and went as he pleased, a free, idiosyncratic creature who preferred to make his own domestic arrangements. His nest was made from old newspapers, any letters that were left about and clothes he collected from the bedroom floor, hoisting them up to the nest by stuffing as much as possible into his mouth and carrying them in a series of difficult backward leaps from the chair back, to the picture frame, and then to the secure heights of the wardrobe.

When the first light came he left his nest and leapt to the bed, biting at Emmie's ear. She rolled over, complaining, and Mo flung himself back on the pillow in his boxing position, kicking invitingly with his hind legs at the palm of her limp, warm hand.

Emmie came wide awake, rolled out of bed and stood, yawning, on the mat. She was growing out of her clothes but only length-wise. Her pyjama jacket barely covered her rib cage and the trousers were two-thirds up her smooth, white calves. She scratched at the bare flesh between jacket and trousers and began to dress, pulling on vest, blouse and jersey in one time-saving operation. Her grey school knickers had disappeared; she lugged a tall stool over to the wardrobe and began to search for them in Mo's nest. Mo chattered at her indignantly: he was by nature a scold.

The noise woke Alice. She looked sleepily at her sister.

39

Emmie's legs were long and white, like bluebell stalks, her behind as narrow and hollowed as a boy's.

'You look disgusting,' Alice said. 'Anyone can see you through the window.'

Emmie glanced briefly at the empty road. 'Let them look. There's not much to see.'

Her unconcerned voice maddened Alice. 'Get down at once.'

'Mo's got my knickers.' She tugged at a loose, grey leg; the knickers came away from the nest tangled up with an old vest of Oliver's and a nylon stocking. 'Yours,' Emmie said, throwing it on the bed.

'He's a pest,' Alice said. 'You'll have to let him go. He'll want to sometime, anyway. He'll want a mate.'

'Do you *ever* think of anything except *mating*?' Emmie said, with scorn. 'Besides, there's nothing to mate with – nothing but grey squirrels round here. Nasty, ratty things. They'd kill him. And he wouldn't go, anyway. If he gets shut out in the garden, he gets in a frightful panic.' Her voice was tender.

'Animals,' Alice said in deep distaste and plumped up the pillows behind her. 'This isn't a house, it's a zoo. Oliver's got that goddamn' hen in his bed again. It's not hygienic.'

'She doesn't smell much. And she can't go out in the run. The others peck at her because she's only got one eye.'

'God,' Alice said. 'My *God*.'

'Don't let Gran hear you, taking the name of the Lord in . . .' Emmie was crouching by the wall. ' . . . vain. The key! I put it under the lino.'

'Here.' Alice fished under the pillow and tossed the key at her. 'I hung *my* clothes up last night. And lugged you out of Oliver's bed. He was half smothered.'

'Did Dad hear you come in?'

Alice yawned artificially and stretched up her arms,

lifting her hair away from her neck. 'No. Only just in time, though. He came up just after. I pretended to be asleep.' She watched Emmie unlock the wardrobe. 'What are you going to do?'

'Throw Oliver's stuff in the pits. It's the safest place. I can't put them back – I don't know where he got them.'

'You'll get caught one day. I don't know why you do it – it's mad. Stark, staring crazy.' Alice thumped her fist on her knee, her fair skin burning up. 'Someone's bound to find out – then what'll it look like? I tell you what'll happen – you'll have to go to court and Oliver'll get put in a home.'

'No one's going to find out,' Emmie said sturdily, but she had gone very white. She went to the chest of drawers and put on her glasses. Her eyes looked back at her from the swinging glass, enlarged and staring. She said softly, 'He'll grow out of it. It's only a sort of game.'

Alice snorted. 'Some game! You ought to tell Gran.'

'I couldn't. She'd think it was wicked.'

'So it is,' Alice said comfortably. She had been feeling uneasy lately about certain aspects of her own behaviour. 'It's against the law.'

'Gran doesn't mind about the law. She'd think it was wicked in a different way – a religious way. And it isn't. He's only little, he doesn't understand.'

'He understands all right,' Alice said. 'It's gone on too long, it's got to stop. If you won't tell, then I will.'

She watched Emmie's face with a curious pleasure. Alice was not a vindictive girl but she had suffered under Emmie's domination. She rejoiced to find herself suddenly in a position of strength. 'I *ought* to tell,' she said virtuously.

Emmie took a step forward. Her fists were clenched. Alice braced herself for a physical assault but after that first step, Emmie stood very still, shaking as if with extreme

41

cold. She said, 'If you did – I think I would *kill* you.'
Anger swelled inside her like a taut balloon that would
burst at a touch. She could have killed Alice at that
moment: her fingers itched to attack that soft, insulting
beauty, to spoil it, to tear at the sunlit hair. But she had a
more effective alternative. She said slowly, 'If you ever tell
anyone, anyone at all, I'll tell Dad about you and Dickie.'

'There's nothing to tell. Only that I've been on his bike.'

Emmie stared at the wall. 'I heard you on the tow-path,
that night last week.'

'Bitch,' Alice gasped. 'Oh – bitch, *bitch*.' She cupped
her hands over her ears and bent forward, bowed with
frantic, unbearable shame. Her mouth trembled and went
square like a child who is going to cry. 'You wouldn't tell
him that,' she said piteously.

'Only if I had to,' Emmie said in a stilted voice. She
showed, outwardly, no lessening of purpose. Inwardly, she
was torn. She had always protected Alice as she protected
Oliver, with a fierce, proprietary pride: they were hers, no
one must be allowed to see their imperfections but herself.
It would tear her in pieces to give Alice away but she
would do it, she would do anything, she suddenly realized,
for Oliver.

She said, 'I only heard what you *said*. I didn't *look*.'

*

She left the room. Oliver's door was ajar. The child slept,
the beautiful little thief, rosily defenceless on his back. His
tortoises scratched in the cardboard box beside his bed.
Emmie closed his door softly and stood, listening. From
her grandmother's room came a consoling murmur that
told Emmie she was in time: Mrs Bean was still safe in
her room and saying her prayers. The old woman slept
very little, though she always lay still in her bed all night,

bony nose pointing to the ceiling. She usually got up before anyone else and said her prayers, kneeling by the bed in her flannelette nightgown, her thin hands meticulously together and pointing upwards like long, narrow spearheads. She had her own religion that bore some resemblance to the Nonconformism she had been raised in, but not much. It was an entirely personal faith that nothing, no doubt or hardship or pain, could touch. Her life had not been easy: she had been born on a farm in Wales, learned to sing in the chapel choir and married a bankrupt theatrical agent who had heard her sing at an Eisteddfod. He had expected her to restore his fortunes: she did not do that but she kept him all his life. She could sing sentimental ballads. She sang them on the music-halls – one season at the Kilburn Empire – a big, curving, healthy woman with firm, bare shoulders and a rose in her hair. She had sung at private parties, in great, gold rooms blazing with chandeliers. She had sung with travelling companies, at pier concerts, bearing her three sons in dismal lodgings in the back streets of grey, gull-haunted towns. An ageing, but still powerful contralto, she had sung to the troops in the desert during the war that had taken two of those sons from her. Her third son was a weakling and a drunk, her grandchildren neglected, each day a mountain that she climbed with aching old legs to find no rest at the end of it, but she still prayed as if her prayer was a tape recording she was sending to a close, beloved relation – a relation who was elderly, like herself, and rather deaf, speaking good and loud so that he should hear. Dear Lord Jesus, she always began. Alice, who was embarrassed by her grandmother and tried to forestall comment by laughing about her, said that she always ended them, Your Humble and Obedient Servant, Emilia Bean.

Emmie crept downstairs. William, the retriever, did not

move when she went into the kitchen. He lay stiff-legged on the rug, his eyes closed. Only the plumed tail thumped faintly on the floor. Emmie went into the pantry, took the saucer off the top of the jug and drank the milk. It was goat's milk, strong-tasting, with a creamy scum that clung to her upper lip like a wisp of silk.

Outside, the ground was still foggy but above the mist the sky was delicately blue. Flaxman, the goat, rattled her chain as she lifted her insolent head to stare at Emmie. Emmie made a face at her and looked at the holly tree. The mother bird perched on the edge of the nest and fed her gaping changeling; the baby robin lay dead and unregarded on the ground. Emmie pushed it into the bushes with her foot, so that Alice shouldn't see it, and went out of the garden, along the tow-path towards the houseboats.

The first two boats showed no signs of life. Water's Edge was owned by an estate agent who let it, summer weekends, to parties from London. Home is the Sailor belonged to an insurance salesman, a little, clerkly man with rimless spectacles and a pale, pudding face who was often away: when he was there he lived alone, without visitors, and spoke to no one. His privacy was absolute. One warm Sunday, Emmie had seen him sitting in a chair on the deck, shelling peas for his dinner. She had said 'hallo', but he had neither answered her nor looked up, though she stood within a yard of him.

On the deck of Riverview, Mrs Hellyer was hanging out washing. She was an enormous woman with a back like a wall and thick, pale legs. As she bent over the basket, the hollows at the back of her knees were visible, white as cold beef fat. She stood up, saw Emmie and called, 'Em, here a minute.' Emmie stopped. 'I've got something for you,' Mrs Hellyer said.

She disappeared inside the boat and Emmie approached

44

the gangplank reluctantly. She was fond of Mrs Hellyer and admired her deeply, but her affection was tempered by physical distaste. To be hugged, occasionally kissed, by Mrs Hellyer was a torment; even the sweets she sometimes brought the children had a curious smell as if from long contact with her heavy, sweating flesh. As Emmie stood on the deck, her nostrils quivered.

Mrs Hellyer emerged, wheezing. She held something in her hand. 'Here,' she said. It was a paper knife with a carved, ivory handle. Emmie looked at it.

'Your Oliver,' Mrs Hellyer said. 'Had it on the tow-path yesterday, Mr Hellyer gave him half a dollar for it.' She mopped her glistening face with her apron. 'Kid said he didn't want it but I said to Mr Hellyer, I said it doesn't do to buy things like that from a child. Not that Mr Hellyer meant any harm, he was playing with it, see, and Mr Hellyer said that's pretty and Olly said, d'you want to buy it? So Mr Hellyer gave him half a dollar for it, just to humour him, like.'

'Oliver shouldn't have taken it. The money,' Emmie said, holding the knife. It was very pretty, the delicately carved handle was cold and smooth to the touch. She guessed it was valuable. He didn't get this from school, she thought appalled.

'He said he picked it up on the rubbish dump but I thought more likely he's found it poking about in the attics, something of the old lady's.'

'It's not Gran's.' Emmie looked up, poker-faced. 'I expect he did find it on the rubbish dump. He goes looking for treasure.'

She held her breath. But Mrs Hellyer, usually so well versed in the wickedness of the world, appeared to believe her. 'He oughtn't to go rootling about there, picking up things, you don't know where they've been.'

'I'll stop him,' Emmie said. 'And I'll tell him to give back the half-crown.'

'No need,' Mrs Hellyer said kindly. Her own children had been much more lavishly supplied with pocket money than Oliver and Emmie: it was her private opinion that middle-class parents were mean. 'I daresay he can do with it, poor little chap.' Emmie turned to go and she added, 'Tell your Gran I'll be a bit late Saturday, my daughter's got to go to the clinic. She's got caught again, that's her sixth and she says she doesn't know how it happened, her husband's ever so particular. She ought to be fitted but she says she doesn't fancy it – I tell her she'll have to stop being so dainty, it doesn't do to leave that sort of thing to the men . . .'

She thought nothing of Emmie's startled, wide-eyed stare. When Mrs Hellyer had been Emmie's age she had been in charge of a family of five younger children and a half-wit elder sister made pregnant by her uncle. At fourteen, she had already assisted at three deliveries and one death bed, her mother's; there had been little, in the practical field, that Mrs Hellyer had not known about life. It had not occurred to her that some girls might know less. Or that over the months she had supplied Emmie, adrift on a sea of ignorance, with a peculiarly one-sided account of human behaviour for a navigation chart.

*

The gravel pits had begun working. On the pontoon the Paxman Engine worked the old Gwynn's Pump and the ballast rattled along the pipe-line, snaked out over the water on the pontoon boats, to the boiling box. The big wheel turned and the sand went up the de-waterer in buckets, over the drum to the hopper; the ballast clattered over the screen with a sound like a giant hailstorm. From where Emmie stood, the noise was not unbearably loud, only hoarse and unremitting: a rasping, coarse, scraping background, so familiar that she did not notice it.

She heard the birds instead. On this side of the road the pits were worked out: tranquil, wide, muddy lakes with sheer, man-cut yellow sides and islands of scrubby bushes. The torn-up trees on the banks were already mossy; across the lakes there were the standing stalks of sailing masts. The pits had been ugly to begin with but then the grass had begun to grow and the birds had come; first the sandmartins and the mallards; then the gulls, flying up-river for an easy living; then the great crested grebes and coots.

Emmie looked for the grebes this morning but only the gulls bobbed on the water, watching her with yellow, vermilion-encircled eyes. At the edge, the water was shallow and treacherously muddy. Emmie climbed on to an old, half-sunk pontoon and moved gingerly along it. The water slapped as the pontoon moved sickeningly in the mud and Emmie shut her eyes briefly and prayed: oh Jesus, don't let me fall in, don't let me drown. Water terrified her, she dreamed of it closing over her head. They said that in the middle the pits were bottomless, that you could hide anything there. She thought of dead men floating under the water, dead women with long hair, fishes eating their staring eyes. Horror raced under her skin. She whimpered out loud and stood, precariously perched on the end of the pontoon. The things Oliver had stolen were in the pocket of her skirt. She threw the pencil case and the pens as far as she could, into deep water, and then hesitated, the paper knife in her hand. It was so pretty; if only she could put it back where it belonged. But Oliver would never tell her where he had got it – he would tell her most things but never that. Most of the time in fact he disclaimed all knowledge of the things he had collected;

if it were not that he made no murmur when they were taken from him Emmie could almost have believed that he was innocent, that the pens and knives appeared in his satchel or in his drawers by some mysterious agency. She sighed and flung the knife into the water. The light caught the blade as it fell, handle downwards, into the brown water. Emmie turned and saw a man standing a few yards away from her.

*

Marjorie's train was due in London at eleven o'clock and Nick was edgy with waiting. He did not know what mood she would be in – tear-stained and silent or nervously bright – nor which he dreaded most. She would be all right eventually, the doctor had said; he must be patient with her. Nick was patient though sometimes when she was not there to be patient with he allowed himself to feel the simple irritation of a practical man: if Marjorie tried, surely she could help herself more? He had woken up feeling this and had gone on feeling it while he bathed and dressed, hardening and arming himself against her. By the time he had tied his tie, he had recognized that this was a pointless attitude and one that he must shake off before he went to meet her.

In Kenya he would have played a round of golf; here there was nothing to do except go out for a walk. The miraculous beauty of the morning struck him, not with any particular pleasure but with a mild sense of recognition: this was the kind of morning that people in England raved about. He walked slowly, without aim except to pass time, slightly irritated by the variegated, incessant noise from the pit machinery but not much – not, in fact, feeling anything very acutely or thinking about anything in particular. The grass glinted at a thousand points like pieces of quartz; he walked along the tow-path and across the Meads, skirting the shoddy wire that fenced the pits. He saw Emmie as she scrambled uncertainly on to the swaying pontoon and watched her vaguely, with half his mind, in the way you watch the only moving thing in the landscape when you have nothing better to do. He saw the knife glint as it turned in air. Then Emmie turned and saw him; she cried out, lost her balance and fell into the water.

*

She had fallen face downwards, her face was cut and she was black and stinking with mud. But she had been in no danger at all; once Nick had lugged her to her feet, the water barely reached her knees. He felt he had made an exaggerated fool of himself, tearing his jacket on the barbed wire and sliming his trousers to rescue a child who was in no need of help – though in fact she seemed badly frightened, not crying, but pale under the streaks of mud and leaning groggily against him as he supported her out of the muddy water and on to the slippery bank.

He scolded her. 'You were all right, you know.'

'The mud sucks you down.' Her voice was soft, gasping.

He said, more gently, 'What's the matter? Can't you swim?'

She shook her head, shrinking away in horror as if he had suggested some terrible indecency. 'I hate water.'

He helped her through the wire, tore up a handful of wet, stiff grass and rubbed at his shoes. 'You'd better clean up too.'

She groped, obedient but blind. Her glasses were spattered with mud. 'Here,' he said, and tossed her his handkerchief. She took her glasses off and he saw that her eyes were beautiful, very large, a very deep, full blue. They regarded him coolly and he had a moment's acute self-consciousness: what did he look like to her? Then she bent and pulled at the grass, scrubbing her skirt. 'It'll never come clean,' she said despairingly.

'You've cut your face.'

She touched her cheek absently. 'It doesn't hurt.'

'Never mind. It should be cleaned up. Where do you live?'

'On the tow-path. Next to the pretty house. Our house is nice too, but it isn't so showy. I'm sorry, I've made your handkerchief all bloody.'

'Where from? Are you hurt anywhere else?'

'Only my hand.'

'Show me.'

She held it out reluctantly, fingers curled with pain, and he saw the deep gash across the thumb. 'It was the pontoon,' she said. 'I caught hold of it.'

It was a nasty cut. Nick said crossly, 'You are a fool, aren't you? Whatever possessed you to go in there? You're not allowed to – there are notices all over the place. Can't you *read*?'

She looked at him blankly, holding her injured hand. It wasn't her look, her gawky childishness, but the sound of his own windy, adult pomposity that disarmed him. He gave a sudden giggle. 'What were you doing, anyway? Destroying the evidence?'

He was quite unprepared for her reaction. She went very red, her mouth hung open. She was terrified. 'Nothing,' she said.

'Oh come on – I saw you.' He looked at her. 'Good God, child, it doesn't matter. I don't care what you were doing.'

She said in a small, obstinate voice, 'I was only watching the birds. I think I'll go home now. Thank you for helping me. I'm sorry about your clothes.'

He took her arm. He felt her stiffen but she didn't pull away. 'Come along, then, I'll see you home.' He wondered what he could say to cover up his mistake. 'Why were you watching birds?'

'For my Diary.' The words came out in a rush of relief. 'You have to write everything down, see? That's the way a proper naturalist works. The time you saw something. And the weather – if there's a wind, that sort of thing.'

'It sounds very serious.'

'Oh yes. There's always a chance you may find out something important. There are so many things people don't know. Children often notice things more than grown-ups because they aren't so busy. My brother often sees things I don't because he's younger. And it was a boy in Australia who found out about bird-anting.'

'I'm out of my depth,' he said, too solemnly.

She said in a dignified voice, 'He saw a bird putting ants between the feathers on its wings. No one took any notice at first because he was just a boy but then he wrote to an ornithologist and it spread, right round the world. Now they know anting is a sort of play. It's something birds do for fun. Like skipping or playing ball.'

Nick felt rebuked. He looked at the severe child, at her aloof, dirty face which was slightly turned away from him so that he could see the line of her cheekbone which was like the line in a Greuze painting: a curious, vase shape that held those surprising eyes and a serious, rather too determined mouth. It wasn't her potential beauty that stirred him suddenly, but her self-possession and her dignity. He had laughed at her and she had put him in his place — not forcefully, but with a secret, confident grace.

He said, 'Is that what you like doing best? Watching birds?'

51

She looked at him gravely. Behind her spectacles, the dark blue eyes shone. He felt transparent as glass.

'I like people better,' she said.

*

Alice and Oliver were at the gate. Their hair shone like barley in the sun. Oliver wore a blue shirt, a red tie and short, grey trousers, Alice, the same school uniform as Emmie, but on her the effect was absolutely different.

She said, '*Emmie*. Breakfast's cold.'

'Bacon's salty,' Oliver said contemptuously.

'Dad's wild – you'll catch it.' Alice took in Nick, standing behind Emmie, and her expression changed completely as did her voice which became higher and artificially accented. 'Emmie *darling*, you're absolutely *filthy*. What on earth . . .'

'You don't have to talk in that silly way. I fell in the lake. He pulled me out.' She looked at Alice scornfully and marched towards the house, back straight as a plumbline.

'How terribly *kind*,' Alice said, smiling brilliantly at Nick, one milky hand curling a strand of hair.

'She was all right, really. The water was shallow. But she's cut her hand. It ought to be seen to . . .'

Alice's face lit with beautiful pleasure. 'Is it a bad cut?'

'Fairly bad, I think. She was very brave about it.'

'I'll see to it,' Alice said. She flashed him a smile, her hair swung on her shoulders, her skirts flew as she ran to the house.

Oliver said, 'She's glad Emmie's hurt. She likes blood. She's going to be a nurse.'

Nick looked at the boy. 'What have you got there?'

'A squirrel,' Oliver said. 'A red one. They're rare. Someone gave it to my mother and she brought it home.'

'Won't it run away?'

'No.' Except for Mr Hellyer who had told him how to feed his tortoises and had promised to show him a badger sett one day, Oliver was not interested in men. He was aware of Nick, but only as an outline, a hollow statue, slightly out of focus. His mind was blank towards him but acutely conscious of a number of other things: that there was a female toad crouching under the broken brick of the wall, that there was a sickly cabbage smell from the boat-house that turned his stomach against food, that his father was angry with Alice.

Nick looked at the overgrown garden, the white goat, the hen run, the Muscovy ducks waddling across the bare lawn. He remembered now who the children's mother was. Jean Rapier had said; *she's always off on some jaunt or other. We call her the Migrant. How she can bear to leave those children, I don't know.* Then she laughed and said the only faintly unkind thing Nick had ever heard her say. *She once wrote a book about a partridge – apparently the partridge makes a wonderful mother.*

Nick smiled to himself and said, 'I expect you keep a lot of queer animals in your house, don't you?'

Oliver regarded him coldly. 'Only indigenous ones. Except for my tortoises, of course. I wish I had an arma-dillo. That would be even better.' His voice throbbed suddenly. 'They have armour, just like the old knights.' His eyes gleamed like a visionary's; he looked, not at Nick, but deep into his shining dream.

Nick was touched and amused. 'Perhaps your mother will bring you one, someday.'

The child's eyes jerked back to Nick's face. He looked surprised as if he had forgotten he was there. 'She won't,' he said. 'She's dead and gone.' He turned his back on Nick and walked up the path, whistling.

53

4

ALICE washed Emmie's hand under the running tap. 'It's a flap come off,' she said. 'I'll pull the edges together with Elastoplast. Look – it's quite easy.'

'I don't want to look,' Emmie said.

Their father stood in the doorway of the scullery. He hadn't shaved, the stubble glistened in the harsh, bristly folds of his cheeks. His pyjama jacket sagged open on his chest, the braces hung in loops at the sides of his trousers. 'I want to talk to you, Alice,' he said.

His eyes were bright and uneasy. He had heard the motor bike stop outside the house the night before and watched, hidden in the laurel bushes, as Alice climbed in through the bathroom window. He had been ashamed of himself, standing there drunk and ineffective while his daughter crept into the house like a thief. His night had been wakeful and tormented. He was shy of Alice and nervous of his responsibility for her. This morning, when he had accosted her on the landing, he had been belligerent and unreasonable and she had been cool and distant, apparently unaware that she had done anything wrong . . .

'Not *again*,' she muttered now, head bent over the sink. 'You've said enough.'

'Not enough, apparently. Emmie's got to listen too. She lied to me last night. Lies I won't have. Though I don't blame Emmie altogether, she's too young.'

Alice said scornfully, 'What a time to choose. Can't you see she's hurt her hand?'

Uncertainly, he frowned, came closer. 'That's nasty.' Emmie's hand lay helplessly on the towel while Alice cut

54

strips of plaster. The edge of the wound was raw as beef. A feeling of sad tenderness came in him. 'Poor pet,' he said, and put his big hand awkwardly on her shoulder. He winced as Alice bound up the hand with assured gentleness. 'She ought to get to a doctor.'

'Oh don't *fuss*,' Emmie burst out, impatient with the pain. He dropped his hand from her shoulder as if it had burned him. 'Listen to me,' he said loudly, 'both of you.'

Neither girl looked up. 'I won't put up with it, d'you hear? Alice mucking about with that boy; you, Emmie, covering up for her. It's got to stop. I'm telling you once and for all. *Alice*.'

They both stared at him, startled. He said, blind with rage at his own uselessness. 'I won't have it, d'you hear?'

'What can you do?' Alice said calmly. 'You can't stop me.'

'I'll take a strap to you . . . you're not too big, you needn't think it.'

Alarmed, Emmie gave a faint moan. 'I feel sick – I want Gran.'

'*Now* see what you've done,' Alice said reproachfully, and led Emmie from the room.

*

She stood in the bathroom, her clothes in a pool at her feet. Her grandmother fastened her clean blouse, Alice searched the airing cupboard for socks and jersey. She disturbed Oliver's hen, who flopped dustily to the ground, clucking indignantly.

'Get Oliver,' Mrs Bean said. 'That hen's not allowed in the cupboard.'

'He had it in bed last night,' Alice said, 'wrapped in a shawl.'

55

'Never mind that. Only not in the cupboard. There are limits. Don't fidget, Emmie. It's gone half past eight.'

Emmie fumbled with her good hand at the fastening of her skirt while her grandmother bent to pick up the things on the floor. The old knees creaked like an unoiled hinge, she put one liver-spotted hand on the side of the bath to help herself up. 'Getting old,' she said to herself.

'*No*,' Emmie stood still. 'You're not old.'

'Nothing to worry about,' Mrs Bean said. 'Only sometimes it takes you by surprise.'

'Mother should be here,' Alice said bitterly. 'It's silly to go off the way she does and leave you with everything.' In her vocabulary, 'silly' was the ultimate condemnation: it meant that something was hopelessly out of tune with her view of how things should be.

Mrs Bean said, 'I can manage. Your mother has a job to do.' Her tone was bleak: it was impossible to tell what she felt.

'She ought to be here,' Alice said stubbornly. 'It's silly.'

'Shut up, shut up, shut up,' Emmie said in a strangled whisper.

Alice looked at her curiously. There was an odd expression on Emmie's face – fixed, stiff, queerly embarrassed. Her eyes were very large and shining.

Alice said, turning to the airing cupboard and muttering so that their grandmother couldn't hear, 'Why should I shut up? *You* just don't care whether Mother's here or not – and Oliver's as bad. Neither of you would care if she never came home again. You're heartless, horrible.'

'*Leave my character alone*,' Emmie said in a loud, desperate voice. Patches of colour burned on each cheek. She turned to her grandmother and said, 'You ought to have Mrs Hellyer for longer. You shouldn't have so much to do. It wouldn't cost much.'

'What it would cost is none of your business. You take too much on yourself, Emmie. It's not right. A child of your age. Put on your jersey.'

Emmie struggled submissively with her sweater, tugged a comb through her hair. Mrs Bean stood in the sunlight that came through the bathroom window, the muddy clothes over her arm, and said irrelevantly, 'A lot of things aren't right here. Both you girls should pay more attention to your father.'

Alice stared at her, utterly astonished. 'We do what you tell us, Gran.'

'That's not the point.' She hesitated. 'It's not enough to do what I tell you. I'm an old woman, you get old and you start to let things go that you shouldn't. You forget what's important.' She looked at Alice's blank, uncomprehending face and felt her responsibility like a heavy load. It was true what Alice said, they were good girls, they did what she said, but she knew with a chill that it wasn't enough. Her mind didn't reach as far as it used to, the horizons were closing in. She said, 'It's important that you should learn to do what your father tells you. I shan't always be here.'

'*Gran.*' Alice's eyes filled. 'Don't talk like that.'

Emmie said nothing. She simply stared and shook. Mrs Bean looked at the narrow, quivering shoulders, the clenched fists, and sighed. It was too late to abdicate. 'I daresay I'll last,' she said. 'Get along – you'll be late.'

'*Oliver*,' Emmie said, and fled.

*

Oliver's body was in his room with his tortoises. His spirit roamed a primeval jungle where giant tortoises moved, armoured, ancient and menacing. Henry was eating a lettuce; Oliver was feeding Murgatroyd with a banana.

The long, wrinkled throat, like an empty sack, was thrust out of the beautiful shell. The flat head shot back as Emmie rushed in.

'You've upset him,' Oliver said. 'You mustn't barge at him like that.'

'You'll be late for school.' She darted round the room, one-handedly seizing his satchel, his pencil box, his cap.

'I'm not going. I was sick.'

'*Yesterday.*'

Seduced by the smell of the banana, Murgatroyd slowly slid out his head. Oliver held the fruit steady, ignoring Emmie. She seized his arm and jerked him to his feet. 'Come *on.*'

'I've got a sore knee,' he complained. 'It hurts when I stand up.' He hobbled in circles, doubled over, his mouth twisted as if in the last extremity of pain.

'Liar. What's the matter? Did you get into trouble yesterday?'

He stopped hobbling and gave her a wary look. 'I got my name in the Black Book.'

'What did you do?'

'Spat in the milk.'

She said, exasperated, 'You won't get in much trouble for that. Only a conduct mark.'

'It wasn't my milk.' The silky eyelids drooped. He looked like a sly young actress.

'Whose was it, then?'

'Michael's. I was putting a curse on him.' He opened his eyes wide and looked innocently at his sister. She shivered as if cold.

'Why did you do it?' she asked softly.

'I took Henry to school and he poked him with a twig. When I spat in the milk, he was frightened. He cried.'

'Stupid,' Emmie said robustly, though in the deep recesses of her mind she was half-frightened, too. Once Oliver had put a curse on a woman who had come to clean the house and objected to the mess the tortoises had made under his bed: she had been taken to hospital the next day with acute appendicitis.

'You shouldn't do it. Though it's just a pack of nonsense, you know that.'

'Miss Clapp put my name down in the Black Book,' he wailed. 'I might get the cane.'

The school they both went to was a gentle, private establishment, run by two kindly elderly ladies who kept discipline by such ineffective methods as conduct marks, staying after school, little talks. Someone had once seen a cane in the study; it had never been used, as far as Emmie knew, but the fear of it made Oliver shrink in his soul. He was a physically timid child who screamed before he was hurt; pain reared up before him like a terrible black nightmare whenever he missed his footing on a tree or stumbled on the pavement. He went quite pale now, his hair was damp. Emmie's stout common sense gave way before his terror like matchwood. The difference between the cold savagery of Oliver's struggle for power and his complete defencelessness when his sins were brought home to him, was something she had never been able to contemplate with detachment.

'It's all right,' she said. 'I'll do something.'

'What'll you do?'

'I'll rub your name out at break. It's only in pencil, nobody'll notice. I'll do it when Miss Clapp goes and has coffee in the staff room.' The enormity of this operation shocked her. 'I mean, I'll try. As long as *you* do something. That half-crown Mr Hellyer gave you. It's not yours – not really. You've got to put it in the Blind Box outside the sweetshop.'

He said meekly, 'All right.' Then he looked at her and his eyes glittered. 'I found the knife on the rubbish dump. I did, I *did*.'

She put her arms round him and hushed him gently. 'All right, Olly,' she said. 'It's all right.'

*

Before Alice went to school she had something to say to her father. He was sitting in the kitchen, drinking his tea and reading the newspaper. She went and stood in the doorway. Her mouth was dry and it was an effort to speak.

She said, 'Dad, Gran ought to have more help. She's got too much to do.'

'Who's to pay for it?' he said, his mouth full of toast.

She ran her tongue across her lips. 'I could leave school.'

'Don't be silly,' he said shortly. Then his expression changed. 'You want to go on with this nursing business, don't you? Or have you changed your mind? Even if you have, it doesn't make any difference. You've got to finish your education.'

Alice let out a long sigh. She had been scared he would say yes, she could leave and get a job. Now she was ashamed for being so scared.

She said, suddenly reckless, 'I could still be a nurse. I could leave and work as a nursing auxiliary now and then train later, when I'm eighteen.'

'There's no need for it. You do it properly.' He looked at her. 'I wish there was enough money for you to be a doctor. I'd like a child of mine to be a doctor.'

She wrinkled her nose. 'I don't want to be. I only ever wanted to be a nurse.'

He laughed. 'I know. You don't have to tell me. When

you were a little thing you were always bandaging your dolls – the poor things were always in the wars, one way and another. Burn cases was what you went in for chiefly. . . .' He poured out another cup of tea, his expression suddenly shy. 'I'm sorry about this morning, Alice. I shouldn't have said what I did. But it isn't always easy.' He looked at her humbly. 'I don't want you to get mixed up with that boy. There are reasons . . .' He stopped, embarrassed. She was so young, so innocent: he thought it better to leave the reasons obscure. 'They're not the right sort of people,' he said.

Alice smiled, touched by his delicacy, his quaint, old-fashioned snobbishness. 'Well . . .' she said, and kissed him lightly on the bald part of his head. 'All right, Dad, I'm late – I must *fly*.'

She left him, quite unaware that he thought he had wrung some sort of promise out of her, and ran out of the house. As she emerged from the Beans' gate, Nick, nosing the car out of the drive next door, stopped to let her pass. Her school straw hat clung precariously to the back of her head; the chaste school uniform, the white socks, reduced her to an artificial childhood. He thought of her as she had appeared last night, and grinned.

'How's your sister?' he said. 'Did you manage to fix her hand?'

'Yes. But it's made me late. And our school lays a *depressing* insistence on punctuality.'

Her weary, would-be sophisticated drawl tickled him. She dragged off her silly hat and swung it gently backwards and forward, flirting with him, not just with her eyes and her smile but with her voice and her young, rounded body. She was not particularly attracted to Nick but any man would do to practise her newly discovered talents on. She even swayed her hips as she passed the road sweepers who were all harmless inmates of the local lunatic asylum.

'Hop in,' he said amiably. 'I'll take you there.'

'That's *terribly* kind of you.'

'What about your sister?'

'She's gone already. Emmie would *die* rather than be late for anything.' She sat beside him, arranging her skirt over her beautiful, bare knees. She smelt of soap. 'Emmie's a perfect schoolgirl.'

'Emmie is a pretty name.'

'It's short for Emilia. That's my grandmother's name. She's called Emilia Clemence. Clemence after my mother. She's supposed to look like her.

'Indeed,' Nick said. A faint recognition drifted through his mind, thin as smoke.

'Emmie's her favourite,' Alice said, not resentfully, but in a bright, chatty tone as. if she expected that he would naturally be interested in her family. Her openness was attractive as was the refulgent smile with which she turned to him and said, with a ludicrously elderly air, 'Really, the traffic gets worse every day. It's almost impossible to sleep at night. One has to pull the bedclothes over one's ears.'

'Trying on a hot night.'

She blushed a little and said quickly, 'The school's down here, to the right. You'd better stop before we get to the gate.'

'Teacher won't approve, is that it?'

She blushed again. 'They have such awful *minds*.'

As she got out of the car, a middle-aged woman in a sad brown coat went past them on the pavement. She glanced at Alice, at Nick, then averted her gaze with haste as if she had inadvertently happened upon a pornographic spectacle. 'I see what you mean,' Nick said.

He watched her down the road and into the gate. She

was charming, he thought, with her pretty face and her
pretty, innocent lechery. But as he drove away he was
thinking of her sister, Emmie. She reminded him of someone. He was half way to London before he realized that
she reminded him of a photograph of his wife, when she
was young.

*

Martin Bean came into the kitchen where his mother was
clearing the breakfast dishes and said, 'Have you got any
spare cash on you?'

His manner was determinedly jaunty; his nervousness
only betrayed by the way he kept tugging at his jacket
sleeves to pull them down over his shirt cuffs.

Mrs Bean said nothing. She piled some plates together
and carried them, chinking, out to the scullery.

'D'you hear me?' he repeated in a louder voice. 'Have
you got any spare cash?'

She came back into the kitchen, wiping her hands on
her apron.

'There's been a lot of bills,' he said. 'Rates, gas, nothing
but money, money, money. What it costs to keep this
house going . . .' His voice rose with adventitious indignation. Her answering silence enraged him. 'Oh, for
God's sake,' he said under his breath. She couldn't hear
that, she was really very deaf, but her sharp, inquiring
look made him feel guilty.

He said, 'On top of the bills, I've had some unexpected
expenses.' That sounded silly, shouted out at the top of
his voice. 'I'm in a difficult position, Mother,' he went on
lowering his tone but speaking clearly and persuasively.
'I've got a chance – a new idea – for a series of articles. It
has to be handled carefully, put across in the right way. I
shall have to take a man out to lunch.'

63

She was standing on the opposite side of the table, watching him. Her expression was exactly what he had known it would be. She despised him, she had always despised him, he thought, and it made him tremble. He thrust his big, shaking hands into his pockets and nerved himself to face up to her.

'It's the way these things are done, Mother. Entertaining people – being in the right pub at the right time. I can't do that without money, can I?'

He was crawling, he thought, *crawling*. And all she could do was to stand there as if she had a bad smell under her nose. Did she think he liked crawling to her for money? The unfairness of his position maddened him, he began to shout and turn out his pockets, pulling out the lining so that shreds of tobacco, old matches, bus tickets, flints for his lighter, spilled out on the floor. 'How am I ever going to get a decent chance with all of you hanging round my neck like millstones? I'd just like to see something of what goes into this house. D'you know what I found Emmie feeding that damn' squirrel the other day? Mushrooms.' His face went dark. 'Mushrooms,' he repeated.

'Martin.'

His mother sat down in her chair and smoothed her apron over her knees. Her voice was thin, a whispering thread but her eyes sparked with anger. She was old, worn away, but she could still crack the whip over his head.

'I'm sorry,' he said. 'I'm sorry. Only sometimes I feel such a bloody failure, that's all.'

'Failure is not a sin,' she said. 'Only lack of trying. "Whatsoever thy hand findeth to do, do it with all thy might".'

His face twitched. 'Oh,' he said. '*Oh*.' He looked at his mother and thought of what she had done to him over the years, what she had done to his father, to his wife. Of what

64

she had made him do to his poor, foolish girl. He said, 'You're a hard woman. I thought one of the chief things in your religion is charity. The greatest of these is charity. Remember that when you're having your next cosy chat with your Maker – or do you work on a one way system? He's simply expected to listen to you, is that it?'

'One day, Martin, we shall all stand before the Judgement Seat,' she said.

He said, under his breath, 'Oh God. Oh my God.' He closed his eyes. Injustice made him angry, made him beg. He wanted her to think well of him – for so much of his life it had been the one thing he wanted. He said, 'I do my best, Mother. I can't do more. No one can do more. I don't ask for money for myself. Only for the children.' He opened his abused, bloodshot eyes and stared at her. He hated himself. His begging and feebleness! Oh – how weak and contemptible he was.

His mother said, 'I have never doubted your good points, Martin.' She stood up, knees creaking, and went over to the dresser. She opened the drawer and took out her cracked, brown purse, opening the wallet. She counted out notes. 'Will five pounds be enough?' she said.

'Yes. Thank you, Mother.' He added, in a low voice, 'Forgive us our debts as we forgive our debtors.' He had gone very pale.

5

'WHAT did you do with the dead man, Gran?' Oliver lay limply on Mrs Bean's lap, head against her shoulder, legs spread-eagled. As soon as he had asked the question he slid his thumb, his one clean digit, back into his mouth.

Emmie looked up from the table. 'That's the end, there isn't any more. They'd all been watching this tramp and feeling scared, then when he knocked at the door he fell down dead.'

Oliver said in an outraged voice, 'But they couldn't just have *left* him there. On the doorstep. What happened after, Gran?'

'What happened after isn't suitable,' Mrs Bean said. She tipped the child gently off her lap and he crumpled bonelessly to the floor. He sighed and yawned, eyes filling with tears.

'You're just greedy,' Emmie said. 'Stories have to stop somewhere. They can't go on and on.'

Her protest was simply for discipline's sake; this was the time of day she liked best, sitting in the comfortable, fuggy kitchen, doing her homework and listening to her grandmother. Mrs Bean's stories were always about the time before she left the farm to marry her rogue of a husband and become a singer, a time that was now more real and vivid to her than anything that had happened since. The rest of her life had become a trackless waste through which she had simply trudged, remembering no landmarks: the country of her girlhood was as green and familiar as yesterday. She was a good raconteuse, acting out all the parts with zest and energy and a kind of macabre humour. The people in her stories were all a little larger than life, eccentric and more, half mad: the man who shut his wife in the sty at night and drove the pigs up to the best bedroom; the farmer who had his mother's corpse embalmed and kept it in the porch to frighten visitors; the crazy *revenant*, who talked his way into half a dozen front parlours one morning and took the furniture apart claiming that he was looking for his dead sweetheart's love letters, while the occupants watched, unable to stop him, bewitched by his flow of talk.

Emmie could have listened to her all night; she was proud of her grandmother and wished that the whole world could know how marvellous she was. But her sense of duty compelled her to grumble. 'It's time he was in bed. You never used to let us stay up after our bedtime, Gran.'

'You get easier as you get older.' Mrs Bean avoided Emmie's eyes. The truth, as they both knew, was that she spoiled Oliver because he was male and therefore weak; she stiffened her granddaughters for the more important role they would have to play in life. She stood up, Oliver tugging at her skirt. 'I want another story. Tell us about the time you played the harmonium in the workhouse.'

'No,' Emmie said. 'Supper.' She started to gather up her books. Oliver lay on the hearthrug, his head on the dog's fat, pale stomach. The dog, William, was old and loving and silly. The children treated him with affection but without respect: his personality did not command it. Mrs Bean stopped at the door of the scullery.

'Where's Alice? You know what your father said.'

'Gone next door. She said someone ought to say thank you properly to Mr Sargent because he brought me home this morning.' Emmie spoke scornfully. Alice's new obsession with polite behaviour was ludicrous to her.

'She's right,' Mrs Bean said. 'Alice knows what good manners are.'

'She hasn't gone because it's manners,' Emmie said. 'She's gone because it makes her feel nice.'

*

Emmie was right. As she rang the doorbell, Alice was feeling a deep, voluptuous admiration for her own graciousness. She had put on her best skirt, a clean blouse, and her face wore the smile she had recently been practising in front of the mirror – mouth drawn up to one side, head tilted, eyes sleepily narrowed. It made her look slightly defective mentally.

When the door was opened, not by Mr Sargent but by a strange woman, she was discomfited, but only a little. As Oliver disregarded men, Alice did not usually notice women except to get ideas, to measure up, as it were, the competition. This was was well worth studying; a tallish woman with a clear, glowing skin, a shining, dark head. Her breasts were rounded, her hips narrow. She wore velvet slacks, a black blouse, and looked slender and patrician, rather like a dark greyhound.

'I want to speak to Mr Sargent,' Alice said, in her most cultivated voice.

The woman blinked nervously. She said, rather shyly, Alice thought, 'You'd better come in, then.'

She moved gracefully, from the hips. Attempting to imitate her, Alice saw with wonder that she had almost no behind at all. In the drawing-room, Mr Sargent was on his feet, frowning.

'Alice . . .' His voice was quick, rather irritated. Alice wondered if she had interrupted something. 'Darling, this is one of our neighbours, Alice Bean. Alice, this is my wife, Marjorie.'

'How do you do,' Alice said, smiling pleasantly.

Mr Sargent said, 'How is your sister's hand?'

'All right, thank you. It hurts a bit, she says, but I dressed it again this evening and it looks quite healthy.' Encouraged by her own competence, she went on, 'That's why I came. I wanted to say thank you. For rescuing Emmie. And for my lift this morning.'

Mrs Sargent said, 'You seem to have been busy, darling.' Her voice was low, marvellously husky, but something in the tone of it made Alice uncomfortable.

Mr Sargent said quickly, 'Not at all. We couldn't have you being late for school, could we?' He laughed in a very hearty way. 'Would you like a drink?'

Alice shook her head and blushed like a poppy. 'Gran doesn't allow us.' She was a little shocked by the offer. Mrs Bean had impressed upon her that no nice woman ever touched alcohol. Alice knew that her grandmother was old-fashioned and queer in some ways but she behaved herself at one flash from her watery old eyes. When Mrs Bean made rules, Alice kept them. She did not find this difficult since there were wide areas of conduct in which it had never occurred to the old woman to offer guidance.

Mr Sargent said, 'Doesn't she now? Lemonade for Alice, then.' He chuckled suddenly as if something had amused him and said to his wife, 'What about you, darling?'

'Whisky,' she said. As her husband handed her her drink she caught his hand and stroked her cheek on it for a second. Alice looked away, slightly embarrassed by this intimacy, but storing up the gesture for future use. If Dickie... She sipped her lemonade dreamily, and answered Mr Sargent's polite questions – how old was she, how old was her sister, did they all go to the same school? – with only half her mind. Now she had done her social duty, she was bored. She had a sudden desire to stretch herself, to run somewhere fast, uphill. She talked, smiled prettily and wondered how soon she could leave. Dickie would be waiting in the boathouse. She thought of Dickie, waiting, and felt giddy with excitement. She glanced at the clock and said, 'Goodness, I must *fly*.'

*

Marjorie said in a high voice, 'You don't waste much time, do you? I thought we were going to be on our own here. That's a very beautiful young woman, isn't it?'

Nick took her hand, 'Don't start something, there's a good girl.'

'Was I going to?'

He looked at her, at the rigid set of her head, her bright, exalted look. He recognized the signs: she was spoiling for a fight. He said slowly, 'I don't know. I never know.' He played gently with her long fingers, spreading them out on the palm of his hand. 'Don't let's quarrel – certainly not over that child. You know I'm not remotely taken with her – it's just another stick to beat the dog with. Isn't it?'

'I don't understand you.'

He grinned at her. 'To punish me then, because you're angry with me and with yourself. You're not a jealous person. You're only pretending to be. It's just because you feel things are in a bit of a mess. They aren't really, but because you think they *are*, you want to hit out, smash us up altogether, make everything dirty and broken. Like – like a child whose toy won't work exactly as he wants it.'

'*Professor* Sargent,' she said.

He flushed, both at her tone and because what he had said sounded like a grinding repetition of the things he was always saying, as if the gramophone needle had got stuck in a groove. He couldn't help it though. He couldn't help the feeling that if he could find out what was wrong, he might be able to put it right.

'I'm sorry,' she said. 'Oh – don't look so *hurt*. But you're wrong about my not being jealous. I *am*.'

'No you're not.' He wondered if he really believed this or whether it was just that he regarded jealousy as such a mean emotion that he could not bear anyone he loved to feel it. And he *did* love Marjorie. That was the thing to cling on to.

She looked at him earnestly with her full, dark eyes. 'I never used to be. It's different now. When you look at a pretty girl I feel sick . . . old and ugly and *useless*. It makes me think how useless I am to you and how much I've let you down.'

'You haven't let me down.'

'Haven't I?' She looked stonily in front of her. 'When we were with Daddy in Birmingham, I could *see*. You looked so lost, when he offered you that job you just said you'd think about it. You sounded so beaten down. How do you think *I* felt? I looked at you and thought – it's *my* fault . . .'

He said mildly, 'I've been busy for fifteen years, doing something I enjoyed. Now, suddenly, I'm not. You need time to adjust to things.'

'You blame me for it, don't you? It's not *fair*.' It was the anguished wail of a child. She said passionately, '*I* didn't make you resign – I was just ill, upset – you didn't have to give in to me. We could have stayed, I'd have managed somehow. However miserable I was, I couldn't have been more miserable than I am now.' She looked at him with moist, waif-like appeal. 'You really wanted to come home too, I didn't make you. Did I, Nick?'

He hesitated, torn. He didn't want to hurt her but he hated lies and wasn't sure that they helped her. He wished he knew what she really believed, if she had really forgotten the weeks that had led up to his resignation:

the tears, the hysteria, the times she had told him how much she hated Africa, had always hated it – screamed it at him over and over again until he was sick with shame at having made her suffer. The issue seemed to him simple: she had wanted him to resign but would not take the responsibility for having made him do so. Once the decision was made she had constructed a wall of self-deception that she could not bear knocked down – or perhaps the truth was so buried in the rubble of its foundation that she had forgotten its existence. This troubled Nick who thought it was important for everyone to see things clearly and be honest with themselves. It also – though he tried to discount this – seemed to belittle what he had done.

He said gently, 'I didn't really want to leave, don't you know that? But I don't blame you – I'm not even sorry we left, if it's helped you. I'm only sorry, purely selfishly, for myself. Isn't it possible to hold two opposing ideas in one's head at the same time?'

'Perhaps – I don't know. Perhaps it is all my fault. I just can't bear to hear you say it. It makes me feel so horrible – so guilty. It just adds one more thing to the list . . .'

'What list?'

She said stumblingly, 'The nasty list of things I've just found out I am. Jealous, hysterical, mean – oh I hate myself. You must hate me too.'

She shuddered suddenly and he took her hands and held them tight, shutting out the treacherous thought that this was the part of their relationship that she enjoyed most now: the emotional recital of her own shortcomings. He said, 'Listen, I don't hate you. Get that into your head. If you were everything you say you are I wouldn't care. I'd love you if you were a fat, greedy old woman with no more finer feelings than a cow.'

She laughed, though rather shakily. 'I wish I could believe that.'

'Don't you?'

He looked at her. This was probably not the right moment but she was very lovely, sitting straight-backed beside him, a hectic flush on her cheekbones. He put his hand on her breast and said, Darling.' As he kissed her, she turned and slid her knees up on to the sofa in a willing gesture. She lay for a moment, not refusing him but not responding either, though he could feel by the stiff trembling of her body that she wanted to. He said, puzzled, 'This isn't a terribly connubial sofa, is it?' and she twisted away from him suddenly and stood up.

'You can't just put things right like that,' she said and he knew he had been right, he had picked the wrong time. They hadn't quarrelled badly enough. She hadn't cried. It was always all right when she cried; once she had got to that point, whatever demon it was that possessed her had been driven out and they usually ended up in bed.

The colour had gone from her face. She said wildly, 'You always do this, don't you? Insult me, humiliate me – then make love to me. Haven't you any feelings?'

He said stiffly, 'I would have thought I was doing my best to express them.'

'Oh,' she said. 'Oh *you*.' She let out one scream, a high, shrill scream like a train whistle.

He tried to put his arms round her but she pushed him away. He said, 'Darling,' and then, trying the cold water treatment, 'Marjorie, pull yourself together.'

She stared at him blankly and then laughed. She said, in a low, almost conversational voice, 'D'you know, Nick, that is exactly what you said to me after the baby died. Do you remember? You stood there in your white ducks – it was November the eleventh – you stood there in your

73

white ducks, looking just like Sanders of the River, and said, 'Darling, do try and pull yourself together.'

She turned on her heel and left the room. A second later he heard the back door slam. He sat down, feeling very tired, and stared into the fire.

*

It was dark in the garden and darker still in the boathouse. It had once been a Victorian conceit, a curious, pagoda-like summer-house, but the whole of the wooden super-structure had rotted and was now only held together by a rustling sheath of ivy and climbing vetch. The boathouse itself ran under the tow-path, a vaulted roof on concrete pillars supporting the bank which had been built up over it. A half-sunk dinghy floated in a narrow channel be-tween two platforms; the only light came from a grille at the end against which the refuse from the river lodged. The place smelt of rotting vegetation and wet wood, a sweet, damp, brackish smell. Alice and Dickie Hellyer sat on one of the platforms on a pile of old punt cushions. The glow of Dickie's Woodbine brightened and died in the darkness.

Alice said, 'It smells mouldy. I don't think it used to smell like this. We used to play here when we were small.'

'Kids like somewhere. Somewhere private to hide.'

'We used to make spells. We had a brick oven over in that corner and we boiled things up in a saucepan.'

'What sort of things?'

'Snail shells. Dead frogs.' She added daringly, 'Do you know what we boiled them in?'

'No.' Dickie was not very interested. He was nineteen and his own childhood had been very short and a long time ago.

'Piddle,' Alice said. 'Emmie and Oliver piddled into the saucepan.' She blushed deep red in the darkness.

'Dirty little beasts,' Dickie said with real revulsion. He was fanatically clean, washing himself daily from head to foot with a pan of hot water, in the cramped kitchen of the houseboat; paring his nails down to the quick and digging painfully at the oil with matchsticks.

'Weren't they?' Alice giggled. 'They said the spells didn't work otherwise.' She remembered the two serious faces, one dark, one fair, turned towards her in the gloom of the boathouse. And her own disgust and unwilling acceptance. Emmie had made her do it. Emmie had always taken the lead. Alice said, 'Oliver used to carry bottles of the stuff about with him. He said it was medicine – old ladies thought he was sweet.'

'Funny the things kids get up to,' Dickie said.

'It wasn't really funny,' Alice said. 'They believed in it. Especially Oliver.' She looked into the shadowed corners of the boathouse and shivered suddenly as if something dark and silent and half-forgotten still lingered there. 'I'm cold,' she said.

'Here . . .' He put his arm round her and she moved close to him, feeling his warm, firm shoulder. He kissed her tentatively, sighed, and fumbled for his cigarettes.

'Don't smoke,' Alice said in a motherly voice. 'It's bad for you.'

'Keeps away the midges.' He grinned and sat upright, his free hand planted firmly on his knee. 'I'm getting lodgings,' he said. 'Fixed up today with a man at work. Three pounds a week. And I've signed on at evening classes. You can't get on in the pits unless you're a Mason. I want to get a proper apprenticeship.'

'I'm glad,' Alice said warmly. She enjoyed the feeling that she was encouraging Dickie in his ambitions.

'I ought to have pulled out before,' he said. 'I've only hung on for Mum's sake.'

'Does she mind?'

'I dunno. Not much good if she does, is it?' He spoke bravely, finding it impossible to express his deep misery and shame. 'I daresay I feel a bit of a rat. But I can't do anything. And you have to look out for yourself sometime. She ought to have left him years ago.'

'When we're married, we'll have her to live with us,' Alice said. Her vision of their neat bungalow, the clean curtains, the shining, ordered life was a little like a film advertising a detergent. It had no reality, nor was it what she wanted. Behind her dreaming eyelids she did not see Dickie, marriage, children, but her dedicated future; the white she wore was uniform, not a bridal veil. 'When I'm trained,' she said, comfortably in the future, 'I can get a night job at a hospital. You can get two pounds a night.' The prospect filled her with a deep, glowing pleasure that had nothing morbid in it. She longed to be part of a hospital, part of the glorious tidiness, the calm, conventual life. When she had had her tonsils out even the smell of the ward had seemed marvellous to her, so clean, so aseptic, in beautiful contrast with her home which was a collection of smells, individually tolerable but collectively disgusting: the smell of dog, of bird cages, rabbit sawdust, of damp upholstery, of stuffed birds.

'I wouldn't want you to work nights,' Dickie said. There was a note in his voice that made her shiver pleasantly.

'Kiss me,' she said. They kissed, rather inexpertly. Very gently, Dickie rubbed his cheek against hers.

'You're prickly. Dickie . . .'

'Yes?'

'I won't break, you know.'

'What d'you want me to do? Pull you along the ground by your hair?'

He rolled her over on the damp cushions. They scuffled,

shaking with silent laughter. Alice became rough and
hoydenish, scratching his cheek. He held her down. Her
hair spread out like moonlight. Dickie said, 'Don't fight. I
don't want to hurt you. I don't ever want to hurt you.'
He was breathing quickly. 'I seen enough of that.'

In the dimness, his fair, pleasant, ordinary face looked
different; sad and much older. It excited Alice. She was
fond of Dickie and sorry for him and interested in him but
not as interested as she pretended to be: basically, she saw
him as an antagonist, someone to try her strength on like
the parallel bars or the ropes in the gymnasium. She said,
'Dickie, have you ever – *you* know . . .'

'Have I ever what?'

She swallowed. 'Gone the whole hog with a girl?' There
was a heavy, sick feeling in her stomach. He let go of her
and she sat up. 'Dickie.'

'It's not the sort of thing you should ask.' His voice was
rough.

'Why not? How're you ever to find out?' Her heart was
pumping in her throat. She said, 'I don't know anything,
only talk and books. I asked my mother once and she said
human beings were disgusting. She said they did it all the
time. She said animals were cleaner. It made me feel sick
when she said that.' Luxurious tears welled up in her eyes
but at the back of her mind she had a distant feeling of
shame. She was not telling the truth: her mother's nervous prudery had shocked her but not much, nor for long.

'Why on earth did you ask *her*?' Dickie said, astonished.
'That's not the sort of thing you ask your parents.'

'You have to find out, don't you? All the girls in my
class . . .' She paused and muttered hotly. 'Sometimes I
feel such a fool.'

'*Do* you?'

She raised herself on her elbow and looked at him

boldly. He was watching her, silent and rather stiff. Instinct warned her she was trying him too far; she wasn't sure whether this was what she wanted or not. Was it, or wasn't it, just a game? He bent over her, hard and dangerous, and she was frightened. She whispered, 'No, I didn't mean . . .'

There was a noise outside the boathouse and they froze.

'It's Oliver,' Alice said, appalled. 'He listens – he listens at doors . . .'

Oliver's wail lifted like a sad siren in the night. 'Emmie, he's gone, he's gone —' He sounded very close, his feet thudded on the steps the other side of the boathouse door. They heard Emmie's voice, indignantly summoning him, 'Olly, come here this minute.'

'Ssh,' Dickie said. He covered the side of Alice's head with his big, warm hand and pressed it against him. Alice cried a little into his shoulder. 'It's all right,' Dickie soothed her, though his own nerves were shaken.' He'll go away.'

They waited, clinging together. Slowly Oliver's cries retreated. Alice was shaken with audibly painful sobs. Dickie felt for her chin and lifted her face to kiss her. Her mouth was warm and trembling, her breasts crushed flat against him. She stopped thinking with an almost anguished relief. 'All right,' Dickie said breathlessly. 'All right. Oh Alice.'

6

OLIVER had lost Murgatroyd. Before supper, he had been playing with the tortoise on the patch of sour, spiky grass which, before the Beans moved into the house, had been a lawn. Now it was covered with rabbit droppings and the white marks left by their movable, wire runs. Investigating the slugs and thin, fascinating worms that wriggled in the dead, crushed grass, Oliver had remembered it was a long time since he had looked for ants. The most rewarding place for ants was under the bricks that edged the border where the flag irises grew. He moved a brick and saw the ants fling themselves into frantic action, rushing their pale, long eggs to safety, tugging, thrusting them into neat, dark holes. Oliver was particularly fond of ants. Watching them his mind narrowed, became blank to everything except the red, scurrying bodies, the network of thread-like black tunnels, the marvellous, intricate city. If he squatted quite still and concentrated, he could feel that he was an ant. For about half an hour he had lived in a world completely his own; only the small movements of his face, the eyes glancing quickly from side to side, the mouth opening and closing in a pincer movement, betrayed the fantasy spinning out inside him.

'I only took my eyes off Murgatroyd for a second,' he said defensively.

'Liar,' Emmie said. 'You've forgotten about him for hours. But he won't hurt. Not for one night. It's not cold.'

'He hates to be in the garden. He hates it. He's a house tortoise.'

Emmie ignored the despair in his voice. 'Come on in, it's late.' She held his shoulder, pushing him towards the kitchen, and he turned on her, face distorted, eyes tight shut. 'Damn you – oh damn you.' His arms flailed like a small windmill's. She held him off, laughing; then one fist landed in her chest and she lost her temper, rolling him on the ground. He wriggled beneath her, whimpering, but she only leaned on him more heavily, digging her nails into him, until he began to cry in earnest. Her anger vanished, she gathered him into her arms and crooned, 'There, there,' holding him to her flat breast. 'It's all right, love, Emmie's here.'

'I hate you,' he screamed suddenly and thrust his hard knees into her stomach. She let him go and crouched on the ground, winded. He went into the kitchen and came out a few minutes later, still shaking, but with his tears dried, holding his grandmother's hand.

Mrs Bean said, 'Emmie, get up off the ground. You'll get rheumaticky. We'd better find this old tortoise.'

Emmie stood up, reproachfully holding her stomach. 'It's dark. We won't be able to. Anyway, Oliver ought to be in bed.'

'Bed's no good if he won't sleep. Where's the lamp?'

The hurricane lamp, discovered behind the rabbit hutches, was rusted solid. Emmie said with disgust, 'It's like everything in this house. Nothing works.' She flung it into the hedge.

'Things need care,' Mrs Bean said. 'There's a torch on the nail in the boathouse.'

'It's gone. I looked for it yesterday.'

Mrs Bean gave her a sharp look and went back into the house. The two children eyed each other. Emmie's expression was smouldering, Oliver's shifty. 'I know who's in the boathouse,' he said.

'Oh you do, Mr Know-all.'

'Yes, I do.'

Emmie said quickly, 'Well keep quiet about it, that's all.'

Their grandmother came out with three candles. 'Only one candlestick,' she said. 'Olly can have it. You'll have to mind the drips, Emmie.'

She sniffed. 'Candles aren't much use.'

'Maybe not. But when you haven't the right thing, you have to make do,' Mrs Bean said.

They held their candles straight while she lit them. There was no wind and the little flames rose straight and yellow. Mrs Bean's face was cadaverous and weirdly beautiful, her expression serious and intent as Oliver's. The child's ability to be utterly, completely absorbed in something very simple, a game, a project, had returned to her in her old age. Watching them, Emmie felt a rush of love. Their innocent concentration, so natural to them both, seemed lovely and enviable to her. 'What fun this is,' she said in an affected voice. 'How mad we are.' She met the uncomprehending look in their eyes and laughed excitedly. 'I wish Alice was here. And Dad.'

They trod slowly across the garden, bending low, holding the candles as upright as they could, peering with watering eyes at the ground. Oliver tipped his stick. 'I'm burned,' he said fearfully.

'It doesn't really hurt,' Emmie said. 'Only at first, when it touches your skin. Then it sets and you can peel it off.' She took his free hand and squeezed it. 'I expect we look awfully funny, don't you? But it's fun, isn't it? Don't you love it when we all do things together?'

'He'll be in the flower beds most probably,' Oliver said. 'He likes polyanthuses. The yellow ones.'

*

Marjorie saw them through the hedge of *rosa hugonis* that

divided the gardens; three skinny, bowed figures, three skinny, yellow flames. 'Gracious God,' she said, awed. 'Nick – come and look.'

Her voice was clear and happy. He saw that the storm had blown through her and left her new and refreshed as grass. Once he would have seized this opportunity to conduct a slow, careful post-mortem on the scene they had just endured – why did she say this, what made her feel that? – but now he had learned a little and was simply grateful that she felt better. As he took her hand she smiled at him as if they had never had a cross word in their lives. 'What *are* they doing?'

'I wouldn't know.' He called out, 'Have you lost something?'

The nearest candle paused, then waveringly approached them. Above its flame, Oliver's eyes were dark, mysterious wells; his hair glimmered white in the moonlight.

Marjorie looked at the beautiful child and gasped, 'Heavens, what a face.'

The pale eyelids flickered with what might have been contempt. Oliver said in a neutral voice, 'We're looking for my tortoise.'

'What?' Marjorie's voice bubbled with nervous laughter. She looked at Emmie who had come up behind the boy and said, 'Do you know – we thought it must be some quite extraordinary tribal ceremony.'

She had not meant to ridicule; her shyness with strangers led her into the occasional clumsiness. But Emmie stiffened. She was not unusually sensitive when people laughed at her, but she hated it when they seemed to laugh at her family. Above all, she hated it when they seemed to laugh at her grandmother. A girl at school had once called Mrs Bean The Wayside Pulpit. Alice had told Emmie this as a good joke and ever since she had suffered agonies of angry, helpless pity whenever she saw her grandmother in the street; watching her as she walked along with her queer, high-stepping heron's gait, wearing the fisherman's hat, the ancient clothes, it was impossible not to see that she might appear ridiculous to unloving eyes. Recently Emmie had taken to accompanying her whenever she could as a kind of bodyguard. Tagging along, a pace behind Mrs Bean and on the look-out for criticism, she met the casual glances of passers-by with a hard, fierce glare that made them avert their eyes and hurry on.

She glared at Marjorie now. 'Oliver's devoted to his tortoise. He won't go to bed without it. And our torch is broken.'

Marjorie heard the hostility in her voice, knew she had offended and said humbly, 'Perhaps we can help then. Nick, have we a torch?'

'It's quite all right, don't bother,' Emmie said in a cold, distant voice.

'Don't you want to find Murgatroyd?' Oliver shot her an indignant look and then turned the full glory of his smile on Marjorie. 'A torch would be a great help. Thank you *so* much,' he said.

Nauseated, Emmie turned and walked across the garden. Nick went into the house for the torch. Marjorie leaned across the hedge and smiled. 'What's your name? How old are you?' She was never shy with very young children.

'Oliver Bean. Eight and three-quarters.' He regarded with grave sweetness. 'How old are you?'

'Thirty-nine.' A slight tremor disturbed her smile. To speak her age frightened her; her voice was like a knell. Sometimes she stood naked in front of the mirror and examined her body with a hard, critical gaze that had nothing nervous or self-loving in it, watching almost greedily for the first signs of middle-age. On these occasions she found an odd, masochistic pleasure in noticing the wrinkle across her stomach, the slight sagging of her breasts, pulling faces at her reflection and saying, you hideous creature, you ugly old hag. It was only when she was unprepared for it, as now, that the thought of being old took her by the throat, half-choking her with fear.

'Have you got any children?' Oliver said.

'I had a little boy once. He would be about three years old now.'

'Where is he?'

'He died.'

'Oh.' Oliver eyed her speculatively. 'Are you hungry?'

'What? Oh – not particularly. Are you?'

'Yes.'

'Would you like a biscuit?'

He nodded and said in a brisk, business-like voice, 'Shall I come through the hedge? There's a place just here.'

'What about your tortoise?'

'Emmie will find him.'

She hesitated. 'We'd better ask your grandmother if you can come, hadn't we?'

'She's gone indoors.'

'I'll come and ask her, shall I?'

A thorn caught her blouse as she scrambled through the gap in the hedge. Oliver had blown out his candle. He stood beside her.

'Mrs Rapier always kept special biscuits for me,' he said. 'Lemon creams.'

His innocent greed enslaved her. She took his hand. It was small and calloused, the fingers tightened confidingly in hers.

He said helpfully, 'She kept them in a jar in the sitting-room.'

'Do you like Mrs Rapier?' Marjorie asked.

'Yes. She's awfully nice.' He lifted his face and smiled. 'But not as pretty as you.'

*

They found the tortoise among the polyanthuses. 'What a mercy,' Emmie said. 'Now I can get that child to bed.'

They had been searching for about fifteen minutes; until now she had barely spoken. Nick had thought she seemed stiff and constrained. He said, in a jolly voice, 'Well . . . this is the first time I've been on a tortoise hunt.'

She glanced at him shyly. 'Oliver's awfully silly. An awful baby.'

He wondered if she was afraid he was making fun of her. He said, 'I expect his tortoise is important to him, don't you? You should never laugh at the things that are important to people.'

There was nothing indulgent in this remark. It would never have occurred to Nick to be either indulgent or condescending towards children; he did not consider them as miniature adults of his own race, rather as a different species of it. He approached them much as he would have approached a strange African tribe, with cautious curiosity, complete suspension of moral judgement and a deep respect for a kind of mind that differed from his own, not so much in knowledge, as in the sort of furniture it possessed. The reasoning capacity was there but the conclusions reached, lacking information, were sometimes odd: he had met a Kisii who, watching a European take matches out of his breast pocket, believed that white men brought fire out of their armpits. Nick did not quite count

Emmie as a child – though he suspected that her thinking would still be unlike his own – but he was perfectly prepared to learn that Oliver held any number of queer beliefs. He would not have been surprised to hear that the boy looked on his tortoise as a kind of god.

Emmie grinned at him gratefully. 'He's an awful scrounger, too. Did he ask if he could go into your house? He used to go in to Mrs Rapier and ask if he could have some breakfast. He used to pretend he hadn't had any.'

'Very provident of him,' Nick said. 'Will he do it to us, do you think?'

'I don't know.' She sounded anxious and he said quickly,

'It doesn't matter if he does. Marjorie likes boys.'

'I expect he'll suck up to her, then.' Emmie sighed heavily. 'It's awful that he's so pretty. It's bad for his character.'

When they went into the house, Oliver was sitting by the fire on a brocade stool, a glass in his hand, a tin of chocolate biscuits open in front of him. His smile was milky and satisfied. Emmie gave him the tortoise and he touched the brown carapace with love, murmuring gently. The armoured legs slid out, then the small, ancient head. Oliver said, 'He likes you to stroke him.'

To Nick's surprise – Marjorie disliked animals and would ordinarily avoid touching one – she took the tortoise and stroked the dry, cool chin. The black eyes blinked; suddenly there was a sharp sound and a dark, sticky stream shot on to her blouse.

'*Oh*,' said Emmie, scarlet.

'It's all right.' After the briefest of pauses, Marjorie smiled at her. Her smile was warm and happy; she continued to hold Murgatroyd without any appearance of distaste. 'It'll wash out,' she said.

'Most people would have dropped him.' Oliver spoke graciously, like a kind young king commending a subject. Marjorie's smile trembled a little. 'What a nice compliment,' she said softly. She made him a mocking little bow and put the tortoise in his lap. Sitting on the stool beside him, she said to Nick, 'Oliver and I have been having a long talk. He says they have a boat. Perhaps we could all take a picnic on the river one day.'

'Emmie isn't allowed. She can't swim,' Oliver said scornfully.

'She'll have to learn. We could teach her, couldn't we, Nick? Oh – we could have such *fun*.'

She put her arm loosely round Oliver and he settled comfortably against her shoulder. Over his blond head, her eyes met Nick's. Her expression was childishly excited but slightly defiant and wary – the look of a little girl who knows she hasn't been good, but is hoping, all the same, for a special treat. It struck Nick that she was holding the child against her like a shield – not protectively, but for protection. The thought made his throat feel tight. Was she so nervous of him? Had he denied her so much? It was his fault that there had been no more children after that first, dead boy, but only in a technical sense. That he had been conceived at all was a miracle ; a million to one chance, the doctor had said. A nice man, he had seemed genuinely upset on Marjorie's behalf. Adoption was the obvious answer in most cases but perhaps not in hers : after her illness it might be difficult to find a society that would consider them suitable parents. Perhaps, anyway, the risk was too great. Nick had agreed with simple relief. He did not want someone else's child. The strength of this atavistic feeling had surprised him at first : now, although it had, in fact, made no difference to their final decision, he was deeply ashamed of it. He feared there might be some streak of dark, unconscious cruelty inside him that made him want to deprive her.

Guilt descended upon him, bleak and cold as fog on a November morning. It blanketed out everything else, her variable moods, her sad despairs, her sudden, violent affections that were sweet and generous while they lasted but often demanded an impossible return – all his knowledge of her wild, inconstant heart. 'Of course we can teach her to swim,' he said. 'We can do anything you like. As long as their father doesn't mind.'

'Dad doesn't care what we do,' Oliver said promptly.

*

When the children had gone, she was in a happy mood; her eyes shone, her skin glowed, she was prepared to go on talking for hours. Nick sat on the edge of the bath while she lay in the hot, scented water, talking and smoking and sipping the nightcap he had brought her. 'Did you go inside the house, Nick? You really should have done – it's awful, dark and horrible. Oliver wanted to show me round – you know how funny children are. There are two enormous rooms full of stuffed birds in glass cases – like some old museum that's been shut up for years. And their old grandma must have come out of the Ark – really Nick, she's old as the hills and almost quite gaga. Certainly not fit to look after children. And they *don't* look well-cared for, do they? It makes me want to cry . . . Oliver says he hasn't got any toys. It didn't sound as if he was complaining, just stating a fact, but it made me feel so sad . . .'

He said lightly, 'He has his revolting tortoise. I should think he must be one of the first people in the world to think a tortoise beautiful.'

'Poor little chap.' Her face was wistful. She said, with sudden urgency, 'Oh, Nick – I'd like to give him things.

88

I'd like to rush into a toyshop and come out with my arms laden. For purely selfish reasons, I suppose. But he looks as if he needs something like that – as if he needs someone to make a fuss of him and spoil him dreadfully and wrap him up well and make sure he's careful of his chest.'

Nick smiled. He felt as if his bowels were dissolving with pity. 'Maybe he does need to be careful of his chest. I admit he's got that consumptive, Victorian look – pale and interesting. I'll bet you anything though that he knows what effect it has.'

She looked at him with hurt eyes. 'You think I'm a sentimental fool, don't you?'

He said, 'No, my darling. I just think you terribly need someone to be responsible for – to cosset, to love . . .'

She stood up, water streaming from her long thighs, her glistening body. He wrapped her in a warm towel and kissed her damp mouth. Her breasts felt heavy and warm against him. She whispered, against his cheek, 'Oh, Nick, you're so terribly sweet to me. And I'm making you all wet.'

'It doesn't matter. Shall I have a bath?'

'If you like. But be quick.' She kissed him again, wetly as a little girl and said, 'Oh, darling, if you'd always be like this I wouldn't need anyone else – I could manage just with you . . .'

*

When he went into the bedroom she wasn't in bed, but standing by the open door in her nightdress. She said, in a low voice, 'I think there's somone downstairs.'

Her eyes fixed on him, terrified. He said, 'You're imagining things. There are always odd noises in a strange house.'

'This wasn't – did you lock the back door?'

'I don't remember.' He took his trousers off the chair and began to pull them on over his pyjamas.

'Hurry,' she whispered, and he grinned.

'I can't face a burglar in my underwear. A man has his pride.'

The ground floor was in darkness except for the glow of the street lamp through the fanlight. He went softly to the back door. It stood a little open, the scented air from the garden blew softly on his face. He closed it gently and stood listening.

There was a small, stifled sound from the drawing-room. A held-back sneeze? He marched across the hall and switched on the light. Standing in the middle of the room, Emmie blinked at him. He said, with angry relief, 'For heaven's sake – what are you doing here?'

She said nothing. He thought she looked sullen, almost stupid. Behind him, Marjorie said, 'Emmie . . .' The child looked at her, lower lip stuck out. Marjorie went up to her and touched her shoulder. 'What is it, dear?'

Emmie flinched away from her as if she had raised a stick. Marjorie grabbed at something she held in her hand. It was a pair of silver grape scissors. She held them out to Nick, eyebrows raised.

He said blankly, 'Don't they belong in the fruit bowl?'

'Yes.' She turned to Emmie. 'What were you doing with them?'

Emmie said nothing. Her face was pale and stony.

Marjorie said, more impatiently, 'Come on – tell us. We won't be angry. Were you – were you *taking* them?'

'No,' Emmie said. The word was wrenched from her like pulling out a tooth.

'Then what?'

She stood sturdily, feet planted a little apart as if she were bracing herself against a fifty-mile-an-hour gale. 'I was putting them back,' she said. 'Oliver borrowed them,' she said. 'Just for a little. He saw them while you were warming his milk.' She looked at Marjorie. 'He likes pretty things. Like – like a magpie. He didn't mean to be naughty.'

Nick said, amused, 'I'm sure he didn't. But why creep back into the house at this hour of night? You could have given them back in the morning.'

'Don't be obtuse,' Marjorie said. 'Does he often borrow things, Emmie?'

Emmie looked at her, eyes huge with apprehension. She nodded.

'Often?'

Again that quick little nod. She burst out, 'What are you going to do?'

Marjorie said gently, 'Nothing, you silly child. What did you expect us to do? Call the police?'

'I don't know . . .'

Nick saw this was not just a joke to her. He said, 'Of course we wouldn't call the police, Emmie dear. Not now. On the other hand if you hadn't brought the scissors back, we *would* have been worried.' He felt it would not do to make too light of the matter.

She said, 'Then you won't tell?'

He smiled. 'Not the police, certainly.'

'Not anyone. Not Dad or anyone. Please. I promise he won't do it again. I'll see he doesn't.'

She looked very young, very pale and determined. Marjorie made an impulsive movement towards her and then checked herself. Emmie was too stiff, too proud, not a child who could be easily kissed and comforted. She stood squarely on her own feet, Nick thought. She didn't expect people to make allowances for her, feel pity. An admiring tenderness rose up in him. He was also uneasy.

91

She had as good as told them that young Oliver made a habit of this sort of thing. It might not be true, of course, but he couldn't altogether ignore it.

He said, 'Emmie, we won't tell anyone if you don't want us to. But if he does it again, *you* should tell someone. Your father . . .'

'*No*,' she said, her voice loud with panic.

Marjorie said quietly, 'Don't make too much of it, Nick.'

'All right. All right, then.' He said slowly, 'You could tell us, couldn't you? After all we know about it. We might be able to think of something. Will you promise me?'

She looked up into his face and sighed. 'Yes. I promise,' she said, and smiled.

Suddenly Nick saw himself through her eyes, calm, adult, all-powerful, and was appalled. His intention was real and kind enough, but before her trusting look he felt a fake. Do parents feel like this, he thought? Or do they get used to playing God? He said, half-angrily, 'For heaven's sake, look at the time. You must get back to bed, young woman.'

'See her home, darling,' Marjorie said. 'It's horribly dark.'

'Dark doesn't worry her,' Nick said. 'Burglars like the dark.'

She chuckled and looked at him shyly. 'I've got to get in through the bathroom window. Perhaps you'd give me a leg-up.'

'I suppose I might as well compound the felony,' Nick said.

*

Marjorie said, 'That poor little child.'

'She's not so little.'

'Oliver, I mean. I was right about him, wasn't I? It

isn't just that Victorian look. He does need looking after. Children steal because they want affection.' She sat up in bed, her eyes large and dark with excited pity.

Nick smiled at her and switched off the light. 'It seems an odd way to go about it. Pinching Jean Rapier's grape scissors.'

He got into bed and settled her comfortably within the circle of his arm. 'I know what the psychiatrists say. But they can't really know, can they? It's only a kind of guessing game. You might just as well say Oliver's a natural collector of old silver who just can't afford Sotheby's yet.'

'Idiot.' She giggled. Then she said, 'Of course it may not be true at all. The girl may have been lying.'

Nick found this gave him a cold, flat feeling. He said slowly, 'She didn't strike me as someone who would tell that kind of lie – the kind that would get someone else into trouble.'

'You can't be sure about that either, can you?' She was silent for a minute and then said, with passion, '*I'm* only sure of one thing. If I were his mother, I'd never have gone off and left a child like that alone.'

He said gently, 'No, I don't think you would. But it's not remotely our business, you know.' He thought of something. 'Though it's my guess you're right – he's not a particularly happy child. This morning I asked him something about his mother – I can't remember what or why – and he said she was dead. She isn't – so presumably he does feel deprived and resentful. Maybe even ashamed. So he lies about her. A dead mother is less embarrassing than an absent one.'

She laughed softly. 'Who's being all psychological now?' Then she moved closer, her warm cheek rested against his shoulder. 'Poor child,' she said.

7

By Whitsun, the days were blue and hot. Even the mornings were never really cool, but still and misty with the promise of heat. Sometimes Emmie woke feeling empty and lethargic as if everything had been drained out of her; other mornings, she could hardly wait to get out of bed and begin the day.

It was different from any summer she could remember. Everything seemed to be changing, and this excited and worried her at the same time: she thought about it so much that her face had a permanently screwed up, wondering look. Her father thought that her glasses must need adjusting and said she should have her eyes tested, but no one made an appointment for her, so she didn't go.

It was her family that were changing, she thought: she was just as she had always been. Dad was different; he had not been the same since that night Alice was out and she had gone downstairs and watched him working on his book. She thought he seemed sadder and older and somehow lonely. Sometimes, when he was writing, she hung around in the conservatory to keep him company. But she seemed to fidget him; he would let her stay for a while and then say, 'Run along, duckie, can't you see I'm busy?' He was kind to her, though. He had thought about sending her to the oculist and he was much nicer to Gran. He didn't get angry or shout at her any more.

Gran had not changed in any real way. She was more tired than she used to be, that was all. Often she didn't get up in the mornings, lying in bed while Emmie got breakfast and made her a cup of tea. Once or twice she said, 'It's not right for you to have so much to do, Em,' but mostly she just took the tea and sipped it and looked at Emmie as if she wasn't anyone she knew very well, any more. Sometimes, when she looked at her like that, it seemed to Emmie that she could easily forget what Gran was like when she was well – how she had looked, sitting in the kitchen all last winter, rocking in her old chair and telling them stories and teaching Oliver games to play with her darning eggs. Everything was slipping away, Emmie thought, and it scared her. There was no way of holding anything back. She wrote a great deal in her Diary at this time, chiefly about Gran, about how clever she was and how beautiful she had been when she was young. She tried to remember some of her stories and put those in the Diary too. She explained that Gran had once been a famous singer and that she played the organ and was teaching Oliver to sing.

Oliver sang very little now Gran was too tired to play the organ, though sometimes he sang hymns softly to himself when he was on his own in the garden. He had stopped stealing, or, rather, Emmie thought he had: sometimes she wondered if it was just that she wasn't keeping a proper watch on him. He was off on his own a good deal, playing with his tortoises, or, next door talking to Mrs Sargent. He got himself up in the morning and dressed in the clothes Emmie had put out for him the night before. The clothes were not always very clean, but they were often the only clothes she could find. He was growing like a beanshoot and most of the things he had had last summer were too small. Mrs Sargent had bought him a pair of shorts and some little shirts; Emmie washed these herself because Mrs Hellyer, though kind and willing, was unskilful – clothes came out of her wash-tub a uniform grey, and crumpled. Emmie thought it would be impolite to Mrs Sargent to let her see the clothes she had bought looking like that.

Mrs Sargent was kind; she took them for drives in the car. Once she had taken them to the cinema and Oliver had been sick with excitement and ice-cream. But it was Mr Sargent Emmie liked best. She thought about him a lot. When she went next door she would go into the bathroom just to see where he kept his flannel and what kind of toothpaste he used. Just to see his silk dressing-gown hanging on the back of the door or his watch lying on the edge of the basin, stirred an unfathomable excitement in her. If he asked her to run an errand, to post a letter or buy some razor blades from the chemist, she was transported with pleasure; she wanted to do difficult things for him, to be his slave, his handmaiden. She dreamed, long beautiful dreams. He would fall into the river and she would dive in after him. Fire would break out in the house and he would be trapped in his room, unconscious; she would climb up the ivy at the back of the house and help him to get out. The nature of his peril changed sometimes but her part was always the same. Always she rescued him without regard for herself. She wanted to die, saving him from death.

*

This Whit Monday morning was one of the days when she woke up, aching to begin the day. When Mo chewed at her ear, she woke up instantly, laughing. The bed was uncomfortable and Alice was lying too close to her; the heat of her body made Emmie long for cool water. She moved her limbs away from the valley in the middle of the bed and remembered, with pleasure, that Mr Sargent had promised her a swimming lesson. Mo chattered and pulled at her hair until the water came in her eyes; when she got up, he jumped to the windowsill where he froze, paws folded against his chest, nose snuffling the air. Emmie took her clothes on to the landing and dressed, looking out of the window.

Mr Sargent was in the next door garden, sitting in a deck chair and reading the newspaper. He was always up early in the morning. Emmie looked down at the top of his head; his hair was black and silky and he wore it rather long, like an artist. She leaned out of the window, half-terrified, half-hopeful that he would look up and see her. She always felt like that when she spied on him which she did quite often, watching him through a gap in the hedge, or from the roof of the boathouse.

She heard Mo chatter and Alice's sleepy voice, 'Get away, nasty little thing, get away . . .'

Emmie ran into the bedroom. She picked Mo up and he dived inside the neck of her dress, scratching her, and then lying quiet in the place he liked best, curled just above her waist and held securely by her belt.

Alice said, 'Wretched little beast. He woke me up.'

'There's no need to frighten him. He doesn't mean any harm.' She felt calm and happy and not at all angry with Alice, who looked frowsty and hot, lying in the crumpled bed.

Alice said, 'I don't want to go to school today. Emmie, will you write me an excuse note?'

'I wrote one for you last week. And the week before. It's not safe. Miss Clapp sees the excuse notes and she takes me for English. She knows my writing.'

'Make your writing different. Honest to God, Em, I feel like death warmed up.'

'I try to make it different. But the only way is to do it with my left hand. And that looks funny. Anyway, it's Whit Monday. No school.'

'Thank God for that.' Alice came wide awake instantly. She swung her legs over the bed; they were long and plump and white with a narrow blue vein running round the back of one of them. She yawned, stretched herself, voluptuously enjoying the process of waking up to a lazy day.

'I never saw anyone like you for enjoying doing nothing,' Emmie said.

Alice's eyes were like blue fire in the sun. 'I think I'll go to the pit to see Dickie after breakfast. The manager won't be there on a Whit Monday, only the men who are doing overtime.' She looked at Emmie. 'If you like, I'll take Oliver. He can ride in the skips.'

'He's not allowed. Insurance,' Emmie said primly. 'Anyway, you ought to do some jobs. It's your turn to feed the Muscovy.'

'All right,' Alice said.

'Careful with her water. You've got to put the basin upside down in the middle of the tin or the ducklings'll fall in and drown.'

'I know.' Alice said scornfully, 'They must be the most stupid birds in the *world*. Fancy ducks *drowning*.' She yawned, curled up on the bed and scratched at her ankles. Her feet were small and stubby with soft, puffy toes. Her eyes were half-closed like a cat's in the sun. In another minute, Emmie thought, she'll begin to purr. It was very warm and lazy and peaceful in the room.

Emmie said suddenly, 'Alice, I'm in love with Mr Sargent.' She didn't know what made her say it but she felt proud, a lovely, running excitement went through her, like water.

Alice went on scratching her foot. 'It's a stage.' Her voice was quite kind.

Emmie said, 'He's handsome, isn't he?'

'Too fat. And too old. I don't like old men.'

Emmie frowned. 'That's just your opinion. I think older men are nicer than boys, myself. They know more about things. They're more experienced.'

Alice stopped scratching. Her eyes blazed at Emmie. 'You haven't *done* anything, have you?'

'What do you mean?' Emmie said in an injured-innocent tone. Her breath came a little faster.

'Nothing,' Alice said quickly. There wasn't much she knew that Emmie didn't know, but the little she thought there was, was precious to her. 'Of course he wouldn't take any notice of you. You're just a kid.'

'I'm growing fast.'

'Like a boy. If you cut your hair you'd look just like a skinny boy. You're no more developed than Oliver.'

'Pig,' Emmie said. 'You pig.' She stumped out and went to the bathroom to cry, holding Mo tight against her until he squeaked. After a little, she felt better. She ran cold water into the basin and bathed her eyes.

When she came out on to the landing, her grandmother called to her. She opened her door. The old woman was lying on her back; the only part of her that wasn't flat as a board was the hillocky outline of her feet beneath the bed-clothes. Her white hair was loose and there was pink scalp showing between the strands; her cheeks were flushed and covered with little red threads like tiny wireworms.

Her head moved on the pillow as Emmie came in. Her mouth was a brownish colour and there was a yellow line above her upper lip. She said, 'Emmie, I want a glass of water.'

Emmie went to the bathroom and emptied the brushes out of the tooth mug and filled it with water. Her grand-mother's hand held the mug, shaking a little. She took two sips, then the water ran out of her mouth on to her chin. Emmie took the mug and put it on the night table. Her grandmother's eyes closed, she lay flat and said, 'The Lord giveth and the Lord taketh away.' Her voice was soft and even. Emmie felt very odd: a little frightened but chiefly bored and irritated. She wanted to leave the room but it didn't seem polite.

She said, 'Gran, are you ill?' but there was no answer from the bed.

'Isn't Gran getting up?' Oliver stood at the door of the room. He was wearing the top half of his pyjamas, his pale little tassel dangling between his thin legs.

'Be quiet,' Emmie said. 'She's sick.'

'I want my breakfast,' Oliver said. 'Is she going to die?'

'Get out of here,' Emmie said, scarlet in the face. She felt as if a hard, heavy fist had thumped her in the stomach. 'Get your clothes on.'

'I expect she's going to die,' Oliver said.

He scuttled out of the way as Emmie lunged at him and ran into his own room, banging the door. Emmie looked into her father's room but the bed was still made: he had not come home last night. The water was splashing in the bathroom; she thumped on the door and called out to Alice, 'Gran's ill. I'm going down to get her breakfast.'

She laid a tray with a cloth and the teapot and slices of bread. She put two pieces under the grill to toast. 'I want bacon,' Oliver said from the doorway. He was dressed and had smarmed his hair down with water so generously that the droplets ran down his forehead and soaked into his shirt. 'Not now,' Emmie said. 'Haven't I got enough on my plate? Have some bread and butter.' She cut two pieces, clumsily, and thrust them at him.

'Doorsteps,' he said disdainfully.

'You're getting too fussy. Go on, get out in the garden. It's a lovely day.'

Blue smoke rose from the grill, she snatched the toast away and scraped off the burnt part. There were some ragged robins in a jar on the windowsill; she put the jar on the tray and thought it looked nice.

Gran's eyes were closed. Emmie put the tray down on the bed and shook her gently by the shoulder. 'Look, I've brought your breakfast,' she said.

It was very hot in the room already and there was a musty smell. Emmie felt a little sick. She went to the dressing table. There was a pewter tray with hair pins and the little yellow pads her grandmother wore to puff out her hair, her coral and amber beads, a china pot with dead-white face powder in it and a silver-topped bottle of lavender water. Emmie opened a drawer, found a handkerchief and tipped a little of the toilet water on to it. She went back to the bed and touched her grandmother's forehead with the handkerchief. Her skin felt dry and rough; her hands, lying on the counterpane, were withered and light as dead leaves.

She opened her eyes. 'Emmie,' she said, in an ordinary voice.

'Are you better, Gran? I've made you some toast, nice and hot. I'll sit you up on the pillows and you'll be nice and comfy.'

She poured out a cup of tea, buttered a piece of toast. She thought: Gran isn't really ill, she's only had a bad night. She thought of Mr Sargent and the swimming lesson and willed her to feel better. She said encouragingly, 'You feel better now, don't you, Gran?'

'Just a little bit.' She smiled at Emmie.

Emmie wanted to talk to her. 'What was grandfather like, Gran?'

'What do you want to know for?' she grumbled. 'Oh – a big man, not fat, you know, but tall. Dark like a gypsy, black eyes, black hair. Weak character, couldn't stick to anything.'

'Did you love him very much?'

'I did my duty by him.'

Emmie thought of Mr Sargent. 'Did you want to die when *he* died?'

Mrs Bean sighed. 'He'd been ill a long time. I had the boys. Your father was a baby. It was no use me dying.' She pushed the tray off her knees and lay back on the pillow.

'Drink your tea, don't you want your nice tea?' Emmie said.

'Not just now. I'll lie a bit.' Her eyes had a lost, drifting look. Emmie took the tray and put it on the floor. Feeling suddenly hungry, she nibbled at the buttered toast. Then she went to look for Alice who was out of the bathroom and sitting on the edge of their bed, brushing her hair. She said, 'Gran's ill. And Dad didn't come in last night – I looked to see. She ought to have a doctor.'

They looked at each other. The Beans had never had a family doctor. Mrs Bean didn't believe in them. When the children were ill, she dosed them with herb teas that she brewed herself. Some of them were so nasty that they had learned to disguise most symptoms of ill health from her.

Emmie said, 'You saw a doctor when you had your tonsils out.'

'That was a specialist, silly, at the hospital. Dad took me.' She stood up and twisted her hair round her head in a long rope, pinning it high. 'We'd better ask Mrs Hellyer. She's always at the doctor's with her leg. She'll know what to do.'

'You'll have to look after Gran, then.'

'I'll take her temperature and tidy her up.' Alice's face shone. 'It'll be marvellous practice,' she said.

*

'I'll pop in at the doctor's when I go down for my shopping,' Mrs Hellyer said.

Mrs Bean gave a mocking ghost of a laugh. It was like the wind rustling through dry sticks. 'I've run down, Mrs Hellyer. Like an old watch. Did you ever know any doctor who could do anything about that?'

There was a yellowish tinge on the tight-drawn skin that reminded Mrs Hellyer of her mother, who had died of cancer. Maybe it wasn't that, maybe it was any one of a dozen other things. It didn't much matter. There was only one thing that mattered in the end. She smoothed the old lady's pillows with her scarred, puffy hands and tucked her up more firmly. 'Now you mustn't talk like that, dear. My doctor's a nice young man, takes no end of trouble. Not like the old one – bottle of pink medicine and out through the door before you can say knife . . .'

'I don't want any young whipper-snapper pushing me about.'

'Perhaps he'll just give you a nice tonic. You've fallen away something shocking. Don't eat more than a bird, I daresay.'

'I'm dying, Mrs. Hellyer.' The two women looked at each other. Mrs Bean's eyes held a gleam – faintly malicious – of humour. In Mrs Hellyer's, tears sprung.

'Now dear,' she said. 'We'll have you up and about in no time.' Even to her own ears, this had a hollow ring. Death-beds are not easily mistaken and Mrs Hellyer had sat beside a few.

'It's the children I mind for,' Mrs Bean said.

'It always is,' Mrs Hellyer said. 'I remember my own poor mother. But as I said to her – I said, God will provide.' The thought of herself, expressing this pious sentiment, brought the tears coursing down her cheeks. It meant more to Mrs Bean.

'I trust He will,' she said. 'I've brought them up in the fear of the Lord.'

'I know, dear,' Mrs Hellyer said respectfully. She wiped her eyes with the back of a grubby forefinger and added more practically, 'You don't have to worry about them, I'm sure. Their Dad'll see they're all right.'

'He's a weak man . . .'

'I don't know about that.' Mrs Hellyer knew all about weak men and she did not include Martin Bean in that category. 'Anyway, he's their Dad,' she said more firmly. Weak or not, in her opinion men should be given their rights as the dominant sex. She looked at the strong old face, the arched bone of the nose, the imperious, high forehead and thought: I bet she's been a tartar in her day. She said, 'And their mother'll be back, I daresay.'

'No,' Mrs Bean said. She coughed a little, with pain. The coughing exhausted her and Mrs Hellyer had to lean forward to catch what she said. 'My daughter-in-law's not fit. She's a whore. Not fit to live under the same roof.'

The word she had used shocked Mrs Hellyer deeply. It didn't sound right, coming from an old lady. She said, reproving but still gently indulgent, 'I'm sure you don't mean that really. You're just feeling bad. I tell you what I'll do – I'll pop downstairs and put the kettle on for a good cup of tea.'

*

Oliver was on the tow-path, squatting beside Mr Hellyer. They were both still and quiet, looking at a toad in the rough grass on the bank; its body was swollen, its legs stiff and straight so that it stood high on its toes, looking like a little table. 'Look,' Mr Hellyer whispered, and Oliver saw the grass snake, swimming just under the bank. He touched the toad and it inflated jerkily, its throat moving in and out like bellows. Mr Hellyer said softly, 'You see? He blows himself up so the snake can't get hold of him.'

Oliver touched the toad again, but this time nothing happened.

'The snake's gone away,' Mr Hellyer said. 'He won't do it again.' They watched the toad, deflating spasmodically. 'It's a wonderful thing to see. You don't often get the chance.'

Oliver looked at him, rapt. Mr Hellyer knew more about animals than anyone else in the world. He had been a gamekeeper's son, and until his father died had lived all his life in the country. He had seen things that Oliver longed to see.

He said, 'Tell me about the hedgehogs. Rolling on the apples.'

'I've never seen that,' Mr Hellyer said. 'But my grand-father did. He saw the old hedgehog rolling round among the windfalls early in the morning. All I ever saw was the apples with little sharp pinholes in them. You won't see it round here. No orchards.'

'I wish I could,' Oliver said. 'Tell me about poaching pheasants.'

'We only did that once, when I was a kid. Pinched some of my old Dad's plum brandy and soaked raisins in it and left 'em in the clearing. The old pheasant came along and in half an hour there he was, drunk as a bloody lord . . .'

'So you picked him up and chopped his head off?'

'That's right.'

'Did he run round after his head was chopped off? Gran says hens do that sometimes.'

'Maybe they do. But there's no need for you to think about that sort of thing,' Mr Hellyer said. Unlike his wife, he had rather prim ideas about what things were suitable for children's ears. He added, indulgently, 'Tell you what.

If you're a good boy I'll take you to see the badgers one day. There's a sett up on the common.'

'Round *here*?' Oliver's eyes were wide.

'I said so, didn't I? Funny things, badgers. You'll find them right up close to towns, sometimes. He doesn't care, the old badger.'

Oliver looked along the tow-path. 'There's Emmie. Don't tell *her*, will you? We can have a secret.'

Emmie and Nick were walking towards them, rolled towels under their arm. Mr Hellyer grinned amiably at them both. Nick saw a stocky, lively-looking man in a cloth cap and baggy trousers, who had bounced up from his haunches eager as a puppy. A fox terrier puppy, he thought, meeting the bright, inquisitive stare of the raisin eyes.

'We've seen a toad all puffed up,' Oliver said. 'So the snake couldn't get it. Mr Hellyer found it.'

'Kid likes that sort of thing.' Mr Hellyer winked at Nick, man to man. 'Got a passion for animals. Animals and hymn singing. I was brought up Methodist myself so I know a few. Get on well together, don't we, Olly?' He tweaked the boy's ear and Oliver looked at him with love. Mr Hellyer said, to Nick, 'The name's Hellyer. Bert Hellyer.'

'Mine's Sargent,' Nick said. 'How do you do?'

'Pretty well, thank you. You've got the Rapiers' house, haven't you? That's a nice place, all right.' Nick got the impression that he was running round them, wagging his tail, wriggling his hindquarters, barking his tinny flatteries, his dubious sincerities.

'We find it very comfortable, thank you.' It sounded stiffer than he meant. He said, to Oliver, 'We're going swimming. Want to come?'

Oliver looked at him, absently scratching his groin. 'No. My stomach's empty. I haven't had any breakfast.'

'Marjorie will give you some,' Nick said.

Oliver glanced at Mr Hellyer, who laughed. 'Off you go,' he said. 'Never refuse a free meal, that's my motto.' He grinned at Nick and Emmie. 'Bye-bye for now.'

They walked back towards the houses, the clownish little man and the thin child – watching him, Nick thought he looked thinner than he had done a month ago. 'Do you often go out without breakfast?' he asked casually.

'There isn't always time,' Emmie said. 'Alice is a lazy slug and Gran's not been well. We have to get to school and there's the rabbits and things to feed first.'

'You need feeding too. Children should have three square meals a day.'

She didn't answer: Nick saw in her face the struggle she always had with herself before she went in the water. Since that first morning at the gravel pit she had not once admitted her fear but she always looked white and tense and, although she could manage a few strokes now, she swam clumsily and jerkily, keeping her head high.

They ducked under the sagging wire and made their way round the back of the lake. Here there was a natural beach, bordered by a thin band of scrub: beyond it was the council rubbish dump. The lorries came and went on a service road near the town; on some days the bulldozer clanked back and forth, crushing the rubbish into the soft, orange earth. When the wind was in the west a sickly smell floated over the pits.

Emmie pulled at her blouse and Mo came to life. 'I'd no idea you had that animal with you,' Nick said.

Mo chattered at him from Emmie's shoulder. 'He doesn't like men. It's tobacco smoke. Put your pipe out.'

Nick put his pipe in his pocket obediently and the chattering died away.

'See?' Emmie said.

She stood, laughing at him, her arms brown against her

childish white vest, the squirrel peering round her neck. Suddenly she seized him and held him toward Nick. 'Kiss him,' she said.

The squirrel squeaked as Nick put his face close, a needle sharp nail caught the side of his mouth. 'Now kiss me,' Emmie said and bobbed against him, hardly a kiss, no more than a puppyish thrust of affection, but she turned scarlet. 'I'll get undressed,' she muttered and stalked off behind a bush.

Nick slipped off his clothes and edged his way into the water. He swam across the lake towards the silted-up island in the middle where a pair of swans nested. When he was tired, he turned on his back, spouting water.

Emmie was standing on the beach, hands crossed over her breast. 'Come on in, funky,' he called and swam towards her, a slow, lazy breast stroke.

She felt as she always did, not fear, but a kind of cold, dead calm, the way you might feel in a car in which the brakes have gone the moment before the crash. She went in slowly, gasping as the water crept up her thighs. She held on to a root that jutted out from the bank, clinging to it as long as she could, then letting go with a despairing moan and sinking, shoulder deep, in the water. She began to swim with her nervy, graceless stroke and Nick watched her sympathetically. She had achieved this much simply by courage; her mouth was screwed up, there was no pleasure in it. He swam up to her. 'Put your hands on my shoulders. We'll go out to the middle of the lake.'

'It's terribly deep,' she said, looking pinched.

He hesitated, then said firmly. 'You'll be quite safe.'

She shut her eyes briefly, then stretched out thin, trembling arms. Her hands, white to the knuckle-bone, rested lightly on his shoulders. He swam carefully, on his back. Her eyes were half-closed, her expression martyred.

Watching her, he was slightly nervous of what he intended to do.

In deep water, he said suddenly, 'Now swim on your own for a bit.'

She cried out. He twisted away from her, she went under, choked, and came up again. He was beside her holding her up but she pushed him away. 'I'm all right, I can swim,' she said.

'Go slow then, *relax*.'

He saw with pleasure that she looked cold but not frightened; she was beginning to swim more slowly and for the first time with trust, as if the water were a friendly and not an alien element. 'Good girl, you're doing fine,' he encouraged her, but she ignored him. Then, as they approached the bank, she drew a deep breath, dived, and came up beneath him, grabbing at his legs. He laughed and caught hold of her. She kicked and wriggled but he held her firmly and carried her out on to the bank.

'I wanted to pay you out,' she said. 'Beast – what a beastly thing to do to a poor girl. What a dirty, filthy *trick*.' Her hair was sleek with water, she looked skinned. She jumped at him, half-laughing, half-serious, and pummelled his bare chest. He held her at arm's length until his muscles ached. She was as strong as a little horse. She butted him in the chest with her head and he slipped in the mud and fell on his back. She lost her balance and fell on top of him, giggling. He gasped, winded, and she twisted off him quickly and sat up, legs drawn up to her chest, chewing her wet knee.

He rolled over on his elbow to get his pipe out of his trouser pocket, and lit it. For a while they were silent, letting the sun soak into them. Then Emmie said, 'I'm going in again, I'm all gritty.' She slid into the water and struck out across the lake with her new, easy stroke, her long hair floating like dark weed behind her. Just as he was beginning to get worried in case she had gone too far, she turned and swam back. Water streamed off her as she waded through the shallows; in spite of the sun, she was cold and shivering.

'Enough for one day,' he said, and threw her a towel. She rubbed at herself inneffectually and he had an impulse to do it for her; if Oliver had been with them, he would have dried them both, enjoying the feel of their lively, vigorous little bodies, but on her own, without Oliver, she seemed too grown-up, not a child any more. She put the towel round her shoulders and sat down beside him. She said, 'I never thought I'd do it. I never thought I'd be able to swim.'

'What made you so scared? Did anyone ever push you in or something?'

'No. I don't know.' She was sucking her knee again, staring thoughtfully over the lake. 'When I was small, I fell in the water butt. I would have drowned only the milkman found me. Gran said it was my mother's fault. But that's not true. She was up in her room, writing a book.'

He said gently, 'Has your grandmother always lived with you?'

She shook her head. 'It was after that she came. After I fell in the water butt. Gran said my mother wasn't fit to look after children. She didn't like her much. Dad says two women in a house always make trouble.'

Her matter-of-fact voice shocked him a little. He said, 'Do you miss your mother?'

She glanced sideways at him. 'I don't know. Gran's always been there . . .' Her expression was queer – panicky and somehow furtive. 'I'm frozen,' she mumbled. She stood up and ran over to the bush where she had left her clothes.

8

AFTER he had had breakfast with Marjorie, Oliver felt very comfortable. He had eaten cornflakes and eggs and bacon and toast and butter and drunk a pint of milk. He rounded off the meal with a bar of chocolate and went to look for Mr Hellyer. He liked to divide his spare time between the Sargents' house and the boat, equally indifferent to the ordered comfort of the one and the shabby squalor of the other. He liked Marjorie but Mr Hellyer was his soul-mate : their interests, in several ways, were similar.

But Mr Hellyer was nowhere around and Alice, when he went back to his own house, was busy. She was wearing the white apron she had for cookery classes at school and was tidying up the house because the doctor was coming. She gave Oliver sixpence to take a letter to Dickie.

He crossed the road and went into the gravel pit. There was only a skeleton staff on duty and no one took much notice of him. He stood by the plant for a while, listening to the noise of the big shaker where the shingle was washed and sorted through different sized screens into the hoppers. The lorries waited under the hoppers to pick up their loads and after a little, one of the lorry men told him to go away. Oliver scowled at him and went behind the plant, muttering a spell he had made up that morning. But nothing happened to the man; disappointingly, when his lorry was full he simply climbed into the cab and drove away.

Oliver walked away from the plant and followed the pipe-line down to the edge of the water. It ran across the lake to the pontoon. He walked out on to the pipe very slowly and carefully. He was very sure on his feet and there was enough rust on the pipe to make it gritty. In some places the water was deep, in others it was silted up in little, narrow islands of spiky, brown reeds. On one of the islands he saw a shaggy water rat; he shouted at it and it slid into the water and swam away with only the top of its head showing. When he got to the pontoon, he saw Dickie, sitting in the cabin working the winch that raised the end of the pipe, to clear it. Dickie's engineering text-book was open beside him. He didn't hear Oliver, there was too much noise on the pontoon from the engine and the pump. Oliver peered down the greasy ladder into the tiny engine room. There was a bench at one side of it with empty tea cups on it and some comic papers.

He went into the cabin and tugged at Dickie's arm. 'I've got a letter for you,' he said.

Dickie looked at him. 'Here Sid, take over, will you?' he shouted. A man came up the ladder from the engine room and Dickie opened his letter.

Oliver said, 'Gran's ill. Alice has got to stay and mind her.'

Dickie's glance was suspicious. 'How'd you get here?'

'Along the pipe.'

'Silly young fool,' Dickie said angrily. 'That's not allowed. The police'll be after you.' Oliver said nothing. Dickie said, 'If they catch you, they'll take you away and lock you up. Don't you know there are special prisons for naughty boys?' Oliver still said nothing. Dickie relented and pulled out a packet of mints from his pocket. 'Here,' he said. Oliver undid the packet and put two mints in his mouth, one in either cheek. Dickie jumped off the pontoon into the flat-bottomed boat moored alongside, and lifted Oliver down. He punted the few yards to the shore. He said, 'Tell Alice I'll see her this evening. The usual place. Can you remember that?'

Oliver said, 'Mr Hellyer went to prison, didn't he? What did he go to prison for?'

'You shut up,' Dickie said. His grey eyes were cold.

Oliver said. 'Do they beat you, in prisons?'

'I guess so,' Dickie said. He beached the boat and lifted the little boy on to the shore. Oliver felt so small in his hands that he was suddenly sorry for what he had said. You had to frighten kids to make them behave, but there was no need to scare them too much. He said, 'You won't go to prison. Not for walking the pipe, though the manager'ud tan your backside if he caught you. You only go to prison for stealing and things like that.'

'Do you go to prison for killing people?'

'Sometimes. If they don't string you up.'

Oliver's mouth hung open. Dickie thought he looked half-daft. 'Get along home,' he said. 'Now. Don't mess about at the plant.'

*

The district nurse had been, and the doctor. He said he would make arrangements for Mrs Bean to be taken to hospital, but that he would prefer to talk to her son first. Martin Bean did not come home. His mother slept. All afternoon there seemed to be nothing to do but wait.

Before lunch, and afterwards, Marjorie came to see if there was anything she could do. Her imagination was stirred by the thought of the three children alone in the house with a sick woman. That she was dying, neither she nor Nick suspected; all the same, Marjorie was eager to help and was disappointed because the two girls seemed so competent and unperturbed. On her second visit, Oliver fell down on the path and grazed his knee. He cried very loudly and Marjorie flew to him, with relief. The way he clung to her was very sweet. She said, 'Would you like to come to tea? If you like, you can spend the night with us.'

The idea pleased him. He stopped crying at once and

went to get his pyjamas and his tortoise box. He ate a large tea and Marjorie played snap with him until it was time for bed.

An hour after he had fallen asleep, he woke up, screaming. Marjorie went to him and took him on her lap. 'Does your knee ache?' she said. He shook his head and went on sobbing, his eyes tight shut.

'I want Emmie,' he said, at last.

'Emmie's busy,' she said, hurt. She went downstairs and brought up the only sweets she had in the house; a box of liqueur chocolates.

'Marjorie's here. Don't you love Marjorie?' she said, holding him close. He sighed and nodded, biting into a chocolate. The brandy trickled down his chin.

*

Mrs Hellyer's sister had come to visit her, turning up as she often did, without warning and in tears. 'Sometimes the house gets on top of her,' Mrs Hellyer explained when she dropped in to see how the girls were managing. 'Poor Nelly. She was never very strong as a girl – weedy little thing without any go in her. Now, since her husband turned the way he did, she's a martyr to her nerves.'

'Is that the one whose husband went for her with a chopper?' Emmie said, interested.

'That's right. He's out next Wednesday week – that's what's getting her down, really. She says she'll never feel comfortable with him again. I tell her – she's got to pull herself together. Not that I could ever do anything with Nelly, she's soft as they come and bone-idle. That was the trouble really – you should see her house. As I said to her, a man likes his house kept nice. What else does he keep a wife for? Bed's all right when you're young and silly but our Nelly's past it now.'

'Is her husband a very bad-tempered man?' Emmie said.

'Not him. He's more the quiet type. But they're the ones you have to look out for – they'll turn on you, sudden.'

'Oh,' Emmie said.

Mrs Hellyer looked at her. 'Sure you'll be all right now? I'd stay a bit till your Dad comes home if it wasn't for keeping Nelly company. She gets a bit down on her own.'

'We can look after Gran,' Emmie said.

*

At eight o'clock, Mrs Bean was still sleeping. Her face was flushed, her mouth slightly open, her teeth lying in a glass on the night table. She looked like a shrunken old witch, Emmie thought – so small, she had never seen a grown person look so small. Alice said they should leave her alone and sent Emmie into the garden to feed the rabbits and shut up the ducks. When she came back, Alice had changed into a cotton skirt and a white blouse that was too small for her. The sleeves cut into the flesh at her armpit. 'Oh God, I'd like some decent clothes,' she said, combing out her hair in front of the kitchen mirror.

'One of the ducklings is dead,' Emmie said. She had found the bedraggled black and yellow object floating in the flat tin of water in the Muscovy's run. 'It's your fault. You saw to them this morning. You didn't put the basin upside down in the water.'

Alice looked at her angrily. 'I suppose you always do everything right. I suppose you always do everything so right that you can't imagine making a mistake.'

Emmie didn't answer. She sat in her grandmother's chair with Mo on her lap. The old dog, William, lay with his head on her foot.

The kitchen seemed dark and enclosing. Alice felt stifled. She said, 'I'm going out for a bit to see Dickie.'

Emmie still said nothing. Alice walked to the door of the kitchen and saw her sitting there, wooden and silent, two spots of colour high up on her cheeks. 'I won't be long,' she said guiltily. 'There's nothing to do. If Gran wakes, she'll only want a glass of water.'

'Go to hell,' Emmie said.

*

She sat in the chair, keeping very quiet and still. Usually she liked being alone in the house, but this evening was different and not just becuse Gran was ill upstairs. She didn't know why she felt so scared. It was as if the house was slowly coming inwards, pressing down on her. The house was old; her father had said it was about time it was pulled down. He had said that it was neither functional nor aesthetically pleasing and that there was death-watch beetle in the roof. Emmie imagined the beetles busy in the roof, gnawing away at the rafters. Sometime, perhaps tonight, the roof would fall in and the house would collapse. They would all be buried under the beams and the walls and the plaster.

Mo slept in a ball on her lap. Emmie stroked him, but he did not wake up. She thought that she had always believed Mo was better company than any person could ever be; now she saw she had been wrong. She wanted someone to talk to, not just a squirrel or a dog snuffling at her feet. If only Oliver had not fallen over on the path he would not have gone to spend the night with Marjorie and Mr Sargent. Mr Sargent had told her to call him Nick and she had tried, but it didn't come easily. She thought of him as Mr Sargent. She whispered his name over and over: Mr Sargent, Mr Sargent. She wanted to talk to him in a way she had never wanted to talk to anyone before, but he was next door, not here. He was too far away to hear, even if she shouted at the top of her voice. Panic swept over her, squeezing out every other emotion. She crouched forward in the chair, her muscles stiff, as if she had been sitting in the cold for a long time.

She stood up and went slowly upstairs. The only person there was Gran, and she was asleep, but it would be better to be with her than downstairs in the kitchen, alone. She opened the door cautiously. It was dusk; the whiteness of the bedcover shone in the gloom. Emmie tiptoed to the far side of the bed and switched on the lamp. It pushed the night back and made a warm, yellow circle to sit in.

Mrs Bean was awake. She turned her head on the pillow and smiled at Emmie. 'There you are, Harriet,' she said.

Emmie looked at the small, waxy face and felt that she did not know her grandmother any more. 'I'm not Harriet,' she said, puzzled, half-resentful. Her voice sounded very loud. 'I'm Emmie.'

But Gran did not take it in. 'I'm sorry I broke your doll,' she said. Her voice sounded very young and light. Her eyes gazed at the yellow light on the ceiling. 'The sun's come out,' she said.

'It's only the little lamp,' Emmie said. She sat in the wicker chair beside the bed and began, after a little, to feel comfortable and sleepy. It was nice, sitting here beside Gran. The smell in the room wasn't bad any more. The district nurse had tidied the bed and sprinkled the sheets with lavender water; the smell was her grandmother's smell, old and powdery and sweet.

Mrs Bean said, 'Harriet, will you read to me?'

Emmie got up, trying not to creak the chair. 'What do you want me to read, Gran?'

There were two books on the table. One was her grandmother's Bible with a tasselled, leather book mark in it, the other was an American thriller from the library. It had a picture on the cover of a red-headed girl with a green face. There was a pair of hands round her throat, throttling her. Emmie said, 'Do you want me to read a piece out of your Bible, Gran?'

Gran was still staring at the ceiling. Her mouth was a little open and there was a watery trickle running out of the side of her mouth. She said something – Emmie could not hear what it was. She bent over the bed. Her grandmother closed her eyes and said, quite loudly, 'Lord Jesus, I come to Thee.'

Emmie screamed, but the scream was inside her. There was no sound or echo of a sound in the room. She began to back slowly away from the bed towards the door. When she reached it, she felt behind her for the handle. She had the feeling that if she turned her back, something black and fearful would leap at her throat. She opened the door, keeping her eyes on the patch of darkness beyond the lamp. Something moved – she was sure something moved – between the wardrobe and the chest of drawers. She moaned and ran out of the room, slamming the door behind her.

The house was pitch dark. The landing window was cobalt-blue velvet, set with stars. She was afraid to move; on all sides she was menaced by the half-open doors of empty rooms. Below, in the kitchen, William whined to go out, a gentle, quivering, undemanding sound that meant, nevertheless, a fairly urgent need. But she could do nothing about it; she was frozen, inside and out. She stood on the landing, maybe a minute, maybe half an hour, staring at the window. Then, suddenly, the dim blue light was blotted out. She began to scream, high, sharp screams that tore at her chest and hurt her throat.

Martin Bean said, 'Emmie – Emmie, for heaven's sake . . .'
He raced up the last few stairs and took her in his arms.

9

Mrs Bean died in hospital the next day, in the late afternoon. Her son was at her bedside. She did not regain consciousness at any point; it was almost, he thought bitterly, as if it were not worth her while to say goodbye to *him*. For most of the day he sat beside her in stunned reflection. Though he was concerned for his children, he made no plans for the future. There were too many memories and resentments stored up inside his mind and while he sat there, waiting for her to die, he thought about them.

He had been her youngest son; when he was born his two elder brothers were nearly grown, twelve and fourteen, and his father was already an invalid, dying in a nursing home on the south coast. Martin had a dim recollection of a visit to a big, dark house surrounded by evergreens and of a cold, high-ceilinged hall where he had been sat to wait. He turned the pages of an old magazine that was filthy with a skin of grease that came off on his fingers. At the end of the hall there was a door that stood open, disclosing a dilapidated lavatory. If he saw his father on that occasion, Martin did not remember it; all that remained whenever he thought about him was an oppressive feeling of fear and dread associated with this house that had seemed to him dark and prison-like, smelling of dust and disinfectant and wet towels and blocked lavatories – a kind of compound reek of disease and poverty.

When he asked about his father, his mother told him he had been a drunkard and a scoundrel. He accepted this – he was too young to do anything else – but he hated her for saying it. When she warned him that if he was not careful he would grow up like his father, he felt rage and shame and dismay. He took his revenge by telling himself that she was a cruel and wicked woman to let his father die in that dreadful place. Even when he was older and realized that the nursing home had probably not been as bad as his childishly fastidious senses remembered it and that, anyway, she could not have afforded anything better, he was still unable to forgive her.

It comforted him to have some definite complaint against her; everything else he felt was so vague and somehow shameful. He believed she did not love him because he was like his father but he could not blame her for this because he knew he was unlovable. He was lazy, he wasted his time, he was an ugly, pale little boy with a permanently running nose. Worse still, he was ungrateful: everyone told him that his mother had had a hard life, that she worked her fingers to the bone, but it meant nothing to him. The knowledge of his own ingratitude convinced him that he was wicked and worthless.

All his childhood he had been frightened of his own shortcomings. He was also physically frightened of his mother. She was a powerful voice and an iron hand: she brought up her sons to be, in her own phrase, Soldiers in Christ's Regiment. It was a terrible sin for his elder brothers to smoke or drink, or for Martin to go to bed unwashed or with his homework undone. She had forced him to live against the grain of his own nature which was weak and pleasure-loving and stubborn with it, so that when she beat him for laziness or lying, he became more determinedly idle and sullen. He was a bright boy, good at his lessons, but she told him that cleverness was only a virtue if you worked hard and used it to good purpose. He remembered the summer that he had failed his last school examination. His mother had been singing with a company playing in a northern seaside town and he had lain on his bed in the boarding house, biting his nails, sunk under a terrible inertia. It seemed to him now, that she had planted inside him the dark seed of failure: that from it, everything else had flowered, his inability to keep a job, his uselessness, his drinking, his failed marriage.

It had always astonished him that his children were not afraid of her; now he saw that it was the gulf of the generation between them. It wasn't just that she had grown older and softer or that they were harder than he had been. It was just that she was not a parent but their grandmother, whose character was fixed and unalterable. They accepted her as she was. Her rigidity, the granite outcrops of her joyless faith were part of the scenery of their lives: they simply went round them.

He sat by his mother's bed, biting the skin at the side of his nails, and thought that of all the grudges you bear, the grudges you bear against your parents are the ones you live with always – you cannot fight them any more than you can fight heat or cold or some virulent infection in the blood.

*

Emmie said, 'I ought to go home. Dad'll want some supper.'

'Marjorie will see he has something. Don't worry.'

Emmie yawned. 'I ought to go though. Have you finished your letters?'

'Yes. The rest can wait.'

She was sitting on the sofa, surrounded by old copies of the *New Yorker*. She looked very pale, there were coaly smudges under her eyes. Nick said, 'It must be nice to be so young that when you're tired it only makes you look prettier.'

It was the first compliment anyone had ever paid her. She acknowledged it with a shy, ducking movement of her head and a slight deepening of colour on her vase-shaped cheekbones.

She said, 'If you've finished your letters, can I post them?'

'They're mostly postcards and I've only got threepenny stamps.'

'Gran used to put threepenny stamps on postcards. She said it – it helped the government.'

'Not many people feel like that about the government.'

'Gran did. She said they had an awfully difficult job and we ought to help them as much as we could. Putting extra stamps on postcards was one thing she did, and collecting used envelopes. And not using too much water. She said being extravagant with water was awfully unfair . . .' Her eyes were dilated with tiredness.

Nick said, 'You're getting garrulous. What you need is sleep. Why don't you tuck down with Oliver? There's room.'

'I couldn't go to sleep.'

'I'll get you a hot toddy.'

'That's whisky, isn't it?'

'A little whisky. Not much for the young. Mostly lemon juice and hot water and sugar.'

She looked worried. 'Gran didn't like people to drink. But I think I'd like a cigarette.'

He frowned. 'I'm not sure that's a frightfully good idea. are you?'

'Because I might get lung cancer? You have to die sometime, don't you? Gran didn't smoke and she didn't drink.' Her tears came slowly and painfully, in the middle of them, she yawned.

Nick said, 'She was very old, darling, and tired.'

'I hadn't talked to her properly for weeks. It just seemed a bore she was ill. There was so much to do.'

He sat beside her and held her. She shook in his arms. 'I've made your shirt all wet. Salt water. Does salt water stain?'

'I've no idea.' He wanted to say something to comfort her. 'Everyone always feels bad when someone they love dies. There's always something you think you could have done or something you could have said. Here – blow your nose.'

She took his handkerchief and blew. She said in a muffled voice, 'It seems so awful that people grow old and die and no one remembers what they were like. Gran was lovely – I know she was old and had awful clothes, but everyone loved her and she had a lovely face, like a statue.'

He chuckled softly. 'You are a romantic child, aren't you?' She looked at him doubtfully and he added, with an odd little spurt of irritation, 'You really believe your grandmother was wonderful, don't you?'

She said stubbornly, 'She *was*. It's not just me . . .' She looked anxiously into his face. 'It's hard to explain, just telling you like this. I wrote it down in my Diary, it's much easier to write things.'

He said, contrite, 'I wish you'd let me read your diary sometime.'

'Would you like to, really?'

He nodded gravely. She gave a deep sigh. 'You can if you like. No one else has read it. I started it – I mean I started the nature part – for my mother.' The colour rose in her face suddenly. He waited for her to go on, he did not want to question her. But all she said was, 'You've been so nice to me – Oh, you're so *nice*.'

He felt guilty, a little sad. 'I'm glad you think so. But

being nice is hardly a virtue, you know. It's something you do to please yourself.'

*

Marjorie said, 'Emmie wants to come home.'

Martin Bean was sitting at the kitchen table. His tie was loose and he was in his shirt sleeves. His eyes were glassy with gin.

'So you've come to see if I'm in a fit state to come home to, is that it?'

'You might have wanted to be alone.'

'My – aren't we tactful? It doesn't matter, you know. Emmie's seen me drunk before.'

'Yes, I guessed that. Though what she *said* was that you sometimes had what she called 'bad turns'. I think she hoped we'd think it was a kind of illness.'

Martin grinned. 'Good old Em. My favourite Dickensian character. Dad goes off to the gin shop, gallant daughter stays up to put the old soak to bed.' His grin faded. 'I'm a flop, you know. A failure from beginning to end. As a father as well as everything else.'

Marjorie hesitated. She was not nervous of Martin Bean. It was impossible to be nervous of someone you were sorry for, and she was sorry for him. She said, 'I think I'll have a drink too.'

He raised his eyebrows in a way that was neither friendly nor unfriendly, simply negative. 'Help yourself.' He pushed the bottle across the table but made no move to get her a glass. She went uncertainly to the dresser and fetched a dusty tumbler.

He said, 'My wife kept this house going for years. Then my mother took over. She had some money – not much. It ran out. I drink everything I earn, which doesn't make me much of a drunk I might tell you.' He looked at her

124

and said in a hard voice, 'I don't suppose you know what it's like to feel simply damned useless.'

'Yes I do,' she said.

As soon as she had spoken, she felt embarrassed. It sounded false. Perhaps because *she* was false, she thought, frightened. She thought of the dream she had sometimes in which she was leaning over a bridge and watching herself drown, watching herself slip down under the clear water and not giving a damn. She said awkwardly, 'I mean, it sometimes helps to know other people feel the same way.'

He said, 'Thank you.' His tone was stiff, a little surprised.

She forced herself to think of how he must be feeling. 'I'm terribly sorry about your mother.' She saw his glass was empty and filled it. He looked at her vaguely, but did not drink.

He said, 'I think I ought to tell you that I do not grieve for my mother.' It sounded oddly formal. He added, 'I don't want your sympathy on false pretences.'

'I'm sorry,' she said absurdly.

Their eyes met and he laughed a little. 'Have another drink.' She felt that the atmosphere between them was suddenly much easier although he said nothing for a moment but kept on looking at her as if he were turning something over in his mind. Finally he said, in a burst of indignation – or sadness – or both, 'She broke up my marriage. She hated Clemence.'

The intense, personal feeling in his voice shocked her. Since her illness, other people had become shadowy to her, characters in a book or a play. They had no real existence except as and when their lives touched hers. Even Nick had become someone who could never be hurt – to be treated as a child treats a parent, with love but without consideration. She had been so deeply involved with her own emotions that she had lost the imaginative sense that is necessary if you are to see other people as independent entities, locked in their private worlds. Sitting in the Beans' kitchen that sense began to come back to her; not suddenly but slowly, a slow prickle of pity and curiosity, like life returning to a deadened limb. 'Tell me,' she said.

'Tell you what?'

'Why did your mother hate your wife?'

'She despised helpless women. That's one reason. And my poor Clemence was about as helpless a female as you'd find in a long day's march.' He grinned. 'I daresay that's what appealed to me.'

'When did you meet her?'

'Just after the war. I had a job in television. I interviewed her for a nature programme. She was so scared she could barely utter – you've no idea. The programme was a shambles and I took her out to dinner to cheer her up. It turned out that she needed it. She wasn't just scared of the cameras, she was scared of everything – scared to go home. She loosened up after she'd had a bit to drink and told me about it. She had a husband, a great brawny brute of an ex-R.A.F. pilot who knocked her about. *And* her child. Funny – I remember that I was more shocked about the child. That was Alice. Anyway – to cut a long story short, she flattered my masculine vanity.' He blinked his boiled eyes and looked suddenly shy. 'Or to cut it even shorter, I fell in love. She lived with me while we waited for her divorce. That's what started it, I suppose – the way my mother felt about her. She wouldn't meet her until we were married. Whenever she met *me* she talked about her as your "fancy woman".'

'If she felt like that, then why did you have her to live with you?'

He said simply, 'I didn't have any choice. I'd thought

Clemence was helpless, but then any girl would've been, in the fix she was in. What I didn't know – what the situation disguised, if you like – was that the poor girl really *was* helpless, plain silly when it came to anything practical. She simply couldn't keep house – not that that mattered so much – but she couldn't cope at all with the children. It wasn't that she didn't love them – or *want* to – she just couldn't. You know, in a way I think she was just bewildered by how long the human young hang about the nest. She knew a lot about birds – she'd have been perfectly able to do a short stint, teaching them to fly and so forth. But she just forgot – she'd forget to change their nappies, she'd even forget to feed them. We had a succession of God-awful nannies we couldn't afford – Clemence's books hadn't started to sell at that point – but the upshot was that I left for work late, came home early. I wasn't in the sort of job where you could do that, so I lost it. Then there was a patch when I tried free-lancing, then my father-in-law died and we moved down here. He didn't leave any money, but he'd paid the rent in advance for six months. That was nine years ago, just before Oliver was born. Clemence was ill, my mother came to help and stayed. It seemed the obvious answer – she was old, she needed a home, if she was there Clemence could write her books – go off on her trips. Only it didn't work. It was bloody hell.'

Marjorie said, 'But surely, once your wife started to make money – she *does* make money, doesn't she? – surely your mother couldn't complain about her being helpless any more?'

He laughed shortly. 'My mother had earned money all her life and brought up three children at the same time – seen their noses were wiped and their morals sound. Besides, by the time Clemence was doing well, the pattern was set.

She thought Clemence an incompetent fool. The only difference her success made was that she thought her an incompetent fool who was lucky enough to make a bit of money.' He looked at her vaguely as if he wasn't sure who she was or what she was doing there. 'I see now, of course. Half the time it wasn't Clemence she was getting at – it was me. I was her oafish idiot of a son who couldn't be expected to make a success of anything – not even of his marriage.'

'It sounds an abominable situation. Couldn't you have done something . . .'

He said tiredly. 'People live with abominable situations all their lives. Anyway, what could I have done? Told my mother to get out? Where could she have gone? She'd got a pathetic little bit in the Post Office – she helped us all out from time to time – but not enough to set up anywhere. Anyway – apart from any chivalrous instincts I might or might not have, I've never done anything so decisive in my life. I just hoped things would get better. When they didn't, I just drank a little more. Isn't that more or less how most people go on?'

He looked at his big, hammy hands, lying loosely on the table and suddenly doubled them into fists. 'Of course I should've done something, think I don't know it? Only I was just scared – I could have broken her in two with my bare hands and I was scared to death of her. If I'd ever done anything – made anything of myself more than a third-rate free-lance – it might've been different. But if I got mad sometimes, shouted at her, it was just bluff. And she knew it. So did Clemence. She thought she'd married a pair of muscular, sheltering arms and what she'd got was a snivelling kid still frightened of Mummy. Not that she really complained. Partly because she was a bloody saint – I *mean* that – and partly because it wasn't, really, so important to her. She'd got her work – chasing round the world after birds – and that was what she cared about. She tolerated my mother because the children loved her and that left *her* free, d'you see?'

'Do you mean she was glad her children loved someone else? I'm afraid I can't understand a woman like that,' Marjorie said.

'I'm not asking you to,' he said coldly. Then he looked at her and smiled in a shamefaced way. 'Sorry. Only I loved her – you've no idea.' He seemed fascinated by his hands; he was flexing the fingers rhythmically and gazing at them as if they could tell him something important about himself. 'I thought she loved me, in her funny way. Until a few months ago.'

Marjorie said softly, 'And then?'

'Oh – she went off.' He took his hands off the table and thrust them into his pockets.

'For good?'

'Yes.' He stared at her almost angrily, as if she had trapped him into a confidence he would have preferred not to have made. 'I don't blame her. Nobody in their senses'ud blame her. Only I couldn't believe it. I'd never guessed – she went off with someone else, d'you see, I'd never guessed she wanted that.' His voice was loud with grief and anger. 'She'd never wanted *me*, not for years. She'd turn her head away when I kissed her. I've seen her kiss a dog. It made me feel sick – as if I'd had a clout in the stomach.' He stood up abruptly and went into the scullery. She heard him turn on the tap and drink a glass of water noisily. He came back, blundered against the table, and stood by the window, staring out. He said huskily, 'The kids don't know. She's in East Africa – not due back for a couple of months. So there's no need for them to know.'

'You'll have to tell them some time.'

'No,' he shouted. '*No.*' He turned to her. 'I can't tell them – it's a terrible thing. A terrible thing for children to know. What do I tell them? Your mother's a bitch . . . ?' He leaned on the table and bent forward, his face very close to hers. 'I tell you – it would be better if she were dead. I'd rather she was dead. I didn't blame her, I told you I didn't, but when she told me I could've killed her . . . I wanted to . . . oh God how I wanted to . . .'

For a moment, Marjorie was frightened. He was standing, his head sunk between his shoulders, his red face beaded with sweat. He looked dangerous, like a bull. It was true, she thought; in spite of his gentle, drunken ineffectiveness, he could easily be a violent man.

Then he began to cry. At first she couldn't believe it; she had never seen a man cry before. Fear left her and she was filled with tenderness. He was crying because he was hurt, because someone he loved had hurt him. He didn't care what she thought, he had no defences, he wasn't proud.

Not like Nick. Nick was too reasonable, too cold. She had never once seen him cry, not even when the baby died. He had never felt anything like this – he was a lay figure, a lump of synthetic wax beside this man who had the humanity to cry. Tears were a kind of emotional richness that only a man who was really warm and human could afford. Suddenly, she wanted to hold him in her arms and feel his warmth against her. It would be like the blessed relief of a coal fire after the dull, dry heat of an electric bar . . .

She stood up and went to him, putting her hand gently on his arm. She was trembling with an odd mixture of pity and sexual excitement. She leaned her head against his shoulder, wanting him to kiss her. He did kiss her, on her forehead, and then stroked her hair gently, as if she were a child or a kitten. She said, 'Martin, I'm so sorry – I can't help. I'm such a fool.'

'You're all right,' he said. 'You're a bloody marvel, a marvellous girl.'

His fingers tightened on her head for a second and then released her. He muttered, 'We'd better go and fetch Emmie.' He took out his handkerchief and blew his nose loudly. 'Sorry about all this,' he said. 'I'm a maudlin, pot-bellied old fool.'

*

Alice said, 'Dickie was ever so kind. He took me to the pictures.'

'How could you? On a day like this . . .' Emmie was deeply shocked. Someone might have seen Alice there.

'It was a sad picture. Not a comedy.' Alice's voice shook a little. 'I had to do something, didn't I? You had the Sargents making a fuss of *you*.'

'All right. As long as Dad didn't know. He'd be *mad*.'

'I don't see that going to the pictures is any worse than getting drunk. And he didn't know. I came in when he was next door, fetching you.' Alice added, rather pathetically, 'I don't see why you should think you mind more about Gran than anyone else.'

Emmie felt guilty because she did think that. She felt in the bed for Alice's hand and squeezed it, to make amends. They lay for a little, amicably holding hands.

Alice said generously, 'Perhaps it is worse for you and Oliver, really. After all, Gran wasn't my real grand-mother.'

To Emmie this remark seemed both heartless and smug. It left her speechless.

Alice said, 'And – it's awful, I know, but I can't help *thinking*. I can't help thinking it'll be nicer now, when

Mother comes back.' She waited for a minute and then added, apologetically, 'Gran was foul to her, you know that.'

Emmie stared into the darkness with hot eyes. This was something she could hardly bear to admit. She had loved her grandmother; she had tried to believe, as an article of faith, that she loved her mother equally. Whenever the two women were together, the conflict of loyalties had torn her in two. She muttered, 'They just didn't get on. It wasn't anyone's fault.'

'All right, have it your own way,' Alice said, quite kindly. She had no interest in abstract justice and there was no other reason for arguing about it. She added, 'All the same, it *will* be nicer, won't it?'

'Perhaps she won't come back.'

'Why ever not?' said Alice, simply surprised.

Emmie's mouth was dry. She licked her lips. 'She hasn't written, has she, not since she went off, just before Christmas?'

'She doesn't, often. She can't. Do you think there are post offices in the jungle?' said Alice, whose geography was bad.

Emmie felt frightened as if she were just going to jump into deep water. She said, 'Do you remember when she went last time? We went to bed – she was going to catch a plane and Dad said it was too late for us to go to the air-port. Well – there was an awful row . . .'

'What's new about that? They were always having rows.'

Emmie didn't answer.

Alice sighed, turned over in bed like an old seal, and plumped up her pillow. 'Well – *I'm* going to sleep,' she said, and did. Emmie thought she could probably go to sleep in less time than anyone else in the world.

She slept deeply; sometimes she gave a comfortable

little sigh. Emmie lay stiff and still beside her. The night hung over her like a big, umbrella, black and stifling.

*

The thing that had woken her, that night, was Oliver crying. When she got out of bed, she found him sitting on the top stair, listening to Dad and Mother downstairs in the kitchen, and crying. He wouldn't go back to bed. She had tried to pick him up but he had clung to the banister rail like a leech and butted her in the chest with his head. He was always like that when there was a row – he cried, he didn't want to hear, yet somehow he had to listen. Emmie understood that. It was always better to know what was going on than to lie in bed with the door shut and wonder what was happening. So she stayed with him, on the dark landing, holding his shivering little body and trying to comfort him. The row went on and on. They listened, frozen. They couldn't hear what Mother said most of the time, but Dad was shouting. He said terrible things; Emmie wanted to stop her ears and couldn't. She prayed to make them stop, please God, make them stop.

It was very cold. After a little while, Oliver was so cold that he couldn't hold on to the banisters any more. She picked him up in her arms and carried him back to bed. He was very tired and yawning. When she tucked him up, he said, 'Perhaps he'll kill her. Someone was hanged yesterday for killing someone. I read it in the paper.'

She scolded him. 'You shouldn't read the newspapers, a little boy like you – all about prison and that. It's silly to read about wicked people.'

'It's true,' he said stubbornly. 'It's true what you read in the newspapers.'

'Oh shut up and go to sleep,' she said.

She left him and went back to the landing to listen. It

was suddenly terribly quiet and she was frightened. She thought about what Oliver had said and how silly he was and then she thought that things *did* happen, and not just to wicked people. Mrs Hellyer and her family were not wicked people: she knew them. She waited on the landing a long time, hating the awful quietness and longing for them to start shouting again so that she would know everything was all right. When she was so cold that her bare feet began to stick to the linoleum, she went back to bed and tried to stay awake. She wanted to stay awake to listen for the taxi coming to take them to the airport. If she heard the taxi, then she would know everything was all right. But the taxi didn't come.

In the morning, everything was just as it always was when Mother went away; much pleasanter, with nobody quarrelling even in that dreadful quiet way of just looking and going out of rooms when other people came into them, and Gran told them several good long stories in the evening. It was as if nothing special had happened the night before – no more than a bad dream that stays at the back of your mind long after you have woken up. The only thing that happened was that Dad came into the kitchen where Oliver was crying because someone had broken the jar in which he kept his stick insects and said, 'What's the matter, old chap? Moping after your mother?' Oliver hadn't said anything but he looked at Emmie.

It was difficult to know what she really believed – if, indeed, she believed anything. She merely had a dark and formless and terrible idea. She dwelt on it remarkably little, she never mentioned it to Oliver and he never said anything to her. It was the best thing to be quiet and say nothing – to push it all away into a dark place like the cupboard under the stairs so it could be forgotten like an old raincoat or last summer's shoes.

10

OLIVER said in a distraught voice, 'Henry's got tonsilitis. His eyes are all gummy. I gave him a piece of tomato.'

'Shouldn't give him too much tomato,' Emmie said. 'It'll make him loose.'

'He didn't eat it.'

'Oh *God*,' Alice said. She had been painting her nails; she spread out her hands, like plump white starfish, to admire the finished effect. Her hair was done up in fat rollers and there were white dabs of anti-wrinkle cream under her eyes. In front of her, on the kitchen table, there was a collection of tiny bottles and tubes. For over a year she had been cutting out coupons from magazines and sending off for make-up samples that she had kept hidden in a small suitcase in the boathouse; since her grandmother's death she had brought them indoors and experimented openly, primping all day long, leaving streaks of grease everywhere, on the table cloth, on the bathroom shelves.

'It's a wonder you didn't wear lipstick to Gran's funeral.' Emmie picked up a jar and sniffed suspiciously. 'Hormone cream,' she read in disgust. 'That's for old women over thirty.'

'You can't start too soon to take care of your skin,' Alice said. 'You can have this foundation if you like. It's the wrong colour for me. I need more of a magnolia colour.'

'I don't want to make a spectacle of myself, thank you very much.'

'Prig,' Alice said. She began to fit her cosmetics into a lacquer box.

'That's *Gran's* box.' Emmie gazed at her reproachfully.

'Dad said I could have it. There's no sense in just keeping things . . .'

'*Oh.*' Emmie choked and went red.

Oliver said loudly, 'Don't either of you care about Henry?' Tenderly, he put the smaller of his two tortoises down on the floor. 'His poor throat's so sore. He ought to see a vet.'

'Mad,' Alice said. 'Raving mad. It's pitiful.' She escaped into the garden with an incredulous sigh.

Emmie rounded on Oliver. 'Who d'you think's going to pay for it?'

'Don't be mean. You can't just let Henry be ill. He might *die.*'

Emmie said, 'I can't ask Dad for money for a *vet*. For a *tortoise*. We owe the milkman for three weeks. And the grocer. He sent a bill.'

Tears stood in Oliver's eyes. Emmie felt sorry for him and angry at the same time because he made things so difficult.

She said, 'You just don't see all the things there are to do in a family. It costs so much – do you know what you eat costs? And then clothes and shoes and the dinner money for school . . .'

Oliver said, 'If I don't have any breakfast for a week, would that pay enough to get the vet for Henry?'

'I don't know. Anyway, you can't not eat breakfast because then you'd be ill.' Suddenly a black rage burned up in her. 'If you keep asking for things you'll be too expensive to keep – we'll all just starve to death or you'll have to be sent away to a Home where they'll lock you up. They won't let you have your tortoises there, you won't be able to have anything.'

'I could have a mouse. Prisoners have mice. They feed them with crumbs and make friends with them.'

'Only in dungeons. They don't have dungeons in children's Homes. Or mice. It wouldn't be hygienic. They block up the holes and kill the mice with poison.'

Oliver was fairly proof against Emmie's attempts to frighten him but this ingenious touch was too much. The look on his face made Emmie feel bad and ashamed. But it was a good thing to scare him, just a little, from time to time. He got spoiled with Mrs Sargent always buying him things and everyone letting him do what he wanted. If she didn't try and make him behave, no one else would.

He said, 'I'll ask Marjorie. She'll let me have the money for the vet.'

'You're not to. If you do I'll – I'll break your arm.' She advanced on him threateningly and he retreated behind the table.

'She won't want Henry to be ill. She loves Henry.'

'She doesn't, then. She only pretends, to please you. And you mustn't ask her, anyway. She's done enough for us, taking us out and giving us tea and things.'

'She's much nicer than you,' Oliver said. He grabbed his tortoise, ducked her swinging arm and ran out of the room, up the stairs.

Chasing him, she banged her funny bone on the doorpost. She came back into the kitchen, rubbing her elbow. It ached, her head ached. It had been very hot all day; they had had exams in the morning and she had done badly because she felt so tired. She felt tired a lot of the time. Sometimes she went to sleep in class because she got up so early to get everything done. Alice was supposed to help but she always woke up too late because she had been working for her exam; Emmie had to shake her for nearly five minutes before she came up, moaning, out of a deep well of sleep. Mrs Hellyer only came once a week and though Dad did some of the housework, shuffling round in the mornings and yawning, almost everything had a skin of dust over it and smelt mouldy, like furniture stored in an attic. It didn't really matter, of course. Emmie only minded because sometimes when Marjorie came in she looked round her in a funny way, sharp and frowning and asked Dad if Mrs Hellyer couldn't come more often. Emmie was always frightened that he would say they couldn't afford it and try to borrow money, but usually he just laughed and said there wasn't any need, the girls could manage.

After that, Emmie tried hard to keep the big kitchen clean; Marjorie could hardly go poking round the rest of the house to see what it looked like. She was washing the flagged floor one Saturday afternoon when Marjorie came in with a basket. 'Emmie, darling, I've brought you some vegetables.'

'Vegetables?' Emmie said bewildered, regarding a purplish bundle of asparagus, a crisp Webb's Wonder. Beside them, on the table, was the remains of their lunch, a packet of sliced bread, a dish of butter and an empty tin of Grade Three salmon. Marjorie carefully avoided looking at them. She said, 'Emmie dear, do you have to scrub the floor on a hot afternoon like this?'

'I like it,' Emmie said quickly. 'Mrs Hellyer can't get down to it because of her leg, but it's all right. I love scrubbing floors.'

Marjorie laughed, and though she was very kind, washing the lettuce and leaving it ready in the colander and telling her how to cook the asparagus and make a butter sauce, Emmie felt humiliated. When Marjorie went back into her own garden, Emmie stood at the door and heard her say, 'Nick, it's too ridiculous, they can't go on like this, that child's worn out. Really, their mother ought to be told – Nick, you must speak to Martin . . .' Mr Sargent had said something then and she lowered her voice so that Emmie couldn't hear her any more.

Emmie had stood in the doorway, biting her nails. Then she had gone into the garden and played cricket with Oliver, running up and down and laughing very loudly so that they should hear her next door and know she wasn't tired at all. In a queer way, though Marjorie was so kind, Emmie thought of her as an enemy. She had the terrible feeling that if she told her too much, gave her an excuse to poke and pry, somehow, all the safe fabric of their lives would be rent apart.

*

All afternoon, Martin had been hammering away in the conservatory. The door was locked. At about four o'clock he opened it and yelled to Emmie to fetch the Elastoplast. When she brought it, he was sitting at his typewriter, sucking his damaged thumb. He winced as she dabbed disinfectant on the cut and covered it up for him. 'I'm a lousy workman,' he said.

'Did you do it with the fretsaw? What are you making, Dad?'

There was something on the workbench, covered up with a cloth.

'Is it for Oliver's birthday?'

'Never you mind.' He sat frowning at his typewriter but Emmie could see he was in a good mood. He was usually in a good mood when he started to make something, though he didn't often finish it. Years ago he had made a doll's house for her; he had made it beautifully with proper wallpaper in the rooms and a tiny lavatory but he never got around to making the roof or putting hinges on the back. She was too old for a doll's house now so it didn't matter, but she hoped he would finish what he was doing for Oliver. Oliver wouldn't understand that it was nicer of Dad to make him a toy than to buy him some dull old thing from a shop. Oliver liked things to be finished and shiny and to look as if they cost a lot.

She said, 'What are you writing, Dad?'

He smiled at her. 'I'm not really writing yet, just roughing out an idea. It's an account of the early days of television – that hasn't been done yet. I've got a lot of interesting stuff – after all, I was in on the ground floor. It should sell like hot cakes if I knock it into the right sort of shape. That's the trouble of course, I've got a mass of fascinating stuff but I've got to be selective.' He frowned and lit a cigarette.

Emmie looked at him. The sunlight shone through the glass of the conservatory and showed up the piece of gold in his front tooth, the little, gingery hairs in the folds of his red cheeks, the grey ones in his drooping moustache. He looked as if he felt bright and cheerful and full of youthful strength, but he looked old, too. Emmie felt a rush of protective feeling for him, the feeling she had, sometimes, for Oliver. She wanted him to be safe, not to be in trouble; she wanted him to finish this book.

'I expect it'll come out fine, Dad,' she said.

'Well – we'll see. I just need time. If I'm not bothered, I ought to be able to get going. It's important to work when you feel in the mood.'

'We won't bother you.' Emmie shuffled from one foot to the other. 'Can I have some money?'

'Again? I gave you two pounds yesterday.'

'I paid some of what we owe the milkman and I bought some sausages and some bacon from Woolworth's because we owe Whiting's and I didn't want to go in there.'

He sighed. 'Milkman, grocers – did any man ever have to work under difficulties like this? It cuts the flow, Emmie, cuts the flow.' He smiled at her. 'You really mustn't bother me too much, old love, mustn't disturb the goose when he's trying to lay the golden egg, y'know.' He was feeling genuinely enthusiastic, in a splendid mood, but he was nervously aware that it could disappear any minute. He said abruptly, 'How much?'

She closed her eyes. Figures went round and round in her head all the time now. She worked out sums on her way to school and in the bath and before she went to sleep. 'I should think four pounds would do.' That would mean she could buy eggs for supper and pay something on the grocery bill and have enough left over for the vet. It would be seven and sixpence for the consultation if they went down to the surgery.

'I haven't got it, duckie.' He fished in his pockets and took out a ten-shilling note and a little silver. 'I had to pay a couple of months' rent yesterday to keep 'em quiet. This'll have to do to go on with. Only rich men pay bills, old girl, remember that.' He laughed cheerfully, he hadn't felt so cheerful for months.

She took the money and put it in her pocket. He said suddenly, 'Alice ought to be doing this. She's sixteen, old enough to take over the housekeeping.'

'I'm better at sums than Alice.'

Martin turned back to his typewriter. The pile of clean, new paper filled him with excited pleasure. He waited for her to go.

She said, 'Is it difficult to get a book published?'

'Sometimes. Sometimes not. It depends.' He smiled. 'Easy enough if your name's Hemingway.'

'Oh. You mean if you're famous already?'

'That's right.' She fidgeted beside him. He said, 'Why aren't you all at school, anyway?'

'It's a half holiday. Dad . . . ?'

'Yes?'

'You said I was to tell you if I thought Oliver ought to go to another school. I think perhaps he ought to. He's getting spoiled. The teachers spoil him because he's so pretty and Marjorie spoils him too.'

He said severely, 'She's very good to you all, just remember that. There's no harm if she spoils Olly a bit. It gives her a lot of fun.' He looked at his daughter. 'You've got a bit of your Gran in you. You don't think people ought to enjoy things.'

Emmie shut her mouth in a tight line. 'She's got him so I can't handle him any more.'

'Stop worrying about that.' He spoke sharply; he suddenly saw Emmie growing up like his mother, stern, conscience-mad, depriving everyone of their fun. On the other hand, she was possibly right. Little as he wanted to do anything about it, the boy's babyishness, his Fauntleroy air, embarrassed and distantly annoyed him: it seemed to reflect on his own manhood. 'I'll think about it. You may all have to leave anyway. It's all nonsense, paying for what you can get free.'

Emmie's heart bumped. She said, 'Mother paid the fees, didn't she?'

'Mmm.' He glanced at her, brightly but bored, his pale eyes restless. 'Now run along, there's a good girl . . .'

*

Nick was walking in the garden with his father-in-law, a tall, lean, bald-headed Scot who had flown down to London for a couple of days and come out to see his daughter between one business appointment and another. Nick was uncertain what he was doing in London, he only knew that whatever it was, his father-in-law was bound to make more money out of it. He was that not uncommon thing, a philanthropist who always made money. Whatever he backed or took over – insecure but deserving commercial ventures, a struggling publishing firm, an inefficient factory which he refused to modernize because it would make some workers redundant – always miraculously turned the corner and became financially successful. This undesired Midas touch depressed and even disgusted him; he was not interested in money. He believed that people should spend as little as possible on themselves and think as little as possible about themselves – no more, indeed, than the little thought that was needed to keep them usefully alive. On the other hand, he believed implicitly in a father's financial duty towards his children. The allowance he gave Marjorie was more than generous and she would be his sole legatee. Within his cold limits, he was also fond of her.

He said, 'Marjorie seems well. She's put on weight. It seems a good thing that she should occupy herself with these children next door. She needs occupation. Though she won't tire herself, I hope.'

He said this, not because he thought it was likely she would tire herself, but because he was aware of a certain lack of sympathy in his own nature and tried, conscientiously, to redress it by saying the things other people said.

Nick smiled. 'I don't think so. Though of course she's not supposed to do too much.'

Her father cleared his throat. 'There's been no return of her illness?'

'No, thank God. But of course the thought of it worries her.'

'You must try not to let her worry. That's always been the root of the whole trouble in my opinion.' He fixed his bleak grey eyes on Nick; they were very close-set, on either side of his long, red, bony nose. 'Of course I'm not a medical man,' he went on, 'but I am absolutely convinced that a lot of mental ill-health springs from not having enough to do.'

'That's true,' Nick murmured hopelessly. It wasn't true. Marjorie's illness was glandular. But they had had this conversation so often and to such little purpose that he had long ago abandoned his part of the dialogue. He sometimes felt that if the last bomb fell, blowing to pieces all the anxious and tentative opinions and reflections of mankind, there would still be, booming on among the wreckage, his father-in-law's assured and confident voice.

'It's a vice of this Modern Age,' he continued. 'Women suffer from it more than men – especially women who have been brought up to think that it is enough just to look beautiful.'

Nick could hardly suppress his laughter. When Marjorie was a year old, her mother had run off with an Armenian. Until she was eighteen, her father had educated her himself; he had dressed her in navy serge and black stockings and made her read John Stuart Mill for an hour every evening. She had not been allowed make-up; if she had, at that age, developed any idea of herself as having rights simply by virtue of being a pretty girl, it must have crept in between the covers of some acceptable book. At one time, thinking of her childhood, which must have been a grey business, rather like a long, dull, cold Sunday, he had been furious with his father-in-law. Now he knew that he had given her what he had, and no one could give more.

He was saying, 'Occupation is all important. Not for its own sake, naturally, but because apart from any useful function that may be fulfilled, it encourages a proper disregard of Self. Of course this can never be true if the occupation has been entered upon for what one can get out of it – one must never expect virtue to bring a reward.

I hope that Marjorie is not just amusing herself with these children. That she might not be thinking of them, but simply indulging herself, is the only factor in the situation that would worry me at all.'

Nick smiled. He had long ago decided that his father-in-law's conversation was so ludicrously irrelevant to anything that he understood as fact, that he barely listened to him. Only occasionally he would say something that struck with a vague sense of warning, like the sudden, cold wind that blows along the ground just before a change in the weather.

*

After he had taken the old man to the station, Nick sat in the garden and read. It was hot, very humid. Emmie watched him from the end of the garden, knee-deep in damp, sweet fern. She liked to watch Nick unobserved. Sometimes, when he went for a walk, she followed him; if he stopped to look at something she stopped too and when he walked fast, she walked fast to keep up with him. If he glanced back, she would dodge into hiding, her heart thumping. One Saturday morning she had waited for an hour and a half outside the dentist's where he had gone to have a troublesome tooth fixed. She had imagined herself going up to him when he came out and asking if he was all right. Perhaps he would take her into Tommy's Bar and buy her a cup of coffee. But when he did appear a suffocating shame kept her rooted to the spot. She watched him along the road and then ran in the opposite direction, singing a high, careless tune, breaking off now and again to laugh rather wildly, so that several people in the street turned to stare at her, surprised.

Nick closed his book, put it down on the scorched grass beside him and got out his pipe. The heavenly smell wafted towards her. She came slowly out of the fern bed. He looked up, saw her, and smiled. He had a lovely smile, she thought. There were white lines in the brown flesh at the side of his eyes because he smiled so much.

'Mr Sargent,' she said. 'Can I talk to you?'

'Of course.' She shifted from one plimsolled foot to the other and he said, encouragingly, 'What is it, darling?'

'I want to ask you about my Diary.' She looked down at her cotton skirt, pleating it with small, brown fingers.

'All right,' Nick said good-humouredly. 'Go on.'

'I wondered – I wanted to know if people of my age ever did get books published. I mean, if anyone would *pay* them for it?'

Nick looked at her, surprised. He had read and enjoyed her diary though there were things in it that he was sure he had not known at fourteen and that he felt, uneasily, were not quite suitable for her to know. Whereas Mrs Hellyer saw her as much older than she was, he saw her as younger than she was. But on the whole there was a simplicity and directness about the way she had written that had pleased him, and occasional bits of unintended humour that had made him laugh, though the way she had written about her family – her grandmother in particular, had made him think her unobservant. He had thought that children were supposed to be sharp and unsentimental and though Emmie had not written in a sentimental way exactly, she had written about her family as if they were perfect. It had puzzled him and made him very slightly jealous.

He had never supposed that it was publishable or that Emmie cherished ambitions of that kind. He had thought her too childish, too unspoiled. He recognized, reluctantly, that this was probably how he preferred to see her.

He said, 'Do you need money?'

146

She hesitated, but not long enough to show him that this was the simple truth. 'No. Dad gives us money.' Ashamed, she hung her head and scraped a pattern on the dry ground with her toe.

'Then what do you want to get it published for?'

'I don't know.' She looked at him through her lashes, almost sullenly. What other reason could there possibly be? 'I just thought people did get books published,' she said lamely.

'Well – obviously. Sometimes very young people do. There was a book called *The Young Visitors* that once made a lot of money.'

She looked up. 'Is my Diary as good as that?'

'It's not quite the same thing.'

She sighed deeply. 'Oh, I see . . .'

Her evident disappointment hurt him. He had a fond, parental desire to give her something. Perhaps there was something in it, after all. He didn't pretend to know what the market would be. Queerer books had been published and sold – at least, he saw them on bookstalls. At least, one could ask . . .

He said, 'If you like, you can give it to me. I know a publisher. I can ask him about it.'

'*Oh*,' she said. Her eyes were luminous with joy. 'Oh – you are nice.'

Her happiness removed his doubts for the moment. When she came back, clasping the diary, her excitement was so enormous – so gloriously young, that he was completely caught up in it. 'Let's go for a walk,' she said, and he shared with her the feeling that it was impossible to keep still. Hand in hand, they went out of the garden. From the house, Marjorie watched them go.

*

When they came back, Nick settled into his chair and took up his book. Emmie sat at his feet, silently hugging her knees. Very lightly, her head rested against his thigh. She felt his warmth and held her breath. If he had moved, given any sign that he was aware of her, she would have jerked away at once. But he sat still, absorbed in his book. Cautiously, like a shy young animal, she moved closer and relaxed against him.

When Marjorie called to her, she stood up reluctantly. Nick smiled up at her. 'Better see what she wants,' she said.

She went into the kitchen. 'I've got supper for you,' Marjorie said. 'Do you know where Oliver is?'

'No.' Emmie looked at the table with an agreeable sense of hunger. There were raspberry jellies and slices of pink, Westphalian ham.

'Where have you been all afternoon then?' Marjorie said.

There was something in her voice that bothered Emmie. She got the feeling that, somehow, she had done wrong. She said, 'I was indoors for a bit. Then I went for a walk with Mr Sargent.'

Marjorie was buttering bread. The westering sun came through the kitchen window and glinted on her fine, nervous arms, her brown, slender throat. She said, 'You know, dear, we love to have you in and out of the house, but sometimes I think you hang around Nick too much.'

'I don't worry him,' Emmie said. 'I don't disturb him when he's reading or sleeping or anything like that.'

'No. But whenever he looks up – or puts down his book, you're there, aren't you?'

It was very quiet in the kitchen except for the clock in the corner that ticked so loudly that it sounded as if it would burst out of its case.

Emmie said, 'Mr Sargent likes me to go for walks with

him. He says he likes me to show him things – birds and animals. There are a lot of interesting birds on the pits. He likes me to tell him about them.'

'Don't be silly, Emmie. You know quite well that isn't what I mean. Of course Nick likes – we *both* like – you to come for walks and talk to us. But he can't move without you – pouncing on him. Like a cat jumping on something.'

The unfriendliness in her voice struck Emmie like a jet from a cold hose. She gasped, just as if the water had hit her in the chest.

'Don't look at me like that,' Marjorie said. She put down the bread knife and rested her hands on the table. Her arms felt so tired, suddenly, that the muscles in them jumped. 'I'm only trying to help you,' she said in a carefully reasonable voice. 'After all, your mother isn't here and there are some things girls have to be told. You're old enough to learn that you mustn't run after men. It's – undignified, for one thing and for another it can get you into trouble. Or them. You have to think of that. Nick isn't a saint, you know.' She laughed suddenly. Emmie found it a dreadful sound. 'Don't get upset – I'm not accusing you, or anything. It's not as if you were Alice. Believe me, if you were like Alice, then I *would* be worried . . .'

She glanced out of the kitchen door and said quickly, 'That's all I wanted to say. Lecture over. We won't say any more about it.'

'About what?' Nick said, coming in. He looked at Emmie. 'Hey, what's the matter with you?'

Marjorie said quickly, 'She's not feeling very well.' Now she had got it off her chest, she felt heavy and cold with shame. Why did I do it? she thought frantically, oh God I'm not fit to *live*. Her cheeks burned. 'I expect she's been sitting too long in the sun,' she said.

'Yes, she does look mouldy,' Nick said. The forced

brightness in Marjorie's voice disturbed him but he did not want to think about it. He took Emmie's arm. 'Sit down, pet, have a cup of tea.'

'I feel a bit sick' Emmie said. She smiled, a fixed, bright smile. 'I'll find Oliver and tell him supper's ready.'

*

Emmie ran across the fields to the pits, towel and bathing suit flapping from her arm. She was going to swim in the lake, alone, because both Nick and her father had expressly forbidden it. An act of defiance was her only defence, not so much against a world that suddenly seemed black and horrible to her, but against the shame in her own bewildered mind. She was not angry with Marjorie. Marjorie had only told her what she had really always known – or, rather, what she now felt she had always known and hypocritically ignored. She thought of the times she had put her hand into Nick's, how she had sat beside him on the grass only half an hour ago. Hadn't she pretended, deliberately, to be younger than she was so she could do these things under the guise of innocence? And if she knew it, and Marjorie knew it, then *he* must know it too.

'Oh,' she said, aloud, 'I wish I could *die*.'

She pulled off her clothes frantically, tearing her blouse, ripping off her skirt as if it were slimed with something dark and evil-smelling. She flopped into the lake and dived and dived again. Then she swam along the bank until she came to the old pontoon. She pulled herself up and lay on it. In a fit of crazy violence she began to run one arm backwards and forwards on the rusty metal until it began to bleed. The pain made her feel better; she slid back into the water and swam slowly, feeling calm and suddenly relaxed. Nothing had happened, she told herself dreamily, nothing had *happened*. Then everything came back in a wave of anguish and she ducked her head under the water and made herself hold her eyes open until they smarted with pain.

She swam slowly back to the beach and lay, limp on the yellow mud. There was still heat in the evening sun and it warmed her slowly. She lay still, arms spread wide; one strand of dark hair lay across her cheek like a line drawn in charcoal. After a little, she rolled over on her side and dug a hollow channel in the mud. She dug down to the water's edge and the water flowed into it. She made a harbour with a jetty and when it was finished to her satisfaction, got up to find pieces of stick to float in it.

11

MARJORIE and the children were sitting on the lawn
cutting out paper lanterns. Dressing to go to town, Nick
could hear their voices through the open window and
Marjorie's occasional laughter, soft and contented as a
cat's purr. He was glad she was happy and whistled softly
to himself as he tied his tie. The return to England had
worked in a way he would never have believed it could.
Since they had come to the house she had grown pro-
gressively calmer, more relaxed. Even her appearance had
softened; the outline of her face was thicker by a hairline
and her skin, tanned to a dark, honey colour, was almost
luminous with health. As he went into the garden, Nick
thought she had never looked more beautiful or more
desirable. She was wearing a low, cream-coloured dress
and her skirt was covered with snippets of bright, gleaming
paper. She looked as if she had a lapful of tropical bird
feathers.

'You look very exotic,' he said. 'Out of place in an
English garden.'

Her dark eyes shone. 'Look,' she said, and held up a
finished lantern for inspection.

'Pretty. What are you going to do with them?'

'We're going to hang them on the trees with candles
inside them,' Oliver said. 'After the special supper, we're
going to play sardines.'

'Oliver has drawn up an impossibly long list of games,'
Marjorie said.

Oliver squirmed with excitement, flinging himself backwards on the grass. 'I've been thinking about my birthday
party for weeks. I can't bear waiting another *week*.'

Marjorie smiled at Nick. 'It's going to be such a party! Champagne for some, Coca-Cola for others. And we shall all dress up to kill.'

'What are you going to wear, Emmie?' Oliver said. He rolled over on his belly and squinted at Mo, who was making little running darts at his hair.

Emmie was fitting her lantern together with an appearance of deep concentration. She had not looked up when Nick came into the garden. Suddenly she said, 'Oh – it won't *work*,' and screwed the paper up and threw it away from her.

'Well – what are you going to wear, Emmie?' Nick said. She was scowling and he felt slightly impatient with her. For some reason, he disliked it when she behaved badly in front of Marjorie.

'I dunno,' she said moodily and stood up, balancing on one leg.

'Whatever she wears, she'll look silly,' Oliver said in a dispassionate voice.

'Beast. Foul beast.' Her lips quivered, she turned her back and marched off. Her legs were long and stalky under her short skirt and grimy down the backs.

Marjorie said, 'She's been a bit cross all morning. I expect it's the weather. Or the school holidays. Children get at a loose end.' She spoke casually, not complaining – rather like a mother of six, Nick thought, grinning. He thought that she had been exceptionally sweet to Emmie lately and he was grateful to her. 'You're a nice girl,' he said impulsively.

She looked at him with a tiny frown but said nothing.

Oliver said, 'I expect she's cross because it isn't her birthday. It's always horrid when it's someone else's birthday.'

Nick was irritated by his tone which he thought deliberately babyish, but Marjorie laughed.

'You *darling*,' she said.

Nick wandered down to the end of the garden. It was a warm, soft day and the garden was heavy with all the scents of summer, sweet and faintly cloying like a bowl of pot-pourri. He saw Emmie over the hedge and called out to her. She glanced at him, then turned her head away and ran into the house. He was distantly disappointed; she had seemed shy of him recently and he had missed her, chattering away while they walked or just sitting beside him, quiet and undemanding in the garden. He supposed she was ashamed of her outburst of bad temper and lingered, looking at the roses and wondering if she would come back.

Marjorie called out to him. 'I thought you were going to London?'

He yawned. 'Yes, I've got a lunch date and I'm going to see that man your father wanted me to see. I don't suppose anything will come of it, but it seems worth looking into . . .'

He grinned to himself a little and thought, you cagey bastard. In fact it was almost certain that the Chairman would offer him the job – it was in a pressed steel company of which his father-in-law was a director – and almost equally certain that he would accept it if he did. He was a little surprised at how much pleasure the prospect gave him; the sense of frustration and failure which had dogged him when he first arrived in England had disappeared almost without his realizing it and he had become enormously restive. He had decided not to tell Marjorie until the offer was definite. He was not sure how she would take it, leaving the house before they had intended and moving up north; also, in the last few years he had got into the habit of sparing her any unnecessary decisions or arguments. All the same, he half-wished she would ask him about it, show some interest . . .

But she only said, 'Have fun then,' and showed Oliver the lantern she had finished. 'There, isn't this a pretty one?'

'How many are you going to make?' Nick asked. It struck him that Marjorie was unusually silent. She had often tired him with her chatter, with her bursts of personal revelations, 'Today I feel this – yesterday I felt that,' but suddenly he wished she would talk to him. He was sure that her withdrawal meant nothing except that she was happy and occupied but he felt oddly lonely, as if she had deliberately left him by himself in an empty room.

She answered, with a faint air of boredom. 'Oh – dozens and dozens.' She touched Oliver's cheek with her finger. 'Aren't we, darling?'

*

It was very hot after lunch. Emmie had climbed into her hiding place on the roof of the old summer-house, to smoke. She lay on her stomach on the flat piece of tin someone had put there, a long time ago, to repair the gully in the middle of the wooden roof. It wasn't very safe, the whole of the summer-house was rotten, but it was very quiet and private, screened by the steep pitch of the roof on either side. The tin was just wide enough for her to lie on, but it was very hot and burned her, so that she had to keep moving her bare legs. When she lifted her head, the sun made everything very black or so white that it hurt her eyes. The light bounced off the river and dazzled her. She smoked her cigarette very slowly, trying not to cough and thinking of all the things she was going to do.

She would go and work with Albert Schweitzer. There had been an article about him in the paper. But before she did that she would have to become famous at something else so that it would be extra sad when she renounced the world and went to work in a leper colony.

She would be a great actress or a great painter, or perhaps the first woman Prime Minister. She thought of the long, black car gliding up to the great white building where they were going to hold the conference that would put an end to war for ever. A gasp would go up as she got out of the car, looking very pale and ill. Perhaps she had had polio so that one of her legs would be in irons. Or perhaps she would paint a picture of Oliver and it would be hung in the National Gallery and everyone would come and look at it and weep because it was so beautiful.

She stubbed out her cigarette and yawned. There were so many things to do but at the back of her mind she knew she would never do any of them. The afternoon stretched in front of her, very long and hot and boring. It was too hot on the roof so she got up and slithered down the ivy into the dark, damp place at the side of the boathouse and went indoors. It was dark in the house after the sun and when she blinked, red and yellow lines jumped in front of her eyes. William was lying on the cool tiles in the scullery, panting. He rolled the whites of his eyes when Emmie came in. Emmie filled his water bowl, found an egg that Oliver's hen had laid in the hole under the sink. Then she drank a glass of water and felt it trickle slowly down inside her as if she were a pipe. After that, there seemed to be nothing to do, so she went upstairs and lay down on the bed. Mo was curled up in a bundle under the eiderdown. She lay down carefully so as not to disturb him. It was hotter upstairs than it had been in the garden, but she was too lazy to move.

After a little, Oliver came in. He wanted her to go down to the river with him.

'I want someone to play with,' he said in a soft, coaxing voice, like the voice he used when he was talking to his tortoises. 'Marjorie told me to run away and read a book. I don't want to read a book.'

'Well, run away from *me*,' she said.

'Can I have some tomatoes for Henry and Murgatroyd?'

'If you like. There's some in the larder.'

'It's hot,' he moaned. 'If Henry laid an egg, would it be hot enough to hatch it? Or would I have to put it in the airing cupboard?'

'Oh – go *away*,' she said.

*

Oliver went out, into the sun. He was scowling fiercely, partly because the sky was so blazing blue that he couldn't look at it and partly because he was Moses Arkwright, the famous jewel thief, searching out a rival gang that had stolen the biggest ruby in the world from the Tower of London. Where had they hidden it? If he could find it, his fortune would be made. He crept, bent double, down the narrow, gritty path to the boathouse.

It excited him tremendously to hear voices. There was no very real barrier between fantasy and reality in his mind. Perhaps the gang was really there, using the boathouse; it would be a marvellous hiding place. With great caution, cosh at the ready, he tiptoed out of the garden and on to the tow-path to spy out the land. He was deeply disappointed when he peered over the bank. The gang would have come in a high-powered motor launch, not in an ordinary punt, hired from the boat-yard half a mile upstream.

He sighed heavily. He knew what was happening in the boathouse and it was too ordinary to convert into anything exciting. The boathouse looked completely disused from the river and a courting couple, discovering the unlocked grille, had simply slipped inside for a bit of extra privacy. This happened fairly frequently during the summer and Oliver had several methods of dealing with it. Sometimes he simply hung over the bank and untied the boat, other times he rattled a stick against the boathouse door and shouted in a gruff, common voice – he was a good mimic – 'Who's there? Come out at once.'

This afternoon he had no spirit. He felt too let-down and disgruntled. He went back into the garden and squeezed through the bushes at the side of the boathouse. There was a spy-hole where there had once been a knot in the wood. He applied his right eye to the hole and blinked once or twice to accustom himself to the darkness. There was nothing furtive in his attitude and he would have been quite unashamed if anyone had caught him. Sexual behaviour was both meaningless and basically uninteresting to him : his curiosity was purely scientific. On this occasion it was satisfied fairly quickly. Nothing new was happening. Human beings he found, yet again, were not nearly so interesting as animals and besides, his bare legs had been stung by the nettles that grew thickly round the boathouse. Crossly, he came out of the bushes and searched around for a dock leaf.

When his legs were more comfortable, he decided that he would go down to the town. It was Friday and there would be enough people in Woolworth's for him to be able to pinch a handful of sweets from the counter if he wanted to. He didn't want to, very much. For one thing it was too babyish – Moses Arkwright would never do anything with so little risk attached to it – and for another, deep in the dark of his mind a small seed of moral uneasiness had begun to germinate. For some weeks now, he had not eaten the sweets he stole.

He walked along the road, hands in pockets, whistling like a blackbird. Just before the bridge there was an opening into the gravel pits, not the opening where the lorries went, but the main gate inside which were the central offices, a bleak collection of army-like huts with corrugated iron roofs. Outside this gate, he was surprised to see Mr Hellyer and another man busily engaged, in this sweating heat, in taking up paving stones.

Mr Hellyer glanced up, saw him, and averted his gaze. Oliver went closer. 'Hallo,' he said, smiling.

Mr Hellyer gave a fairly convincing start of surprise. 'Oh,' he said, 'it's you, is it?'

'Yes,' Oliver said. He waited for a moment while Mr Hellyer removed another paving stone and added it to the growing pile in the hedge. Then he said, 'I didn't know you had a job, Mr Hellyer.'

'Well, now you know different,' Mr Hellyer said shortly.

'I thought you didn't approve of manual labour,' Oliver said.

Mr Hellyer straightened up, moved his cap to the back of his head and scratched it. Oliver smiled. Mr Hellyer looked at that sweet, cozening face and, unwillingly, grinned.

'Needs must when the devil drives,' he said. He winked at the other man who was watching Oliver sullenly. 'Here – you run along and let me get on with it.' He began to fumble in his pocket. Watching him, Oliver said helpfully, 'They took up all this pavement last week.'

'Did they now? Well – they didn't settle 'em back properly. Inefficient lot, our Council.' He gave Oliver half a crown. 'Get along with you – buy yourself a lolly.'

'Will you take me to see the badger's sett soon?' said Oliver, driving a hard bargain.

Mr Hellyer sighed. 'All right. Now get along. Or I'll have the supervisor after me.'

Oliver got along, hopping on one foot, dragging the other leg and hunching his shoulders. He was a bird with a broken wing.

*

He had a happy time in the town. He bought a comic, several candy bars and a bag of liquorice all-sorts. In the street market he managed to get a wilting lettuce for Henry and Murgatroyd, reduced to fourpence. After that he went to the pet shop which he despised but which occasionally sold him broken biscuits for William, cheap.

Crossing the bridge on his way home, he thought he would stop and give Mr Hellyer a piece of his Mars Bar, but as he got nearer, he saw Mr Hellyer was gone. The paving stones were still there, neatly piled against the hedge but the two men were not there, only three police officers getting out of a black car. One of them glanced towards the town; his eyes rested, briefly and incuriously, on Oliver.

Oliver, who had a natural distaste for policemen, crossed the road and ran home, on the other side.

*

Nick's publishing friend fitted his glasses more securely on the bridge of his nose and said, 'My dear chap – I thought it was charming. Really, I mean it. I found it the greatest fun. Odd, of course, a bit zany, but the odder the book the better it tends to do nowadays. If it wasn't for the law of libel we could probably make a very nice little thing out of it.'

160

'It's mostly about birds. They don't sue,' Nick said shortly.

Will giggled. He had become rather giggly, Nick thought, arch and giggly. Perhaps it was simply being a publisher. Every trade had its mannerisms.

'I suppose not. But one would have to cut out a lot of the nature stuff. It would be quite a considerable editorial job. The best bits are about people. That's where the libel comes in. I should guess that your little friend has a splendid knack of observation but no fictional powers. Those people in the houseboat, for example. My dear chap – you couldn't put them in a work of fiction. No one would believe a word of it.'

'Couldn't you cut them out?'

'No. No, that wouldn't do at all. They're very important, part of her background – of what you might almost call her mythology. Perhaps I'm using the word loosely but it conveys what I mean. These people in the houseboat are almost the only people she knows outside her family. One gets the feeling that she bases her deductions – all her knowledge of the world, in fact, on what she knows about them.'

'I see.' Nick found he disliked this idea very much.

'And of course they're a splendid contrast to her own family – the gifted children and the marvellous old grandmother.'

'*They're* mythical if you like,' Nick said. 'They're not in the least like that. The father's nice enough, but a bit of an old soak and the grandmother was a dragon. I found it a bit odd that a sensible girl should write about them in that – that romantic way.'

Will said gently, 'It's not a bad thing to have a few illusions. Especially about the people you love.' He took of his glasses, put them on the table and flipped them a short distance. 'I'm sorry,' he said. 'I hate disappointing people. Sorry on my own behalf too. It would be the *greatest* fun to produce, a good, classy production, *illustrated* in the right way, I should think . . .'

'I'm sorry you're depriving yourself of so much pleasure.'

Will gave a slightly nervous laugh. 'I have overdone it a bit, haven't I? I almost mean it, though.' He picked up his glasses and rubbed them up on the tablecloth. 'What's the girl like?'

Nick smiled. 'A little, half-grown, black cat.'

'How old?'

'Fourteen.'

'Nubile?' Will sighed gently. 'I suppose we're getting to the age when we'd envy our sons if we had any.'

Nick said savagely, 'She's a child. Absolutely sexless. Thin as a rake and flat as a board. And plain as a lemon.'

Will raised his eyebrows.

*

Driving home, Nick saw her as he went through the village. She was standing on the pavement waiting to cross the road. She had a heavy bag of vegetables.

He stopped the car. 'Jump in.'

She flushed brightly and fidgeted from one foot to the other. 'Oh – don't bother,' she said.

'Don't be a silly ass. Get in. We're holding up the traffic.'

She glanced nervously over her shoulder and pursed up her mouth. Then she got in and sat beside him, her shopping bag on her lap. He drove off slowly and stopped at the lights.

He said, 'Have I done anything wrong?'

She shook her head so violently that her hair flew.

'Well then – what's the matter? Aren't you a bit huffy? Has Oliver been up to anything?'

The lights had changed without his noticing. He said 'Damn' and ground the gears. They moved off jerkily.

'I don't think so.' Her voice was neither offended nor embarrassed, simply stiff. She added, more naturally, 'He's not thinking about anything except his birthday. And his old tortoises, of course. Henry ate some apple today. Usually he doesn't like fruit.'

'He's getting daring. Henry's the intelligent one, isn't he? Ah – he's a Deep One, our Henry.'

He waited for her smile but she was looking at him with a serious, strained expression. She said, 'You think we're a pack of fools, don't you?'

He said quickly, 'No. I'm sorry. I didn't mean to laugh at you.'

She said, 'Oliver loves his tortoises, Like I love Mo, only they're more real to him than Mo is to me. They're people to him – not human people, but the same sort of thing, only different. Much more important, too. He loves his tortoises much more than he loves people. I used to feel like that. I don't now. I mean Mo is only a pet, isn't he? Just a squirrel?' She sounded sad and resigned as if she had lost something.

'You're growing up,' he said cheerfully. 'You couldn't grow up believing animals mattered more than human beings, could you? You'd be a very funny sort of person.'

'I don't see why. People aren't so very marvellous, are they?'

He laughed. 'Perhaps not. Perhaps animals are much nicer to live with. They don't sweat and whine about their condition, they don't lie awake in the dark and weep for their sins.' She was staring at him blankly. He said, 'A poet wrote that. I forget the rest. All the same, you wouldn't

163

want to live without people, would you? I mean – you love Oliver much more than you love Mo.'

'Yes. But I love Mo too. And William.' She grinned suddenly. 'I'd like to have hundreds and hundreds of dogs one day and show them at Crufts.'

'Maybe you will.' He was relieved by her change of tone. He hated it – he was astonished by how much he hated it – when she seemed unhappy or depressed. He said encouragingly, 'It's nice to be as young as you. To have everything ahead of you. You might do anything, breed dogs or be a naturalist – or you might write books.' He glanced at her sideways. It had to be said sometime. 'Though I'm afraid we haven't had any luck with your first book. I showed it to a friend of mine and he thought it was splendid – he really did – but he says he can't publish it. Apparently there are technical difficulties.'

'Oh.' She looked at him quickly and then stared out of the window. Her cheek was flooded with colour.

He saw shame was her chief emotion and felt sick with pity for her. 'Don't mind too much, darling. You're awfully young. You'll have to go on trying, that's all. Perhaps you'll be a famous writer some day.'

Her reaction surprised him. She turned on him, red-faced and scowling. 'Oh *do* shut up. You don't have to go on and on, as if I was some silly kid. I don't want to be any of the things you said. I'm not like Oliver and Alice. I don't want to *be* anything. Why should you think I want to write books?'

He looked at her sullen, furious face and was irritated. 'You might have said that before,' he said coldly. 'It would have saved me a lot of trouble.'

*

When Emmie got home she felt very miserable. She had

been angry with Nick because she hated herself but that wasn't his fault. She wanted to be happy with him and for everything to be as it had been before but it didn't seem possible. Her love for him now seemed shameful and foolish; she imagined Marjorie saying to him, 'That silly kid's crazy about you' and could almost hear his laughter in her ears. When he had stopped the car to pick her up she had been terrified. But there had been nowhere she could run to, no place to hide. The only thing she could do was to assume an air of indifference.

She went up to her room, put the Diary in her drawer and stood for a long time, breathing on the window and drawing faces. Nick was saying to Marjorie, 'I picked up poor Emmie in the town. Poor child, it's terrible that she loves me so much.'

'Poor child,' Emmie said scornfully, aloud. 'Poor silly Emmie. Poor silly skinny *hideous* Emmie.' It was a relief to think these things and say them aloud. It helped to destroy the love which was becoming so hateful to her.

After a little, she went to Oliver's room and found a Nux Bar in his satchel and ate it. It made her feel a lot better. She sat on the edge of his bed, eating the Nux Bar and wondering how she could make some money. An idea came to her and she felt better still. She went down to the kitchen. Her father was helping Alice get tea. Alice looked cross. She said, 'There you are, you've taken your time, haven't you? Did you bring the tomatoes?'

'They're in the bag. I was a long time because everyone was gassing in the shop. Some men pinched all the wages at the gravel pit. The man came back from the bank in a van and the other men stopped it at the gate and grabbed the money.'

'Was that why there were policeman all over the road?' Alice said.

'I expect so. They said in the shop that the men who did it had been pretending to take up paving stones – nobody thought anything because it looked as if they were from the Council.'

'You'd better not tell Oliver,' Alice said. 'You know how revoltingly morbid he is. Especially if someone's been killed. Was anyone killed?'

'The man who was driving the van got hit on the head. I don't think he was killed.' Emmie's interest in the story had evaporated during the telling of it. She had something more important to think about. She said, 'Dad?'

'Yes?'

'You remember you said it was easy to get a book published if everyone knew your name?'

'Mmm.' He was pouring boiling water on to the tea. He held the kettle in his left hand and looked clumsy.

'Dad. A publisher would know Mother's name, wouldn't he?'

'I expect so.'

'Have we got any paper and string?'

'In the drawer,' Alice said. She watched Emmie turn out tablecloths, dirty napkins, grubby candles. 'Oh God, don't make a *mess*.'

'I'll clear it up,' Emmie said. 'I always do.' Clasping brown paper and a roll of Selotape, she left the room.

'Untidy pig,' Alice said, and began to throw things back into the drawer.

Martin watched her. She looked tired; there were purplish marks, like bruises, under her eyes. He said, 'You feel all right, Alice?'

'Of course I feel all right.'

He put the brown teapot on the table and covered it with a patchwork cosy. He said hesitantly, 'D'you remember when you made this? You gave it to me, one Christmas.'

'*That* old thing.'

'You made it very nicely. You were only a little thing.'

She turned to the table, yawning so that the tears came into her eyes. She set out butter, jam, milk jug. She was absolutely indifferent to him, he thought, and it hurt him suddenly.

He said, 'You were a funny little girl. You had round red cheeks, just like a wooden doll.'

She smiled at him in a distantly friendly way. 'Don't get sentimental, Dad.'

He wasn't sentimental, he thought stubbornly. Unless it was sentimental to want to remember a time when he and this girl had not been strangers to each other. It hadn't been easy at first; he wasn't her father and all she remembered of her own father was blows and shouting. She had been a rosy, stocky little girl who had stared at him with a bright, vacant face, her finger in her mouth. When Clemence had gone into hospital to have Emmie, she had cried because she was left alone with him. 'Mummy, I want Mummy,' hitting him and butting him in the stomach with her head, like a little goat. Half-frightened of her, he was clumsy, fumbling with her buttons, hardly daring to brush her hair. Then, one day, he had visited the hospital; he had nowhere to leave her except outside, sitting in his old car. When he came out, it was snowing. He drove half-way home before the windscreen-wipers packed up and then trudged the last two miles, through blinding snow, with the child tucked into his overcoat, her cold face buried in his shoulder, her small, cold hands round his neck. She went to sleep, she was so heavy that he thought he could barely carry her another step but he got her home and set her down in the warmth of the

167

kitchen. She woke and cried, her fists in her eyes. He took off her outdoor clothes and sat her on his lap. He said, 'Don't cry. Daddy's Apple-Pie.' When she stopped crying, he made her a potato man with matchsticks for legs. She laughed. 'Make it a mouth, Daddy.' She had never called him Daddy before. He made a mouth with his knife and a piece of carrot. She said she was hungry; he fed her with cornflakes and afterwards she went to sleep, her fat cheek squashed against his waistcoat button, her pink mouth dribbling milk. He had sat for hours, holding her. The discomfort was very sweet to him. He loved her. He loved his wife and he loved her child. He was, then, a big, overgrown, shy man of twenty-eight who had never loved anyone before and it made him feel happy and strong and confident. He held the sleeping baby and was alternately happy and tortured with fear that something might happen to her.

There was a time after that when she was the most important thing in his life. Emmie was only a baby, a wandering-eyed little animal, belonging entirely to her mother. They lived in a basement flat in South London then, he, his wife, and the two little girls. When he was expected home, Alice would stand at the top of the area steps watching for him. When she saw him, she started running, fat legs pumping. Once she fell and when he picked her up, her front tooth was broken. It had hurt him, as if someone had smashed a fist into his own face. It hurt him to think of it even now; he looked at the tall aloof girl, calmly cutting bread and butter, and felt as if something was bleeding inside him.

She cut bread, spread butter, then Marmite. He went up to her and touched her shoulder awkwardly. He said, 'You'd better have a rest after tea. You look rotten.'

'You're very considerate all of a sudden.' She wrinkled

her nose, laughing at him. 'You must have been at the whisky bottle.'

Her face was bright, kind and empty. He was no more to her, he thought, than a tiresome old man, an old fool. Suddenly he was overcome with self-pity. No one wanted him. He was finished. His decision to stop drinking, made two days ago, now seemed futile, a pathetic old man's gesture. He was nervy and on edge. It was supposed to be a bad thing to cut it out just like that. It made you depressed and unreasonable. Mentally, he counted out the change in his pockets. After tea, when the children were settled, he would go down to the pub and get half a bottle.

Alice said, 'You might call the children and tell them tea's ready.' She was sitting down at the table; he thought she really was looking very ill and wretched but his tender pride kept him silent.

Emmie was typing in the conservatory. He said, 'You're not supposed to touch my typewriter.'

She looked up at him pleadingly. 'I'm being awfully careful, Dad. Really I am.'

'What are you doing?'

'Nothing. Just a letter.' She spread her hands secretively over the page.

'Well – your tea's ready.'

When he had gone, Emmie read over what she had written. '*Dear Sir, I am sending you my new book. I am very sorry it is not typed out, but my secretary is ill.*'

She took the sheet out of the typewriter and wrote underneath, *Clemence Bean.*

12

It was a warm evening, but when Emmie went up to bed Alice was lying with the blankets drawn up to her chin, grey as a rat in the face and shivering.

Emmie said, 'Whatever have you got all those bedclothes on for? It's too hot to live.'

'I feel sick,' Alice said pathetically. She leaned her head over the side of the bed and was sick on the floor.

'Oh dear God,' Emmie said, and went to the bathroom for rags.

'I'm sorry,' Alice said. 'Filthy thing to do.'

Emmie mopped the floor, retching. 'You can't help it. Have you eaten something?'

Alice shook her head weakly.

'When did it come on?'

'After I'd put Olly to bed. He was awful. Going on about his birthday as if it was the Second Coming.'

'He's greedy. Natural to be greedy at his age. Are you going to be sick again?'

'I don't think so. I'd better have the potty just in case. That dreadful, flowered thing of Gran's. It's under the bath.'

When Emmie came back, Alice said, 'Can I have Mo in bed with me? Just for a little?'

'I thought you couldn't stand him.'

'I just want him,' Alice said fretfully.

Emmie got a chair and climbed up to Mo's nest. He chattered at her, sleepy and indignant as she dived for him among the dirty linen, the old letters, a moth-eaten scarf. But he was quite acquiescent. He settled down under Alice's chin and went to sleep again.

'That's nice,' Alice said. 'Thank you, Em.'

Emmie began to get undressed. She said, 'What am I going to wear for this old party tomorrow? I haven't a thing. I'm bursting out all over but it's worse in the chest.'

Alice said, 'You can have my green thing. It'll be too big for you but you can get a belt at Woolworth's.'

Emmie looked at her, astonished. 'What's come over you? Lending clothes . . . You *must* be ill.'

Two tears spilled out of Alice's eyes and slid sideways into her hair.

'*Alice,*' Emmie said. Her own mouth quivered in sympathy.

'It's all right,' Alice said. 'I was going to have a baby but I'm not any more, so that's all right, isn't it? Only I feel so miserable I could die.'

She wept with her eyes closed. Her fair hair was dull and dark-looking. Emmie crept to the bed. She felt sick and awed. 'Oh, Alice – didn't you think – you might not have been able to do your training. Not if you had a baby.'

'Oh don't.' Alice opened her eyes. They were pink-rimmed, her nose was pink and glistening slightly. 'Don't *you* start on that. It's been bad enough walking about with my insides falling out and knowing people were looking and having to keep on behaving like a healthy young virgin who's never had anything to do with a man. Without you . . .'

Emmie felt her stomach cave in. 'All right,' she said frantically. 'I'm sorry. Only I just thought . . .'

'D'you think I didn't? What d'you think I've been thinking about all the time? I was thinking that if I couldn't be a nurse I just wanted to die . . .' She cried for a little but comfortably, with relief.

Emmie said, 'Are you all right? I mean, shouldn't I get a doctor? Things sometimes go wrong, don't they?'

'Nothing's gone wrong. I didn't *do* anything. It's just nature taking its course.'

'Would you rather I went to sleep with Olly?'

Alice nodded. 'I wish Mother was here,' she said.

*

Emmie could not sleep. The bed was too narrow and Oliver muttered in his sleep and ground his teeth and thrashed about with his fists. She stared at the car lights going by on the ceiling and thought about her Diary and wondered how much they would pay her for it. It was nearly a week now since she had sent it off. They would surely write back soon and send a cheque. They still owed the grocer and Dad said he had had to pay another month's rent. She thought that she hadn't realized before how important money was. If they didn't pay the rent they could be turned out of the house and have to sleep in a ditch. Perhaps the police wouldn't even let them do that, perhaps they would treat them like gypsies and move them on and on and not let them stop anywhere. She thought that the first thing she would do when she earned some money would be to buy a house or a caravan like they had in Turpin's Field, so that whatever happened they could all be together, safe for ever and ever.

When she did go to sleep, she had a nightmare. Two years ago one of the lorry men had found a baby on the council dump, dead and rolled up in newspaper. Emmie had forgotten about it until now. Several times in the night she had this bad dream and once she woke up on the floor. She had banged her elbow and the sheet was twisted round her, dragged off the bed. It was almost light. Oliver slept in the middle of the bed, naked, his eyes fiercely shut as if he were trying very hard to think about something. His fists were doubled on his chest. Emmie climbed back into bed and fitted herself round him. When she woke, it was late and the sun was coming in through the greasy, grey window. Oliver was crouching by the tortoise box, holding Murgatroyd up to his face and murmuring, 'It's my birthday, wish me a happy birthday, Murgatroyd.'

Murgatroyd gave a faint squeaking, like a very old, rusty door; his beautifully armoured legs with the long, spiky nails slid slowly out of the shell, the black, shiny eyes opened.

'He's talking to me,' Oliver said with glorious pride. 'He *knows*.'

'Shut up,' Emmie groaned. 'Oh – be quiet.'

'Don't you know what day it is?' Oliver said indignantly.

'Your birthday. Many happy returns. Now – can I get back to sleep?'

She curved herself into a small, tight ball. She didn't want to wake up. She heard Oliver stump out of the room and the sound of water running. Then she felt a beast and forced herself to get out of bed.

Alice was lying propped up on pillows. Her face was peaked but she had slept well.

'More than I did,' Emmie said savagely. 'I fell out and banged my funny bone. It's coming up in a great lump. Where did I put his present?'

'In the wardrobe. Under your plimsolls.'

Emmie rummaged in the bottom of the wardrobe, flinging out old shoes behind her, like a dog digging. She took out the small parcel and ran downstairs. Oliver was playing with his father's present, a wooden model of a tea clipper with full rigging and sails. 'Dad made it,' he said. 'Isn't it lovely? It's my best thing.'

Emmie gave him her present. He tore at the string like a starving man with a food parcel and took out a penknife and a book on tortoises.

'The book's from me,' Emmie said. 'The knife's from Alice.'

He drooled over the knife. He was so excited that the spit flew from his mouth. 'It's sharp,' he said. 'It's lovely – oh, it's my best thing.'

'It's too sharp,' Martin said. 'Too sharp for a boy of nine.'

He was in rumpled pyjamas, the trousers held together with a safety pin, but he had shaved and looked alert and cheerful. He had been much more cheerful lately, Emmie thought, and all her night fears suddenly seemed childish and silly. Of course they wouldn't be turned out of the house. Even if she didn't earn any money, Dad would look after them. He had said he would give up free-lancing and get a regular job on a trade magazine or something. He hadn't got a job yet but he had gone up to London every day this week and come home in a jolly mood. Most evenings now he was very cheerful and joked with her and played games with Oliver; after they had gone to bed he usually went round to the pub to calm his nerves.

He said, 'You'd better take Alice a cup of tea. She's not feeling too good.' He paused and added delicately, 'She's unwell.'

He avoided his younger daughter's eyes. This was a subject that embarrassed him sorely. 'I expect Alice has explained to you about that,' he mumbled.

'Oh yes,' Emmie said. 'Oh yes – she's explained to me all right.'

She took Alice up her tea and a slice of bread and butter.

'Dad thinks you've got the curse.'

'Least said, soonest mended.' Alice heaved herself up in bed and sipped the tea. 'It's not much more than that, anyway.'

'Are you sure? Are you sure you're all right? You ought to go and see a doctor.'

'I will. Do you think I'm stupid? I wouldn't be able to start my training if I wasn't well.' She handed Emmie the empty cup and picked up Mo tenderly. 'He's been so good all night. It's as if he knew.'

'He must be ill,' Emmie said, alarmed. She took him from Alice and looked at him. 'His eyes are weepy,' she wailed. She put him on the chest of drawers and fetched a nut out of his special box. He held it between his paws and nibbled feebly. She rolled him over on to his back and wiggled her fingers invitingly, offering to box, but he lay inert, front paws curled gently round her forefinger.

'Put him in his nest,' Alice said. 'He'll be happier there.'

Emmie climbed on the chair and tucked him in gently. He curled up and nipped her finger half-heartedly. 'Perhaps he's just tired,' she said hopefully. 'I don't expect he slept well last night.'

'I didn't stop him,' Alice said. 'I kept still as still.'

'If anything happens to him, I'll want to die,' Emmie said. Her chest heaved, tears came into her eyes.

'You haven't bothered with him much lately. He probably feels it.'

'*Oh.*' Emmie buried her hot face in his smelly nest. 'Oh Mo, darling Mo. I love you, I love you.'

'It's no good getting sentimental now,' Alice said.

*

The day was hotter than any day that summer, and still. The pit machinery clanked, the iron sound rose to the hot, metallic sky. On the road, the cars hooted, bumper to bumper in the week-end crawl to the coast. Dogs panted in the shade.

Marjorie was going to take the children to the fair in the afternoon, but Nick persuaded her to stay at home. He thought she looked tired and it worried him. 'It's too hot,' he said.

'It depends on Oliver,' she said. 'It's his day. I don't want to spoil it.'

Oliver, waiting with his hand in Emmie's, gave her an indifferent look. 'I don't mind.'

Marjorie smiled at him, though she was hurt. 'I'll stay, then. There's a lot to do for the Feast.' She hesitated. 'Don't I get a birthday kiss?'

He looked at her measuringly. She bent down to him and he touched her cheek briefly. 'That's not much of a kiss,' Marjorie said.

She followed him with her eyes as he walked with Emmie to the gate, very neat and spruce in the white Terylene shirt and blue shorts she had bought for him at Harrods.

'You should have given him his present,' Nick said.

'I wanted him to have it after supper. You remember what birthdays are like when you're small? They start off so large and marvellous, then they dwindle away to nothing. I wanted him to have another peak, just before the end.'

'He didn't know that.'

'No. It was stupid. I'm a fool. And he's angry with me.'

She looked utterly desolate and all of her thirty-eight years; her cheeks seemed to sag and her jaw-line looked heavy.

He said bracingly,' 'Darling, it's not worth getting upset. Naturally he was fed up, he's only a child and he was expecting a present. It'll be all right soon as he gets it.'

She looked at him as if she had barely heard him. 'You saw?' she said. 'He didn't want to kiss me . . .'

The words were bathetic but behind them there was a despair frightening in its intensity.

Nick said, 'You mustn't let yourself get so involved with him. It's not worth it . . . '

He was quite unprepared for the anger with which she turned on him. 'Is that how you really think? That you must only love someone if it's *worth* it? Doesn't it strike you that sometimes it might be nice not to be so emotionally mean – to *get* involved, without reckoning up what the price is going to be?'

He said, trying to keep his voice light and easy, 'I think the price of loving Oliver might be quite high, don't you? If you were a tortoise or a beetle or something you might get some return . . .'

'And you think I expect a return?' Her voice rose, he put his hand on her arm but she shook it off.

'Everyone does,' he said. 'All adults, anyway. We only love ourselves. Or what we see of ourselves in someone else. You have to be very young to be really altruistic in love.'

She stared at him stonily. 'Don't you ever despise yourself?'

'Frequently.' He had a cold feeling in the pit of his stomach. 'Most of the time, perhaps. But I don't see the point in having romantic illusions about myself – or about anyone else for that matter – just because it makes me feel nice and cosy.'

'You certainly don't have any about me, do you?' She turned on him. There were tigerish glints in her brown eyes; it was extraordinary, he thought, how anger made some women more beautiful. Her rage burst over him like hailstones. 'Oh – I'm used to that, I'm used to being criticized, despised. But this is something new. I'm not allowed to love Oliver – it makes me feel too warm, too happy and safe. Too *human*. I've got to be made to realize that I only love him for what I can get out of it. I'm nasty, selfish, probably perverted. Can't you work *that* in too?'

He said helplessly. 'We shan't be here much longer – if I *do* take this job, only another month. I only don't want you to be hurt.'

She stared at him. She was breathing hard as if she had been running. She said in a tone of simple surprise, 'Don't you know that you can't love someone without being hurt?'

*

The fair was small and scruffy, several beat-up caravans clustered on the Meads. There was a coconut shy, a candy floss stall, and one where you got a prize for fishing up a coloured celluloid duck out of a moat of dirty grey water. The children had five shillings each to spend. Oliver spent all of his on the plastic ducks and collected ten prizes. Emmie walked round, having a good look at everything, and apportioning the money in her mind.

She met Dickie by the coconut shy. She would have run past him, but he caught her by the elbow.

'Don't do that,' she said. 'It's sore.'

'Sorry.' He ran his hand through his spiky fair hair, looking very tall and brown; like a sailor, Emmie thought.

'How's Alice?' The words came out rough and abrupt and he reddened.

'She's all right,' Emmie mumbled, keeping her head low.

He said in a lost way, 'Is she? I just wondered.' He jerked his head at the shy. 'Like a coconut?'

He bought three balls and stood on the line. A nut

178

rocked but didn't fall. 'They're fixed,' Emmie said. 'You have to hit awfully hard.' He rubbed his hand down the side of his tight black jeans and aimed again. This time one came off; the man who ran the shy picked it up and gave it to Emmie. 'For the lady, I take it,' he said, and laughed.

'Shall I open it?' Dickie said. He took out a clasp knife and sawed at the nut. The top came off and he gave it to Emmie. She tilted it and drank the sweet, thin fluid. 'Give the nut part to Alice. She likes it,' he said.

Emmie saw that the whole operation had been directed towards this but she was only slightly disappointed. 'I'll tell her you got it,' she said.

She wished he had a letter for Alice instead; it would be more romantic. But he said, rubbing his hand down his thigh as if he had been bitten there, 'Tell her something, will you? I've got a job in Wolverhampton. I've got to go next week. It's an apprenticeship and I get a day off each week to go to school.' He took a packet of Woodbines out of the breast pocket of his cotton shirt and lit one. He was very red in the face. 'I'd like to see her. She can send a note over to the pit any time. I'd come to the house but your dad mightn't like it. I don't want to make trouble for her.'

Emmie thought how nice he was. And then she remembered what had happened to Alice and he didn't seem nice any more, just big and handsome and rather frightening, standing there in his tight jeans and his bright shirt, looking at her. She thought of what he and Alice had done and felt queer – excited and scared at the same time. 'She's in trouble anyway,' she said. Her pulse was thumping away inside her ears and high up in her throat.

'What d'you mean?' he said quickly, eyes staring.

'Work it out for yourself,' she said, and then turned and

ran. She heard him call after her and got into one of the swing boats with a pale, freckled little boy who was hanging nervously on to the rope while his plain, doting parents stood beside the boat, saying encouragingly, 'Go on, Sidney, it'll be such fun.'

Emmie paid her sixpence and grasped the rope. She could see Dickie standing among the people by the boats and knew he was watching her. She shut her eyes and tugged at the rope, sending the boat soaring high up over the scruffy, stinking little fair and the bare-headed people and the wide, comfortable, pleasure-loving river. The wind whisked past her ears, her stomach lurched; she opened her eyes and saw the white, freckled child screaming, his mouth open like a great dark cave, clinging on to the side of the boat with his frail clean-scrubbed little hands. Somewhere down below his neat, desperate parents were bellowing at her to stop but she wasn't going to. The need she had just then for a wild outpouring of physical exertion was stronger than anything else: she wanted to go on, pulling at the rope and screaming with laughter. Then the boat began to slow down. She saw that the man who owned it was hanging on to the side and checking it each time it swung. He was a thin, brown man with a brass stud at the neck of his striped shirt and a sad expression as if he were on the point of tears. His voice was very soft, almost weeping. 'Now you shouldn't do that,' he said, 'the little boy's crying.'

She stood up in the boat. She couldn't see Oliver anywhere, but she could see Dickie, standing some way back in the crowd. His face looked lost and anxious and somehow sad, like someone left behind at a railway station.

The little boy's father was lifting him out of the boat.

'Young hooligan,' he said. 'Kids like that shouldn't be allowed on.' His eyes, pale and hostile, encountered

Emmie's. 'You've got to consider other people,' he said. 'Didn't your mother learn you any manners?'

Emmie gave a loud laugh and jumped, landing like a cat. Without a word or a glance she ran off, shouting, 'Oliver, Oliver,' in a high, affected voice.

*

Oliver had gone home. He was anxious to avoid Emmie. Spending his five shillings had given him great satisfaction, particularly as none of it had been wasted. His pockets bulged with the prizes he had won at the plastic ducks: a packet of fruit gums, a monkey on a stick that broke the first time he made it jump and three engagement rings with glass stones in them. He knew perfectly well that they were not very good prizes and that he would have done better to lay out his money at Woolworth's, but he did not wish to hear Emmie telling him so.

He went towards home, singing softly under his breath. He sang an endless string of tuneful but meaningless words that were only very loosely attached to the long, narrative poem that went on inside his head. The stories he told himself were, in fact, almost wordless; simply a procession of scenes and incidents through which he moved, not as an active participant but rather as a curious watcher in an alien element. It felt rather like swimming under water in a glass tank: on all sides and above him he could see the world, the outer air, but he was not part of it.

He saw Mr Hellyer through this barrier of glass. He was digging in his minute patch of garden opposite Riverview, on the other side of the tow-path. He was wearing a pair of old baggy trousers, a dirty white singlet and a large and handsome red silk cravat fastened round his neck. Oliver paused a little distance away. He eyed the cravat critically and decided that he liked it – in general, he admired and envied Mr Hellyer's casual way of dressing – then crept silently closer and pounced. 'Got you,' he said triumphantly, thudding his small fist into Mr Hellyer's bent back.

Mr Hellyer jumped and swore. When he saw Oliver he gave a watery grin and said 'So it's you again,' in a low, rather grumbling voice. He didn't say anything else. He leaned on his spade and looked at Oliver in a vague, thoughtful way, not smiling.

Oliver turned out his pockets and spread out his loot on the ground. After a brief pause – his mind seemed elsewhere – Mr Hellyer squatted to admire it.

'Diamonds, eh?' he said, picking up one of the rings. 'You'd better get them insured.'

Oliver laughed appreciatively. He was at an age when he could be both inside himself and outside himself at the same time: he knew he was only playing a game, but the game still remained real to him. So though he laughed at Mr Hellyer's joke he was able to say, with perfect seriousness, 'It's all right. No one'll steal them. I've got a special hiding place. I'm going to hide them so no one can find them, ever.'

'That's a good thing,' Mr Hellyer said, quite good-humouredly but with a singular lack of interest. Unlike most grown-ups, he was usually ready to stop whatever he was doing to sit down and talk, and Oliver, who had looked forward to a good gossip, was both puzzled and disappointed when his friend stood up, spat on his hands and went back to his digging.

Oliver sighed deeply, stuffed his treasure back into his pockets and sat down on the grass to watch. Mr Hellyer was digging with extraordinary vigour, the sweat streamed in runnels down his dark, rather engagingly wrinkled face. He looked a little like a damp nut, Oliver thought.

After a while, he said, 'Did you give up the job on the Council, then?'

'Let's say it was a mutual understanding,' Mr Hellyer said. 'I gave it up, it gave me up.' He glanced at Oliver and added brusquely. 'You'd better get up. Ruining your good trousers wriggling about on the ground. You'll get grass stains all over your backside.'

This word, so casually spoken, shocked Oliver. Mr Hellyer, who was in fact too nice-minded to do so, could have sworn, blasphemed, and Oliver would not have turned a hair. But the word *backside* outraged him to the depths of his soul. He stood up at once and began to stalk away but Mr Hellyer called to him.

'Olly.'

Oliver stopped. Mr Hellyer's tone had changed subtly; it was placating, almost wheedling. Oliver scowled, but waited.

Mr Hellyer said, 'To tell you the truth, Olly, I never was on the Council. Not officially. As a matter of fact it was rather a hush-hush sort of business. A bit difficult to explain – I was sort of keeping an eye on things.'

'*Spying?*' Oliver said.

'Sort of.' Mr Hellyer scratched his head. His powers of invention were rather limited. He said simply, 'You'll do me a favour if you don't mention it to anyone.'

He was very red in the face, probably because he was ashamed of using that horrible word, Oliver thought. He said, completely mollified, 'Is it a secret, then?'

Mr Hellyer hesitated. His instincts told him that a child was more likely to keep something dark than an adult – a child has no tiresome misgivings about deceiving even his loved ones – but he was not sure that he dare trust his instincts. On the other hand, he had no choice. He said, 'Yes, it's a secret. Just between you and me.'

'O.K.,' Oliver said lightly. 'I won't tell anyone.'

His casual manner concealed a swelling pride. He said happily, anxious to make some return, 'If you like I'll show you where my secret hiding place is. You might like to hide something there some time. It's a very useful place.'

'I daresay it might be,' Mr Hellyer said, very slowly. He looked at Oliver narrowly, his terrier eyes bright and beady. Finally, he said, 'You're sure it's a good place? Not where your sister might find it if she goes snooping about?'

'It's a *fabulous* place. You could – you could hide the Crown Jewels there,' Oliver said blissfully.

'Big? Big enough to hide something – a suitcase, say?'

'*Anything*.' Oliver glanced at Mr Hellyer and added with regret, 'Not too big a suitcase. A piece might stick out. Though it wouldn't matter. No one goes in the boathouse much and it's a high place. No one'ud look up there.'

Mr Hellyer looked round him, considering. The fields, the river, the tow-path, were pleasantly empty. This comforted him as it had comforted him half a dozen times this afternoon, but his mind remained basically uneasy. He was not a very intelligent man; intelligent men do not go to prison with such sad regularity. It was not wickedness that led him into crime but a cheerfully impulsive nature and an almost complete lack of reasoning power. Like most small criminals he had about as much grasp of the laws of cause and effect as a very young child and rather less imagination. Mr Hellyer was capable of carrying out a simple crime; he was practically incapable of taking sensible steps to avoid arrest afterwards. The money he had stolen from the gravel pits reposed under his bunk in the houseboat. It had not struck him until now that this was an inadequate hiding place.

Oliver would have had more sense and initiative.

Mr Hellyer's gaze rested on the boy's bleached head. It reminded him of something – a picture, a picture in a story book. The rusty wheels of his memory began to work. It was a story about Roundheads and Cavaliers that his mother used to read to him when he was a boy. A man had hidden in a window seat; his enemies had not looked for him there because on top of the seat, someone had laid a sleeping child. Mr Hellyer could see the illustration now. The child had worn a purple suit with a lace collar. His hair, in long, effeminate ringlets, was barley-fair, like Oliver's. Painfully, Mr Hellyer's mind made the connection. No one would bother to look in a child's hiding place.

He grinned cheerfully. 'Well, Olly,' he said. 'Suppose you hide something for me, eh? Just for a bit of fun. We'll have a really good secret, shall we?'

Oliver's face was radiant. He took Mr Hellyer's hand and skipped happily along beside him.

He said, 'When are we going to look at the badger?'

'What?' Mr Hellyer was startled. 'Oh – bad time of the year for badgers.'

Oliver's face fell.

Mr Hellyer said, 'Tell you what though, when we've finished our little job, I know where there's a hare form. Happened on it this morning. Rare bit of luck – you don't often find 'em round here. Beautiful thing, a hare form.'

His enthusiasm was not assumed entirely for Oliver's benefit.

*

Later that afternoon the police, who had been diligently searching certain caravans on Turpin's Field, spread their net wider. A pleasant spoken young constable arrived at Riverview with a warrant and asked if he might look over

the boat. Mr Hellyer gave him every assistance and afterwards went thankfully down to the pub for a few beers.
He had a weak head for liquor which always roused up his
deep, if sentimental, religious feelings. After several pints
he suddenly startled the whole pub by saying in a loud,
benevolent voice, 'And a Little Child shall lead Them.'
He followed this up by a brief speech about his poor old
mother, God bless her sweet soul, and ended by singing
the first few verses of *Onward, Christian Soldiers*, in a light,
pleasing tenor.

13

In the late afternoon, it got even hotter. After Emmie had
had her bath she felt cool and clean for not much longer
than five minutes; by the time she was dressed, she was
sticky and hot again. She had put on one of Alice's bras-
sières under the dress she had lent her, but it looked odd,
so she had to take it off. The green dress was too long; she
was almost as tall as Alice now, but there wasn't so much
of her to fill it out. The bodice hung in folds but when she
pulled the belt good and tight it didn't look so bad. She
put on her white sandals. Then she put lipstick on her
mouth and pressed her lips together the way she had seen
Alice do. The lipstick made her teeth look very white and
her skin very brown. She looked at herself full face, then
sideways, with the hand mirror. The shoes were wrong and
her glasses were wrong. She took off the glasses and
widened her eyes. Her squint was almost gone. It took her
some time to get used to her face without them. She
thought she looked better, but somehow naked. She talked
to herself a little, lowering her voice and drawling carefully. Then she opened the wardrobe and looked for a pair
of high-heeled shoes.

*

She was the last to arrive at the party. They were all
sitting on the stone terrace at the back of the house
when she opened the garden gate and started up the
path.

Martin said, 'Will you just *look* at that child?'

Her ankles turned over a little on the high heels. She
walked in a wobbling, mincing way like a dressed-up

penguin, bulging out like a squashed balloon above and below the cheap gold belt. Her face was set and nervous and white as a clown's with powder, except for her lips which were bright orange.

Marjorie said. 'Emmie, we wondered where you were. You do look nice.'

Emmie made a nervous grimace with her hideous orange lips. The walk up the path had been dreadful. She said in the new, husky voice she had been practising, 'Heavens, it's so hot. I could just do with a drink.'

'Come and get one,' Nick said, from the table.

She hobbled over to him, wincing with pain. 'My feet are bigger than Alice's. They're *killing* me.'

He whispered, 'You sound as if you've got a dreadful cold. And you've got the least bit too much lipstick. Otherwise the effect is splendid.'

She scrubbed at her lips with a not too clean handkerchief.

'Better?' she said in her normal voice, and grinned.

*

Marjorie had opened the long sash windows and pushed the table near them, so that it was almost like eating in the garden. The lanterns, each with a nightlight inside, hung on the trees; as the evening darkened, they shone like fairy lights. There were candles on the table, there was a turkey and tiny peas cooked in butter and baked alaska pudding. Oliver ate eagerly, his eyes wandering to the corner of the room where there was a large, square object covered with a piece of sacking.

'Stop looking,' Marjorie said.

'When can I look?'

'After we've played games . . . when we cut the cake. Alice, have some cheese.'

'No, thank you. It looks lovely, but I couldn't eat another thing.'

'Feeble girl,' her father said. 'Nick – did I ever tell you the joke about the two men who wanted to lose weight?'

Emmie was so excited that she couldn't eat. Nick poured out half a glass of champagne for her and a dribble for Oliver.

'. . . so the doctor gave him some pills,' Martin said, 'and when he woke up in the middle of the night there was a beautiful girl on his bed . . . diaphanous nightie, trailing blonde hair, the *lot* . . .'

Emmie tasted her champagne. It tickled her nose and made her gasp. 'It's *exotic*,' she said.

Oliver choked and had to be thumped on the back. 'Just like fizzy lemonade.'

'. . . so that the end of the week he found he'd lost two stone. Naturally, he told his friends and this other man went along too and *he* got some pills. But when he woke up there was a gorilla beside *his* bed . . .'

Emmie thought her family looked beautiful, sitting round the table in the candlelight. Dad looked lively and happy and young, Alice like some marvellous film actress and Oliver – Oliver simply looked beautiful. His eyes reflected the candles, his white hair fell like silk over his white forehead.

'. . . so naturally, he complained and the doctor shrugged his shoulders and said, well, after all your friend is a private patient.'

Emmie didn't think it was very funny, but she laughed because Nick and Marjorie did. It was wonderful that they should all be sitting round the table, laughing. She loved her father because he could make everyone laugh.

When supper was over, they played games. There was a

game where you blew up balloons and sat on them. Dad was better than anyone; he burst six balloons, one after the other. Oliver said, 'We're going to play sardines, you promised we could play sardines . . .'

His eyes blazed; he picked up a sausage on a stick from the side table where there were extra things to eat, and ran out into the garden. 'My sausage shines the way,' he shouted, and they all laughed again. Emmie thought she had never heard people laugh so much or sound so happy. She wanted to reach out her hands and touch each one of them: she loved them all so much.

Nick thought he had never seen anyone so transparent with joy. It made his heart ache to look at her.

*

Marjorie was to hide first. It was the fairest way, the children said, because they knew places where she and Nick would never find them. They gave her time to hide and threw dice to decide the order in which they should go after her, a five-minute interval between each departure. Martin went first, then Oliver, then Nick. Sitting on the terrace steps, Emmie watched him down the path. She heard the click of the gate; then nothing, except the crickets rubbing their back legs together in the grass.

Alice whispered, 'You go next. I don't think I'll play.'

'Do you feel very awful?'

'Not bad. But not like prowling round in the dark like a kid.'

'It *is* dark, isn't it? No moon. . . .' Emmie hugged her small, hardy knees and stared into the blackness. One by one, the little lanterns on the trees were going out. She was so excited it was difficult to wait. 'Is it time . . . ?'

'Not yet.' Alice lifted her pale, plump arm, peered at her watch.

Emmie said in a low voice, 'I saw Dickie. He's going away. He's got a job.'

She couldn't see Alice's face, only the loose wispy bits of her hair, glinting in the light from the guttering candles behind her.

'Did you tell him anything? About me?'

'No.'

Alice gave a little, gusty sigh. 'Thank God for that. He'd make an awful fuss. He's got an awful sense of responsibility.'

'I should've thought you'd want him to know.'

'Why?'

'I dunno . . . I just thought.'

'Well don't,' said Alice, crisply. Her voice repudiated any further discussion. She had retreated further and further away from them all, Emmie thought. She had been one of them once, but suddenly she had gone a long way away. It hurt Emmie less than it would once have done. 'Time must be up now,' she said, and sprang to her feet.

*

Martin found Marjorie in the boathouse, sitting on the punt cushions and smoking a cigarette. He lowered himself creakily beside her and felt for his own packet.

'What a game. It's pitch black – I barked my shin and took a tumble in a nettle bed.'

'Poor you – and you'll probably get rheumatism sitting here, unless they all hurry up. Do you think Oliver is enjoying himself?'

'Sure to be.' He said, rather huskily, 'I can't thank you enough for this evening. For all you've done, in fact. It goes beyond thanks . . .'

'No. It's I who should thank you. I – I was so miserable when I came here.'

His big, red face was turned towards her, attentive in the cigarette's glow; his moustache, like two orange tusks, made him look like a gentle walrus. The absurd image touched her and made her feel somehow protected and safe: this kind, bumbling man would never despise her. She was a little drunk; the drink and the intimate darkness made it suddenly very easy to talk.

'I'd been miserable for a long time. No one's fault but my own, not even *my* fault, in a way, but that doesn't make it any easier, does it? I've let Nick down so badly – he didn't want to leave Africa, you know. He loved it more than anything, more than he loved me, more than he could ever love a child . . . When he fetched me from hospital after my baby died, we drove home in the dark. It was a long way and we didn't talk. I was thinking about the baby. Then Nick stopped the car and I thought – he's going to talk to me. We hadn't really had a chance to talk – you know what it's like in hospital, so unreal, so sterile . . . There were frogs all round us, bubbling away, and we sat still for a bit and then he said, "That's the sound of Africa – it's one of the things I love best", and I knew he hadn't been thinking about the baby or about me. I felt as if someone had stuck a knife into me – I started to hate Africa then and I went on hating it – I began to hate a lot of things I hadn't minded before, when I was happy. Nick couldn't understand it, he said he couldn't understand why I'd changed so much. It *was* hard on him, in a way. When we got married I was quite different. My father brought me up – he'd trained me to be the nicest kind of boy, tough, self-reliant. Nick liked that, he likes people to be strong and independent.' She giggled suddenly. 'Such hard luck on him – to find he'd suddenly got a wife who was all the things he loathes – hysterical, difficult, clinging . . . I'm not complaining, really. He's had a rotten deal from me and he's been marvellous about it. But he treats me like a child. He doesn't expect, he doesn't *want* me to help him. I'm no good to him, no use. Until I came here I'd got to feel so useless and empty.'

Martin lit another cigarette and gave it to her, silently. His calm, listening presence reassured her. She said, 'So you see – it's I who should thank you. For Oliver.'

He said nothing; he was watching her gravely. She said simply, 'I love him so much. So much that sometimes I can almost believe he belongs to me, that nobody and nothing can take him away. It makes me very happy but it's a frightening kind of happiness. Sometimes it terrifies me because he's not really mine and sometimes it doesn't seem to matter.' She gave a shy little laugh. 'You know – now and again, I have such a silly pipe-dream. I let myself think I might adopt him – oh, not altogether, but just so that he could come and stay with me sometimes and I could do things for him. I'm horribly rich – it seems such a waste . . .'

She caught her breath. She had not imagined she would ever dare say this aloud. She said quickly, 'I expect you think I'm mad. I don't know why I'm telling you all this. I suppose it's just because I feel so comfortable with you.'

It was true. She had an almost childish sense of comfort when she was with him; the comfort of a roaring fire in the grate, muffins for tea, home and safety.

Martin dropped the end of his cigarette on the ground and methodically stamped it under his heavy shoe. 'Why not? I seem to remember that I unburdened myself to you, a while back.' His voice was curiously flat, deliberately unemotional. 'It's wonderful that you should feel like this about Olly. I mean that. If things were different . . .'

He paused, breathing heavily beside her in the darkness. Finally he said, 'I ought to tell you – I was going to, but there hasn't been an opportunity. I heard at the beginning of this week – my wife's coming back.'

The words fell like lumps of ice. She heard him talking distantly. She had written to say she was sorry, she must have been mad, of course she was coming back. It would be easier now his mother was dead – though Clemence hadn't known that when she wrote. They would put things on a proper footing, he would take a job, they would get a good housekeeper. 'I should have told you,' he said. 'The truth is that I couldn't believe it. It seemed too good to be true.' He sighed. 'As far as the children are concerned, it's an enormous relief. I was dreading telling them – you can't imagine. It's a terrible thing – to destroy a child's innocence.'

She said, 'I'm so terribly glad. So terribly glad for all of you.'

It seemed there was nothing for her after all, no warm fire, no nursery comfort, no being needed. Only emptiness and unwanted love and Nick's cold charity. The tears streamed down her face.

He muttered, 'I'm sorry, I'm sorry. You poor, dear girl.'

Tentatively, his warm hand rested on her shoulder, his stiff moustache brushed her cheek.

*

Oliver said, 'They're not in the boathouse. They're *not*.' His voice rose high, he dragged at Nick's arm.

Bewildered, Nick looked down at him. He had discovered Oliver weeping in the conservatory and though he remembered his own childhood clearly enough to know this was the likely end to any birthday, it touched and disturbed him. They had looked together in the sheds, behind the dustbins. Now he wondered if the child was afraid of the boathouse. Perhaps some bogey, some witch-in-the-cupboard lurked there. He marched him down the path and said, brisk as any old-fashioned nanny, 'How do you know? Have you looked?' and thrust open the door.

'Ssh,' Marjorie said. 'Making all this noise. You'll warn the others.' Her voice shook a little; with clumsy pity, Martin felt for her hand in the darkness and squeezed it tightly.

Oliver said, 'They shouldn't be here. It's not allowed . . . it's *private*.' His appalled eyes searched in the shadows. He couldn't see the suitcase but he knew where it was, in the cavity between the walls and the roof. High up for him but not for a grown man – if Nick moved now, only a little, he would strike his head on the jutting edge. He stamped his foot and said loudly, 'Come out, come out *now*.'

No one moved, they were staring at him in astonishment. Frantic, he did the only thing he could. He opened his mouth and began to wail.

Nick said, '*Not* a success, apparently. Emmie's given up too – turned her ankle in those silly shoes.' He bent to the howling child. 'Come on, old chap, we'll go back, shall we?'

They went back to the house. Oliver's tears were genuine now; he sobbed in the dreary, hopeless way of a tired child, his head hanging on his frail neck like a heavy flower. Nick set him down on the terrace and he rushed indoors.

'What's up with him?' Emmie said. She was sitting in a chair, nursing her ankle.

'Dog-tired, poor baby.' Marjorie followed him into the

dining-room. He was sitting on the floor among the cracker wrappings and the crumbs, his shoulders shaking, his eyes tight shut. She knelt compassionately beside him. 'Don't cry, pet. It's all right.'

He opened his eyes and glared at her, very pale and sullen. 'I knew you were there all the time,' he said. 'It was a silly place . . . you shouldn't have gone there.'

'Why didn't you come in then? Oh – never mind. It's a silly game, we won't play it any more.'

She tried to put her arms round him but he fought and wriggled. One flying fist caught her in the throat. 'It's *private* – a private place,' he shouted. 'I *hate* you.'

'Oliver.' Martin glanced at Marjorie's stricken face, seized the child's thin wrist and jerked him to his feet. 'I won't have this. Damned rudeness . . . you apologize to Marjorie this minute.'

Marjorie said thinly, 'Don't, Martin. He's tired. It's our fault – we went on too long.'

'It's more than that. *Oliver* . . .'

Oliver looked silently at his father.

'He hides things in the boathouse,' Alice said in a disinterested voice. 'He's probably got some silly treasure.'

'*No*,' Oliver whispered. He was very white, his face seemed all hollows.

'Then there's no excuse,' Martin said. He felt he would burst with anger and shame. 'All this stupid fuss. What's it about? Come on, Oliver. I want a proper answer.'

He loomed over him, large, heavy and implacable, blocking out the light. The child looked up, transfixed, He was seized, suddenly, not only by the fear of discovery but by a deeper, long-buried fear. Words came to him and he used them. He said, squeakily, 'I know why you went there. You were mating. That's what people always do, they mate in the boathouse.'

Alice began to laugh, hysterically. A grin passed fleetingly over Nick's face. Martin stared at his son. His anger had left him and he was merely deeply shocked.

He said, firm but quite gentle, 'That's enough, Oliver. I think it's time you came home. The party's over. Time you were in bed.' He put his big hand on the boy's shoulder. Oliver gave a high scream and wrenched away from him. His voice fluted, thin with panic as he fled from his father and blundered into Nick, who caught and held him. 'Don't let him . . . don't . . . he'll hurt me . . . he's wicked, a wicked man . . .'

The look on Martin Bean's face stayed with Nick a long time. He picked Oliver up and held him, weeping, against his chest. The child hung from his hands like a puppet. 'Stop blubbing,' Nick said, not over-sympathetically. 'It's all right. No one's going to hurt you.'

Oliver said, his face pressed into Nick's jacket. 'He will, he *will*. Emmie knows.'

They all looked at her. She stood, fists doubled against her mouth, eyes wide and staring. It seemed as if the end of the world had come. 'I don't know. I don't know anything,' she said. 'He's a terrible liar. He always tells terrible lies.'

'I don't,' Oliver said in a stifled voice.

'You do,' she shouted. 'He's upset because he's seen people in the boathouse . . .' She looked round wildly and saw Alice's face, red and stupid with laughter. Emmie hated her suddenly. 'He saw Alice,' she said. 'Alice and Dickie . . .'

*

She ran down the garden and out on to the tow-path. The thunder started as she reached the gate, a great crash and then a long roll of drums. Her legs trembled so they would hardly carry her. She reached the poplars and stumbled into the field behind them, falling flat on her belly, her face pressed into the spiky grass. The rain started, a few heavy drops at first and then hissing spears of water that struck her sharply on the head, on her neck, pricking through the thin stuff of her dress. She shut her eyes to shut everything out. She wanted to die. She hoped she would be dead when the morning came; they would find her, dead, cold and stiff. If she was dead, Dad would forget what she had said and Alice would forgive her. After a little, the rain stopped but the trees went on dripping. Each drop was like a lump of ice.

*

William found her. He came up to her, snuffling, wriggling his clownish hindquarters, letting out little, frenzied yaps of delight. She flung her arms round him, her face buried in his soaking coat.

'I thought he'd track you down,' Nick said. 'Up you get now.'

He helped her up. She was very cold and heavy. She didn't cry but stumbled beside him as he led her home.

'I think you'd better get straight to bed,' he said. The rain had cooled everything down and the Beans' kitchen was cold and depressing. Emmie shivered as if she would never stop. 'You'd better go up and have a hot bath. Quick about it. I'll bring you a drink. Can you manage?'

She nodded and trailed up the stairs. When he brought her a whisky, mixed with lemon and sugar and hot water, she was in bed. Her clothes lay in a heap on the floor.

'There wasn't any hot water,' she said.

'Never mind. Drink this up, there's a good girl.'

She sipped it and made a face. She wasn't looking at him.

He said, 'Don't ever do anything like that again, Emmie.'

She trembled. 'I didn't mean to say that about Alice. It wasn't true. Nothing's true. Oliver's a terrible liar. He can't help it, he makes things up all the time and he forgets what's true and what isn't . . .'

Nick smiled. 'That's not what I meant. I meant, don't run off again.'

'Were you worried?' she asked with a faint gleam of interest. The whisky had brought colour back into her face and her shivering was less violent.

'Terrified. Out of my wits. I thought you had chucked yourself in the river.'

'I didn't mean to scare you. I just wanted to get away. I couldn't bear it.'

'There's nothing you can't bear. You're tough as an old boot. But I was afraid you might feel like that.' He took her hand. It felt very small and icy. 'You're all right now?' he said anxiously. 'Warmer? You don't feel sick or anything?'

'Don't look so worried. I'm all right. I won't even catch cold – you'll see. I'm as strong as a horse. Is Oliver all right?'

'Tucked up snug as anything. With Alice in the other bed.' He grinned at her cheerfully. 'There was a fine shemozzle after you'd gone. Oliver howled, Alice passed out flat on the floor.'

He was relieved to see her smile. 'Trust Alice. Did Oliver get his present?'

'No. But he'll get it first thing in the morning. It's a . . .'

'Ssh.' She put a cold finger against his lips. 'I don't want to know. It's not fair, before he does. Was he awfully unhappy?'

'Pretty.' He hesitated. 'Is he – is there any reason why he should be scared of your father?'

'No.' Her voice was disconcertingly loud. He wondered if she were telling the truth and decided that it hardly mattered. Emmie was fond of her father. She could not, so his simple, adult mind reasoned, be so affectionate towards him if he had done anything very dreadful.

She said, 'I expect Olly's sorry now for telling such fearful lies. He can't help it. It's because he's so clever. He's got an extraordinary imagination, everyone says so. Not like me. I just say things when I'm angry. I was angry with Alice. You know it wasn't true what I said, don't you?'

She looked at him, half-sly, half-pleading, like a child who wants a present it is not entitled to. For a moment, his mind rebelled. She was his straight, his shining Emmie – he could not bear dishonesty in her. Then he saw it was no good. He could not deny her the comfort of this lie any more than he could deny her a piece of bread if she were starving.

'I knew,' he said. 'I doubt if your father did, though.'

She gave a long sigh. 'Was he very angry?'

'A bit.' He stood up to go. This was something he preferred not to discuss with her. He believed – or wished to believe – that she had not understood the implications of what she had said about Alice. 'I'd better get back. Get your beauty sleep. You'll be all right, won't you?'

She nodded. Then she said, casually, 'Do I bother you? Hanging around and getting in the way?'

'Never. Why should you think you do?'

She turned her head on the pillow, so he could not properly see her face, only the Greuze-like line of her cheek. 'I don't know. I just thought . . . I'd hate to be a nuisance to you.'

He felt a wave of almost painful love for her. He said, 'You'd never be a nuisance to anyone. Least of all to me.'

She looked at him, smiling, her eyes bright as if she had a secret. She said, 'If I was older, would you still like me? If you were younger, I mean.'

'That's a lot of ifs and buts.'

'If we were both about twenty-five. Both of us. Would it be different?'

Her voice was deliberately childish; she was acting, he realized, pretending to be several years younger than she was. He was not irritated but touched.

'Just a little, pet,' he said, and bent to kiss her. She twined her arms so tightly round his neck that he almost choked, pulling him down so that he overbalanced and fell on top of her. 'Oh, I do love you,' she said, 'I do love you.'

Her hair was still damp; it smelt like wet grass – a pleasant smell, not sweet like hay but fresher and cleaner. Her thin arms were surprisingly strong. He released himself gently as he could and stood up, half-laughing. 'That was a very strenuous good-night kiss,' he said. Then he looked at her scarlet face, at the awful misery in her eyes and didn't want to laugh any more. He said helplessly, 'I love you too. Now be a good girl and go to sleep. God bless, sleep well.'

*

For some time after he had gone, Emmie stared with smarting eyes at the ceiling, humming casually under her breath. Then she remembered Mo. She climbed out of bed stiffly and pulled the chair up to the wardrobe.

*

He was dead. He lay stiff on her hand, small, cold and useless. A flea jumped off him. She held her breath for a moment and then the tears and the breath burst out of her at the same time. 'Oh Mo . . . Mo . . .'

14

MARJORIE woke him in the middle of the night. 'Nick . . .'

He raised himself sleepily on one elbow and switched on the light. Her face was very pale, her eyes very dark. 'I'm afraid,' she said. 'I can't sleep.'

His stomach quailed. This was how her illness had started in the beginning – with an outbreak of insomnia some months after her child had died. It had been the first definite sign that something was wrong; though she had been moody and withdrawn for some weeks before, he had thought this a normal reaction to her baby's death. He remembered now, feeling sick and cold, that she had barely spoken last night, after the break-up of the party.

*

She had sat silent in a chair, not drinking or smoking, while he and Martin talked. It had been a fairly calm conversation. Martin apologized because he had shouted at Alice in front of them all – he had been no angrier, Nick considered, than any father had a right to be – but after that, he seemed disinclined to discuss her. Nick, who had feared a torridly emotional hour or so was relieved by this; grateful, he had shared half a bottle of brandy with Martin and told him a great deal about the behaviour of adolescents in certain African tribes, a safe subject, and one he was apt to enlarge on when drunk. At some point, Marjorie must have gone to bed; finishing an account of a ceremonial circumcision he had attended, Nick had glanced abstractedly in her direction and been surprised to find her gone. 'I expect she was tired,' he said.

Martin's eyes looked a little glazed. He said abruptly,

rather as if he had been thinking about something quite different all the time Nick had been talking – 'She may be a little upset, I'm afraid. My wife's coming home.'

'Why should that upset her?' Nick said, simply surprised.

The big man stared at him. 'Oh? She didn't – well, I don't know . . .' His skin darkened. He mumbled in a vague, harassed way, 'She's got so fond of the kids. Oliver especially. Must be a bit of a blow to her in a way, Clemence coming back. Boy's own mother. Must look a bit as if everything's coming to an end.'

'She told you that?' Nick was slightly annoyed.

Martin fidgeted in his chair, drained his brandy glass. 'Not exactly . . .'

'I'm sure you must have misunderstood her.' Nick's stiffness was not intended as a rebuff; it was simply an instinctive reaction to the sentimental concern in Martin's voice. He disliked it, when people were over-sensitive to Marjorie's feelings. His attitude, part shame, part protectiveness, was the attitude of a parent towards a loved, crippled child: Marjorie's miseries were his private affair, he preferred others to treat her as absolutely normal. He said, 'I'm sure she's delighted, really. I must say, I am too. She's been very happy with the children but I've wondered once or twice if they weren't rather a strain on her.'

'I'm sorry if they have . . . ' He looked straight at Nick, very red and glistening. 'But I thought – women like to feel indispensable, you know.'

'Yes.' Martin's solicitude made Nick ashamed: it seemed to point out a certain coldness in his own heart. He said, 'It's nice of you to worry about Marjorie. But I'm sure there's no need. If she seemed upset it was only because she was tired.'

*

203

He said to her, 'It's all right. You're only over-tired. You've been doing too much.'

She said, 'Don't pretend. I can't bear it,' and moaned, biting her lip. He remembered, suddenly, how she had looked when he had seen her after her first shock treatment, her lips bitten and bruised.

He said loudly, 'Of course that's all it is. You mustn't think every time you're tired or can't sleep that it's this thing starting up again. It's *normal* to get tired.'

She looked at him and for a moment he thought that this time it was going to be easy, this time she would believe him and go to sleep. He could never be sure; she was alternately a person you could convince of anything, however unreasonable, and a person you could convince of nothing. But she snapped, 'I'm not tired, I'm *not*,' glaring at him like an enemy, and he felt a sour weariness at the prospect of the long, white night ahead of them.

He said, 'You are, you know. You've had a hell of a lot to do – virtually running two houses and now this stupid scene this evening. I was afraid it might be too much for you but you seemed so happy.'

'I was happy,' she said, sitting bolt upright in bed. 'And I'm *not tired.*'

'All right,' he said, soothing her, stroking her long, narrow back, massaging the taut muscles of her neck, 'there my baby, you're not tired, you're all right, you're going to sleep . . .'

She gave an irritated sigh and flung herself back on the pillows, staring straight up at the ceiling. 'You don't have to pretend to love me, Nick. It's an insult.'

He stifled a yawn and smiled apologetically as he met her hard, straight gaze. 'Come on,' he said gently, 'out with it. What part of my character is under fire this time?'

'*Don't,*' she said with such pain in her voice that he

could almost believe it was genuine. He had to remind himself that when she was in this mood she was a mistress of the single, agonized word, the mutely suffering glance.

'Well,' he said, warily humouring her, 'what have I done?'

She muttered something, he caught the tail end, '. . . that girl.'

'What girl?'

'You know what girl.' She said in a detached, emphatic way, 'She's potty about you. And you . . . I've seen how you look at her. You're mad about her.'

'You don't believe that?'

'I've been lying here, thinking about it.' Her voice had a steely, triumphant ring. 'I know you, Nick. Any young girl will do. You can be a splendid mixture of teacher and lover. Gratify both your instincts. What do you do to her? Talk to her in your best, professorial manner, make her think how nice and kind you are and then gently – ever so gently – put your hand up her skirt?'

He controlled his disgust with an effort. 'Stop it. Listen to me. This jealousy – this thing you have about girls is all nonsense.'

'Everything's nonsense when I know what you don't want me to know.' She began to weep. 'Oh God, oh God, I wish I was dead . . .'

Her clenched hands beat on his chest. He caught them and tried to hold her still but she fought him like a spitting cat. 'Dead, dead . . .'

'Control yourself.'

'Filthy dead and rotten . . . you could do what you like then . . . though I suppose you know she's under age, there's a law about that . . .'

'Stop it,' he roared. 'Stop it. Listen. *Listen*. You're not upset about Emmie, you're not that sort of bitch. You're upset about Oliver, because his mother's coming back. You're afraid you'll lose him – you'd pretended to yourself he was yours. But he isn't yours, he never was, it never was any good . . .'

She let out a long, sobbing shriek. 'Oh . . .' And lay still. He looked at her white face and the dark fear in her eyes and felt a brute. Hysteria had nothing to do with reality, it was something you couldn't help, couldn't hold back any more than you could stop flood water finding out the weak places in a dam. She couldn't bear her imaginary fears : to confront her with her real ones was like pushing a frightened child to the edge of an abyss.

He said, 'I'm sorry. I shouldn't have said that . . . it doesn't help. I love you, my baby. I don't love any girl.'

She looked at him with a gleam of defiance. 'You do. She told me.'

He sank his voice to a gently reproachful tone. 'That's a lie, isn't it? Either that – or the girl's mad.'

'*I* was mad,' she said, and came shuddering into his arms.

He held her close, comforting her. She said, over and over again, 'I'm sorry, I'm sorry, I'm sorry . . . ' He kissed her mouth, her hair, her wet eyes.

'I'm a lousy person,' she said. 'I hate myself. Why shouldn't you be fond of the child? I just couldn't bear – oh – the way you look when you're with her, relaxed and happy and younger. *She's* so young – it makes me feel so old and useless . . . you *don't* love her, do you, Nick?'

'No,' he said. 'I don't love her.'

'And then – this evening, when everyone was so upset . . . you only thought of her . . . you went off after her as if she were the only person that mattered to you . . . I felt as if you'd left me . . . as if I was alone on a bridge and there was no safe place at all . . .'

'You'll never be alone,' he said. 'I'll never leave you again, not for a minute.'

*

When she finally slept, tear-stained, he felt no relief, only an enormous exhaustion. She was going to be all right eventually; her illness was physical in origin and the possibility of a relapse, while it terrified them both, would diminish as she grew older. He had only to be patient. To hold on. The grim thought struck him that perhaps he could not hold on much longer. More and more after these scenes he felt worn out, drained – as if his life were being slowly refined down to a point. It was not just that his career had suffered: he would have been an errand boy if it would have done her any good. But he could not watch her terrible despairs without participating in them; increasingly, he found he was as paralysed by them as she was herself. Though he loved her, he felt he was less and less able to help her. She was too much a part of him. Her fears were too much a part of him – like some disease in the marrow of his bones.

Lying in bed, awake, became intolerable. He got up at last and stared out of the window at the empty road and the gravel pits, grey in the dawn light. A single owl hooted. Marjorie turned over in bed with a deep, sobbing sigh, and he felt vaguely and wearily sorry for whatever unhappiness she was feeling in her sleep. He wondered whether she really believed her wild accusations – and then, bracing himself, whether there was not some truth in them, after all . . .

He thought about it, solemnly searching his heart. He knew he was, in some ways, a priggish, unimaginative man: he believed himself to be also an honest one. He felt nothing for Emmie, he could swear, that a father might not feel, or an affectionate uncle. She was touchingly, comically independent, young, undefeated – he was afraid for her and wished her well. The truth was , he thought ironically, that he had got to the age when it was too late to have splendid dreams and nice thoughts about himself; the age when childless people feel the lack of children. If you have a child, your failing aspirations, your narrowing vision, the whole of your shabby middle-age matters less; you can collapse, panting, at the post and hand on the torch. A poor substitute for personal hope and endeavour, he had always thought, listening to his friends besotted by the achievements of little Willy, but perhaps it was a human necessity no one could quite escape from. You have made a mess. You hope your children will do better.

If he loved Emmie, then, his love was only a projection of his need, and even if he found that need curiously weak and shameful, it was common enough. And harmless enough. As harmless as her love for him.

All the same, he had a feeling of guilt as if he had been accused of something in the middle of a bad dream and, waking, could not remember what it was. He had done nothing wrong, nothing at all, but there was no way of proving it, even to himself.

*

Emmie had cried until her eyes were hot and her throat dry and aching. She sat on the back door step, in the morning sunshine, bare feet on William's fawn and white belly, aimlessly pulling at his soft ears. From time to time, a dry little hiccough shook her.

She was thinking about Mo. Her mind was full of him, there was no room for anything else at all. She thought she would never be able to bear it. From time to time, her eyes screwed up in a spasm of misery. He was so quick, so dear, so light. In the spring, they had had a vase of bluebells in the kitchen; he had run up the stem of one full, blue flower and it had barely bent under his weight.

Oliver said, 'You'll have to bury him.' He had wept too but now he calmly awaited a new pleasure. He liked burials, the ritual pleased him and the prospect of having a new grave to tend. He grew flowers on the graves: last winter he had started a cemetery at the bottom of the garden and stuck in a big cross for a sign. On the crosspiece he had painted the words: *Oliver Bean. Undertaker.*

Emmie shook her head. 'I can't – I can't touch him.'

'I'll give you my shoe box. The one I keep my stones in. I'm not going to collect stones any more. I'll get him and put him in for you.'

Emmie shuddered. Death had no horror for Oliver. He could touch dead things, even dead slugs after they had had salt poured over them. He touched them wonderingly, without fear, speculating on what it was that was different. He went indoors and returned a few minutes later with the shoe box. 'I've wrapped him in one of Dad's handkerchiefs,' he said. 'It makes a good shroud.'

'Oh – you *ghoul*.' Emmie dug her toes into William's sun-warmed coat and blinked miserably at the box. 'I can't bear it,' she said.

Oliver said, 'You can have Henry if you like. Tortoises live longer than squirrels.'

The heroic gesture touched her. 'You can't give your animals to me.'

'I don't mind. I like Murgatroyd better than Henry, anyway. Besides, then I can get a female. Then they can mate together. Marjorie's given me a tortoise house for my present, but I don't like it. It's got windows and a pretend door like a human house. It's silly for tortoises.' He looked thoughtfully down at the white box, Mo's coffin.

'William's dug a hole at the bottom of the garden. I can use that for a grave. It'll save me digging.'

'Oh – don't tell me, I don't want to know,' Emmie cried passionately, flinging herself down on top of William who suffered her patiently for a moment and then got up, shook himself and moved away.

'All right. I'll do it,' Oliver said.

She watched him through her fingers as he went down the garden and bent over the hole. Then she flew after him and snatched the box away. 'I'll do it,' she said in a choking voice. 'He's *my* squirrel.'

They firmed down the earth and put a brick to mark the spot. 'I'll make a border of shells,' Oliver said, 'and plant some forget-me-nots.'

'Do what you like.' Emmie turned her back and stumbled up the path. 'It's all done,' she muttered to herself. 'All finished.' The words were exquisite. They filled her with a deep, purple-rich sadness that was almost like happiness. But only for a moment. Then she felt a stab of coldness and terror, suddenly glimpsing the hopelessness of all struggle, of all life, of all love. She gulped back tears and called to Oliver, 'Come on in, can't you? We've got to have breakfast.'

'I've had it twice,' Oliver said. 'Once next door and then I had a second breakfast with Dad. Just Dad and me. Alice was in the bath. He said where were you and I said you were crying over Mo.'

'Is Dad indoors?'

'No. He's gone up to London. On the early train.'

'Did he say anything about last night?' Emmie asked curiously. She did not understand how Oliver could be so calm after what he had said about Dad at the end of the party. If she were Oliver, she could not have borne to look her father in the face.

Oliver stared at her in surprise. 'Of course he didn't. He gave me a shilling for sweets. You can have sixpence of it, if you like.'

*

He had, in fact, had a very pleasant breakfast with his father, eating a third bowl of cornflakes and toast, without for one moment feeling uncomfortable or wondering why his father should be so gently considerate and butter his toast for him. Everybody was, as Oliver knew himself to be, changeable. This meant, of course, that at any moment almost anything might happen but life was like that. What mattered was the present, how people behaved to you here and now. So he had thankfully devoured his second breakfast, simply pleased that his father was being so attentive to him and not connecting this in any way with his own outburst of the night before. He had quite forgotten it, or, rather, it had sunk back to the dark, subterranean level from which it had sprung and on which he really did believe his father might kill him some day. The fact that his father behaved towards him for most of the time with mild, if somewhat unthinking kindness, did not rule out this possibility which is present at some time or other in most children's minds : after all, if you were going to kill someone you would naturally go on being kind to them for the time being, giving them money for sweets and generally keeping up appearances. If Oliver's fear was slightly more explicit than is common, this was merely because killing people was a concept he dwelt upon fairly frequently and with lively interest.

*

'I don't want any breakfast, thank you,' Alice said. She knelt on the floor of the bedroom, a suitcase open in front of her, ramming in jerseys, shoes, underwear. Emmie looked at her, uncomprehending. She didn't understand Alice, she didn't understand anything. Her thoughts were still so full of Mo: she thought that if she tried to say anything, she would have to lie down on the bed and howl.

Alice sat back on her heels and looked at her sister. 'Aren't you interested in what I'm going to do?' she said, cold as stone.

Emmie stared at her.

'Or don't you care? After what you said last night . . .' Alice's calm broke. Her mouth quivered. 'I'm going away,' she said in a high, shaky voice. 'Out of this awful, rotten house. I'm never coming back again. Never, never . . .'

'You can't.' Emmie's tongue felt thick and swollen in her mouth. 'You can't go . . . Dad . . .'

'He's not my father,' Alice said. 'And you're only my half sister. I haven't anyone.'

'That's not true,' Emmie whispered, sick with love and shame. 'You can't leave us. Where can you go?'

'I'm going to stay with Dickie's aunt. She lives in the country. She's a district nurse. I can be a cadet at the local hospital and later on I can do my training in London.' Alice had controlled her tears and her face was pale and stiff with the effort to be sensible and make arrangements. 'Dickie says his aunt is nice. He used to go and stay with her when he was a little boy.' She looked at Emmie and said with distant kindness. 'I expect she'll let you and Oliver come and stay some time. I'll give you the address.'

'Are you going to marry Dickie?' Emmie said. A sodden heaviness weighted down her limbs. She sat on the edge of the bed and leaned her drooping head against the post.

'I'm never going to marry anyone. I'm not just saying that. It's true. I thought I might but it was only a phase.

Part of growing up. There's only one thing I ever really wanted to do. And if there's only one thing you want to do you have to get on and do it. There isn't time to do other things as well.'

Slowly, her words came alive, carrying their meaning fully, and Emmie understood. Alice was dedicated. Emmie had always known it, really, but only as part of the long, beautiful dream she had about all her family. Now she knew it was true, Alice's face looked different to her: set, calm and holy as a nun's. Emmie felt awed and a little lost and lonely, not because Alice was going away, but because nothing she could dream about her any more could be more splendid than the truth.

She said, rather wistfully, 'Do you think you'll be a Matron? With one of those high, white hats, like a cake?'

'I expect so. Not in a big hospital, though. Small hospitals are better. I shouldn't be so busy organizing things, I'd have time to do some nursing if I wanted to.'

Alice shut her case with a snap and stood up, a little flushed, eyes very full and shining. She said, 'You'll have to give me some money out of the housekeeping. For my fare.'

15

'COME on, out with it,' Martin said. 'Where does she live? This aunt? Does she really exist, or have you made it all up?'

Emmie shook her head. She stood very straight, her hands locked behind her back. Like a martyr, her father thought sourly. He had never struck his children but he felt suddenly that he would like to shake this sullen brat until her teeth rattled.

He said, 'This is a fine home-coming, I must say.' He felt a rush of indignant self-pity. 'I go up to London for half a day, get myself a job, and what do I find when I get home, eh? *What do I find?*' Anger bubbled up inside him like a clean spring; he shouted, thumped the kitchen table with his fist until the dirty cups and saucers danced.

Emmie was not at all alarmed. Her cheeks went pink, her eyes shone. 'Oh, Dad – *where*? Why didn't you say? Is it a good job?'

Her pleasure, bright as a new penny, disarmed him. 'Trade magazine,' he said, in a more composed voice. 'Not a bad job.'

The kind of job, he thought, that was simply an admission of defeat. He was to get twenty pounds a week. The editor had as good as told him he was lucky to get it. Sourbutts – Edgar Sourbutts, the name had a kind of freak, Dickensian squalor that went with the small frowsty magazine, the small, frowsty office. Maybe he was lucky. At the moment his shoulders simply felt bowed, as if someone had laid a yoke across them. Someone had. His children . . .

He looked at Emmie. 'You'll have to tell me where she's gone. Or I'll have to get hold of the police.'

She flinched away from him as if he had raised his hand. 'No,' she said breathlessly. '*No*. You mustn't do that.'

'Why ever not?'

His tone was purely surprised. He hadn't meant to frighten Emmie. He saw she *was* frightened and hadn't the energy to wonder why. He was too tired, too worried.

She said, 'I've got the address. Alice wrote it down and I stuck it behind the clock.'

He looked at Alice's round, clear writing. She wouldn't have left this address unless she had intended – hoped? – he would go after her. The poor child. The poor, hurt, silly child. He thought of her with shocked tenderness and a kind of sad humility. He hadn't looked after her properly, he'd been a bad father. Now this had happened he would have to try to get closer to her, make a fresh start . . .

Emmie said. 'You won't tell the police now, will you?'

He looked at her abstractedly. She was a pale little ghost in the dusk of the kitchen.

'No . . . I'm going to fetch her. I'll be some time – several hours. Depends how the trains go. You'll be all right, won't you? Give Oliver his tea, put him to bed.'

'Yes, I'll look after Oliver.'

'Good girl. You're a good girl.'

He kissed her forehead and ruffled her hair, feeling slightly uneasy. She'd been so panicky, looked so pale. 'Give us a smile, pet,' he said. 'Cheer up for Chatham, Dover's in sight.'

At this preposterous saying, one of their small, intimate jokes, she did smile. But it was a mask-like smile that gave her face a waxy, basilisk look.

*

As soon as he had gone, Emmie raced down the garden to

the boathouse. On the punt cushions, Oliver sat where she had left him, in tears. The suitcase lay opened in front of him. The bundles of notes, in their elastic bands, made Emmie feel cold as stone.

'Now,' she said. 'Now Dad's gone, we'll have the truth. Where did you get it?'

'I didn't steal it, I didn't.' Oliver's mouth opened wide and square in a terrible howl.

'Shut up – someone'll hear,' Emmie said, in horror.

He checked his cries, going red in the face with effort. Finally, he sat, silent and quivering, bursting out with only an occasional, suppressed sniffle.

Emmie's voice ached with grief and a queer kind of triumph.

'I might have known – I might have known you hadn't got over it. This is the worst thing you've ever done. The worst thing. I ought to have stopped you in the beginning – I ought to have walloped you good and hard instead of hiding the things and pretending I didn't know anything about it. I ought to have told Dad or someone. It's all my fault. That's what they'll say and they'll probably send me to prison.' Her voice sunk to an awestruck hollowness. Oliver was sitting quite still, his eyes fixed on her and his hands clasped round his knees. His legs were trembling so that his hands wouldn't keep still. She said, 'Then, when I've gone there won't be anyone to look after you any more and they'll find out what a nasty little thief you are. And they'll send *you* to prison too.'

He said in a gasping voice, 'I didn't steal it. I wouldn't steal money. I didn't know it was money. I thought it was treasure. Mr Hellyer asked me to hide it for him. He said – he said we'd pretend it was the Crown Jewels.'

'Oh no,' she said, 'oh no,' in a shocked, incredulous way as if someone had just slapped her in the face. It was as if she had been having a nightmare – terrible, perhaps, but still only a dream in which the money could vanish like fairy gold – and woken up to find it was true. It had really happened. Those bundles of notes weren't fairy gold, or even Monopoly money. They were real. They had been handed over counters, crumpled, made greasy by hundreds of sweaty hands. Mr Hellyer had stolen them.

'You're an Accomplice,' she said.

Oliver gave a small, whimpering sound, but he didn't cry. He said, 'What are you going to do, Emmie?' He looked at his sister, with fear. She was so strong, so old, so terrible.

She said slowly, 'I'm not sure. I've got to think it over. But you're not just going to get away with it, this time. There's been too much of that.'

He was silent. His eyelashes concealed his eyes in that secret, almost coy way he had and she was suddenly dreadfully frightened and angry with him at the same time.

'I've stuck up for you long enough,' she said. 'I ought to hand you over to the police. I ought to have done it long ago. Do you know what they do to thieves sometimes? They cut off their hands so that they go about for the rest of their lives with bleeding stumps.'

He huddled up as if he was trying to roll himself into a ball. His head fell forward on his chest. She said, 'You just sit here and think about what you've done. Don't you dare move.'

She fastened the suitcase without looking at him. Then she came out of the boathouse and shut the door. She was shaking all over, partly because she was so angry with Oliver and partly because she was so afraid. It was growing dark in the garden, but not dark enough – she was naked and exposed under the wide, open sky. As she ran up the garden, her legs felt soft and boneless under her;

she had the terrible feeling that they might collapse altogether if she didn't hurry and find somewhere private, somewhere nice and safe and dark.

She reached the house, ran into the front room and shoved the suitcase behind a big, glass case that had a capercailzie in it. Then she sat down on the floor, in the dark, green room among the birds. She felt them watching her with their dead eyes. There was no sound except her beating heart.

*

Half an hour later, she felt a little better although she hadn't decided what to do. There seemed to be nothing she could do. It would be wrong to give the money back to Mr Hellyer and terrible to tell Dad. He would certainly hand Oliver over to the police; he had said he would tell the police about Alice and this was much, much worse. And the police would do something dreadful to Oliver. Though he had to be punished, of course . . .

She became aware that she was very hungry. She got up off the floor and went into the kitchen. There were two kippers in the larder; she stuck one, tail up, in a saucepan and cooked it. She ate it in her hand and washed it down with several glasses of Tizer. She left the other kipper for Oliver, but decided that she would wait a bit longer before she went to fetch him. She had frightened him properly this time. She hoped she had, anyway. If she left him long enough, sitting in the dark in the boathouse and thinking it over, perhaps he would never do anything wrong again.

In the meantime, she had to decide what to do. She went upstairs and picked up a hairbrush – Alice's brush – that she had left behind on the chest of drawers. Emmie brushed her hair half-heartedly in front of the cheval mirror. A little breeze came in through the open window

218

and set the hanging light swinging, so that her face was now shadowed, now glistening pale in the electric glare. She put the hairbrush down and began to pull hideous faces in the glass, pulling the corners of her eyes down with her forefingers and squashing her nose up with her thumbs so that she looked like an insane pug dog. Then she sighed and squeezed in by the side of the chest of drawers to look out of the window, scratching away with her finger nail at the film of grease on the pane. From where she stood, she could see the road and the front of the house next door. The car was out with its bonnet up and Mr Sargent was there with a flashlight, peering into the engine.

She frowned, thinking. If she told Mr Sargent, would he know what to do? He was kind, he wouldn't tell anyone. It would be difficult to tell him, though. She wondered what she could say. *Mr Sargent. Nick* – he had asked her to call him Nick. *Nick, do you remember what I told you about Oliver a long time ago? Well, something has happened again. Something rather tiresome. Tiresome* was a good word, not too serious. She didn't want him to think it was too serious. Not at first. Not until she had had time to explain that Oliver was only a little boy, that he hadn't really understood . . .

*

'You made me jump,' Nick said. 'Creeping up behind me like that.'

He did look jumpy, Emmie thought. He glanced past her, at the open door of the house and then, rather determinedly, smiled.

'What do you want?' he said.

Emmie blinked at him. Now she was here, she couldn't quite think what to say.

'Alice has gone away.' That wasn't important, but it

was easier to start with something unimportant and then, later on, she could begin to tell him about Oliver.

'Has she? Where?'

'To stay with someone. Dad's gone to fetch her.'

'So you're on your own?' He sounded a little puzzled but not really very interested.

Emmie said quickly, 'That doesn't matter. I mean, I'm used to looking after Oliver.' That was the way, she thought. In a minute she would say she wanted to talk about Oliver and they would go somewhere quiet, where she could explain everything slowly, from the beginning.

'Are you busy?' she said.

'Why? As a matter of fact, we're just going out.' He smiled, his nice, crinkly smile, but his eyes flickered away from her. 'Marjorie's feeling a bit low. I'm taking her out to dinner to cheer her up.'

Something in the way he looked at her, or, rather, didn't look at her, made Emmie embarrassed.

She said, 'Is my face dirty, or something?'

'No . . .' He did look at her then, rather sadly and searchingly as if he were going away for ever and wanted to remember what she looked like. 'No,' he said. 'Sparkling clean. Like a glass of Pimms with a piece of fresh mint in it.' He frowned suddenly, either at her or at himself. 'There isn't anything wrong, is there, Emmie?'

After a fractional pause, she shook her head. For some reason she felt uncomfortable with him. And anyway, there wasn't time to talk. 'Of course not,' she said. 'Why should there be?'

*

The boathouse was very quiet and dark. She said, 'Oliver,' and there was no answer, though she had thought she could hear him breathing. She couldn't be sure, there were

220

so many other sounds: the creak of the old boat in the water, the slap of the river against the grille. Perhaps he was screwed up somewhere small in a corner. It was several minutes before she decided that he really wasn't there.

She came out of the boathouse and stood uncertainly, biting her thumb nail. It was dark and Oliver was frightened of the dark. The memory of all the things she had said to him came back to her and she was suddenly scared. He was so little, so thin – she wanted to get hold of him and hug him tight and safe.

He wasn't in the garden or in the house. In his bedroom, Henry was scraping about in the tortoise box. Henry, but not Murgatroyd. That worried her. If he had run away he would have taken Murgatroyd – he wouldn't have gone anywhere without Murgatroyd.

She looked in the garden again and then went back through the house and out on to the road. She walked a little way along, kicking a stone, and came to the entrance to the gravel pits. The machinery was tall and gaunt and silent. She went in, shrinking fearfully away from the deepest patches of shadow and called, 'Oliver.' The empty echo of her voice alarmed her and she whispered his name instead. 'Oliver, Oliver . . .', creeping along delicate and tense as a stalking cat.

The water of the big lake chuckled gently against the soft banks and against the pontoon boats and the pipe. The pontoon would be a good place to hide. She got into the flat-bottomed boat and tried to push it away from the bank but the pole stuck in the mud and the boat was too heavy for her to move. He couldn't have used the boat, then, but he might have walked along the pipe to the pontoon. He could have fallen in. She looked at the dark, shiny water and shivered.

Then she remembered the skips. There was a rough railway that had been built from the plant to an almost worked-out pit. There was no pipe line there, only a crane and grab. They got the ballast out and loaded it into skips and the loco brought it along the line to the plant. Once, Dickie had given her and Oliver a ride in the loco and another time he had been very angry with Oliver for playing hide-and-seek in the skips.

Remembering this, her heart lifted. She ran along the line, stumbling over the planks, until she came to the old pit and the line of empty skips. Oliver was in the end one, scrooged up in a corner with Murgatroyd on his lap. When she found him he screamed and hit out at her. She had never heard him scream like it, the dreadful sound echoed back from the sides of the skip and his fists were hard as little rocks.

'They won't get me, they won't get me,' he shouted, in between the screams.

Emmie tried to get hold of him but he fought like the baby wild cat her mother had once been given to tame. It had been a pretty little creature, it had looked quiet and gentle and good like Oliver, but as soon as you went near it, it had turned into a clawing, spitting bundle of hate.

'It's all right,' Emmie said over and over again. 'It's all right. No one'll get you. I'm a liar, I told you a lot of lies.'

The awfulness of what she had done came over her and she began to cry too. This seemed to quieten Oliver; his screams died down into long, big sobs that made him shake all over. They cried together until they were warm and salty with each other's tears. Then Emmie helped him out of the skip and along the railway; he clutched her with one hand and held Murgatroyd with the other. He said, 'Don't let them get me, Emmie. Please don't let them.'

She felt wickedly ashamed because she had been so cruel. She loved him more than she had ever loved anyone, animal or human, more than she loved Mo, more than she loved Mr Sargent. Nothing must be allowed to happen to him.

She said, 'I won't. I won't – I promise.'

He began to smile, a rather wobbly, damp smile.

*

'You can't burn it. Not MONEY.'

'If you can think of anything better . . .'

'It's *wrong*.'

Oliver's tone, shocked, febrile, had about as much effect on Emmie as a quotation from Habeas Corpus would have on a crowd of hungry cannibals. Morality no longer concerned her – it never had, overmuch. What mattered was her family, the people she loved, Oliver's safety. With this in question, pale concepts of right and wrong faded into nothingness: she had become atavistic, female, terrible as a lioness with cubs. She would lie, steal, cheat for Oliver: burning a few hundred pounds was chicken feed.

She had no shadow of misgiving. 'We can't burn it in the grate – Dad might come back, we mightn't clean up in time. Get the bucket.'

Oliver stood, finger in mouth and stared at her.

Her eyes flashed at him. *'Under the sink!'*

He fetched it without another word and watched her while she folded sheets of newspaper into firelighters in the thrifty way Gran had taught her. She set a match to them and they smouldered economically.

'Give me the suitcase.'

He sighed deeply but dared not disobey. Tenderly, she laid the first few bundles in the pail and sat back on her heels, blackened fingers curled, like a housewife waiting for the stove to light. In the bottom of the bucket the newspaper burned steadily and undramatically; the edges of the notes curled like live things, went brown but did not ignite.

'They won't *burn*,' Emmie said. 'Paraffin . . .'

She flew to the scullery, lugged back the heavy can.

'Screw's rusted. Oh damn, oh damn and blast.'

She wrestled with it, panting. The lid came off, tearing skin off her fingers. She poured a little into the bucket. A tentative, pale tongue licked round the notes, trembled and died.

'Oh damn, oh damn . . .'

She emptied in half the tin and threw in a lighted match for good measure. The bucket went up in a geyser of flame, yellow and blue and white.

'Lovely,' Oliver said. '*Lovely.*'

Steadily, screwing up her eyes, Emmie fed in more bundles. The bucket was incandescent.

'The suitcase,' Oliver shouted. 'It'll burn lovely.'

'Not in the pail . . . it's not big enough. *Oliver!*'

Too late. The suitcase landed clumsily. The bucket tilted and then, curiously slowly, fell on to its side, six inches away from the open dresser cupboard and the piles of old newspapers Emmie had tumbled out when she made the firelighters. They caught at once, not smouldering, but a crackling, merry fire that swept hungrily up the wooden dresser, devouring candles, paper serviettes and spurting brief but splendid fireworks from a box of matches. For a moment, the children stood paralysed, Emmie with horror, Oliver with a fearful joy. Recovering, Emmie seized the thin old hearthrug and began to beat at the flames. A thick, choking smoke arose but the rug began to burn and she dropped it with a cry. Oliver caught at her skirt. 'Emmie, Emmie – come out!' She hadn't been frightened until then but the high panic in his voice infected her. It also saved their lives. As they ran into the garden, stumbling clumsily against each other, there was a hollow explosion: the flames had reached the uncovered paraffin tin.

They collapsed on the ground, gasping, black in the face, their hair covered with charred paper that was slowly settling like a shower of tiny, black, bird's wings.

Oliver said with a nervous excitement that was not altogether unpleasurable, 'The house will burn down.' The kitchen door, the window, became a yellow sheet. He said, 'It's like a bonfire, like Guy Fawkes night.' Suddenly he jumped to his feet and began to run up and down the garden, shrieking, turning cartwheels, hopping on one leg.

Emmie could say nothing. She felt nothing except a great awe. She began to cough. The earth seemed to shudder underneath her; she clutched at it, tearing up handfuls of dusty grass and retching.

That was how Mr Hellyer found them. He came up the garden shouting something – they did not properly hear him. They only saw him: it was very sudden, just as if he had materialized out of thin air. One moment he wasn't there, the next he was, a shabby, monkeyish little man with his mouth wide open and an expression of horrified bewilderment. They stared at him guiltily. For perhaps three seconds guilt was all they did feel, the simple, shocked guilt they would have felt before any adult. Then they looked at each other and a silent flash of understanding passed between them. Mr Hellyer was not just any adult. His interest in the fire was peculiar. Under his grime, Oliver turned as pale as his own pale hair.

Oliver opened his mouth. His eyes, fixed on Mr Hellyer, had a bright, fanatical look. Emmie saw, appalled, that he was about to tell him the truth. She leapt to her feet with a wild cry and rushed towards the house, tugging at the rusty handle of the little-used back door. (The Beans always came and went through the kitchen.)

'Emmie.' Mr Hellyer was behind her but she was already inside.

'Grandfather's birds,' she screamed over her shoulder, before she disappeared in a cloud of dingy smoke.

He only hesitated briefly. All the same, by the time he was halfway down the passage, she was coming back, staggering under the weight of a large, square, glass case.

'Get another,' she shouted and carried her burden into the garden.

Stunned, he proceeded, coughing, in the direction from which she had come. His bewildered eye was still roving round the museum when she returned. 'This one,' she ordered briefly and was off again before he could settle the awkward burden conveniently in his arms. She made three journeys, he made one. As far as Mr Hellyer was concerned one was enough to make the absurdity of this mission apparent.

'It's a mug's game,' he said, seizing her by the wrist.

'All right,' she gasped, not altogether reluctant. 'I've got three.'

She had rescued the capercailzie, a black-backed gull and a pair of redstarts; Mr Hellyer only a case of passerine birds which broke when he dumped it down too roughly on the path, spilling out the small, dry inhabitants into the larger air they had once so intimately known.

'Fire brigade,' Mr Hellyer said.

'I'll go,' Emmie cried. 'Telephone's next door.'

She was at the gap in the hedge when she heard Oliver shout. She turned back and saw him, leaping up at Mr

Hellyer like a hound at a stag. 'Henry . . . Henry . . . Upstairs in my bedroom. He'll be burned alive.'

*

Why he did it, it is impossible to say. Maybe he didn't understand who Henry was, maybe it didn't matter: the words *burned alive* are highly emotive. Mr Hellyer was fond of Oliver, he was also an unreasoning and impulsive man. In his action, kindness and stupidity were almost certainly inextricably blended.

For some minutes after he had dragged his coat over his head and entered the house through the back door, the children waited, trustingly expecting him to emerge with Henry in his hands. They had no fears for his safety. Even Emmie, though she knew Mr Hellyer to be a thief and therefore in some ways unreliable, was still young enough to see him as grown-up and therefore entirely competent in an emergency. And to Oliver, of course, Mr Hellyer was god-like, invulnerable.

From somewhere inside the house there was a crash, a hideous, tearing sound as if the bowels of the earth had opened. The windows of the house glowed suddenly bright, like the eyes of some monster waking in the dark. For a second or two after the crash, there was no further sound except the steady suppuration of the fire. Then the landing window fell out in a rain of sparks and blackened timber and from the road came the terrifying, metallic clamour of the fire-engine bell.

'Emmie,' Oliver said. His voice was hoarse as a raven's croak.

She turned to him, her eyes lit with pure terror.

'Emmie . . .'

She put her arms round him and held him tight against her. He didn't move, nor did she. A fireman found them, some minutes later. With her long, tangled hair, her wild eyes and her protective stance, Emmie looked like a heroine in a Victorian engraving.

*

When Martin Bean returned with Alice – an Alice who was tear-stained but still young enough for tears to be part of the simple process of healing – Emmie and Oliver did not tell him about Mr Hellyer. They never told him. Neither of them ever mentioned Mr Hellyer's name again.

16

Two nights after the fire, Martin Bean was undressing in his hotel bedroom when Oliver gave a long, despairing moan. He was lying in a small bed next to his father's; after that one, eerie cry, he made no further sound. Bending over him, Martin had decided that the child was asleep when his eyes opened. In the dim light they shone darkly, like deep pools. His hands shot up and fastened tightly behind Martin's neck. For a moment they were uncomfortably – almost painfully – locked together. Martin's face was pressed into his son's neck; inside that incredibly soft, frail stalk he could feel the heart beat like a little pump.

Oliver said, 'Don't let them cut off my hands.'

That was all; immediately afterwards, he released his father, turned over on his side with a long sigh and went to sleep.

Martin sat on the end of the bed, watching him. His heart yearned after his son, but intellectually, he was puzzled. And not newly so. That nightmarish cry was the first sign Oliver had given of any inward disturbance. During the last two days he had behaved with a kind of exalted gaiety, as if the whole sequence of events, the fire, Emmie's removal to hospital, his own stay in the hotel, were an exciting treat arranged for his benefit. Everything pleased him, the soap in the wash-basin stamped with a coloured picture of a medieval castle, the electric contraption that blew hot or cold when you turned a switch, the fascinating choice of cereals for breakfast. The first night he had stayed awake, fiddling with the radio above his bed, until the programmes went off the air. He had only once spoken about the fire. 'We were burning some rubbish,' Emmie said to the doctor who bandaged her burned hands at the hospital and Oliver added, 'We were playing a new game.' He had said nothing more. When Martin asked him about it, throwing out questions in a carefully casual way, it seemed that the boy had suddenly been struck deaf.

It wasn't his secretiveness that surprised Martin – natural enough that he should be stunned into silence by the appalling consequences of a heedless game – but his apparently callous indifference. His home was in ruins and he seemed not to care. Worse still – what showed an even more shocking lack of feeling – he had not once mentioned his pets. The dog, William, had been off on some private business at the time but others had perished: the rabbits, killed in their hutches by a falling beam, his tortoise, his half-blind hen. Once or twice, contemplating his cheerful little son, Martin had felt a cold depression.

He found Emmie's silence more understandable. Her responsibility, and therefore her shame, was greater. Besides, she had been quite badly burned trying to rescue her grandfather's ridiculous collection and was suffering from shock – though Martin, tiptoeing into her hospital room, had been agreeably surprised to find her cheerfully, if rather childishly, colouring the black and white pictures in an illustrated magazine.

It would obviously be unwise to pester her with questions. Indeed it was not until today when Mr Hellyer's body had been discovered trapped under a mess of laths and plaster, that questions had really been necessary. Even so, they were carefully guarded. Not only did the local Inspector have a simple theory which explained Mr Hellyer's presence in the house, but he was also a sentimentally devoted father. 'A child's mind is a delicate instrument, easily damaged,' he said solemnly to Martin. He added, more practically, 'If she knows nothing, then I shall leave it at that.'

*

'When you started this fire, you were on your own in the house? No one else about?'

Emmie shook her head.

'You didn't see anyone? Not in the house? In the garden?'

Emmie shook her head again. Since her first, clouded stare she had not looked at the Inspector but behaved as a very shy, much younger child, would have done, clumsily turning the pages of the magazine with her bandaged hands and pretending to look at the pictures, all the time he was talking to her.

'So you thought you were alone?'

'There wasn't anyone else there,' she said in a clear, rather hard voice.

'Quite sure?'

Colour flamed into her cheeks. 'Why should there be? There was only us – Dad wasn't there.' She flung herself sullenly back on the pillows and lay there, face averted, her body jerking angrily in the bed. The nursing Sister bent over her, smoothing the covers, and then glanced meaningly at the policeman. He got up from his creaking chair and stood, looking down at her.

'Rather daft at your age, wasn't it? Playing with matches? A big girl like you ought to have more sense.'

Martin thought his tone curiously unsympathetic and his pointed reference to her age unkind, though in fact her behaviour had irritated him too. She had always been young for her age but it seemed that she had been pretending to be younger still, deliberately retreating into babyhood. Presumably it was only a kind of defence – all the same, he was puzzled. He lingered, after the Inspector had gone, watching her from the doorway. Her face, now the furious flush had faded, was cold, stony – remarkably *un*-childlike, really . . .

He said, 'Don't worry, pet. All over now. Though you didn't behave very nicely, did you? He was only trying to find out what happened.'

'Leave me alone,' she said. '*Leave me alone.*'

Suddenly, perhaps because she now looked her proper age, or because her passionate tone did not ring quite true – it sounded more like acting than real desperation – an unpleasant suspicion darkened his mind. It was un-formulated, but terrible.

He said, 'It's very important to tell the truth, you know.'

'I have told the truth.'

Her voice had a defiant ring that seemed much more natural. He was eased at once. Of course – that was it. The child was bitterly ashamed, as well she might be, of what she and Oliver had done. The fact that she was old enough to know better embarrassed her. Martin could remember that at her age embarrassment was the most terrible of emotions. And this questioning must worry her all the more because she did not know the real reason for it. She was thinking that it was directed at her own, fearful incompetence. The appearance of a policeman at her bedside may even have terrified her into believing that her stupidity was actually criminal. Poor child – poor little girl. The best thing was to help her to forget it. Or, if that was not possible, to provide as many distractions as he could.

He thought how completely the excitement of staying

in an hotel had taken Oliver's mind off the disaster. Emmie was too old to be so easily diverted but the prospect of finding a new house, of moving to a completely different neighbourhood, would provide her with a great many things to think about. Slowly, with care, the memory of what had happened would begin to fade.

In the meantime, all he could do was to buy her a few books, a new game. He spent an enjoyable half-hour in a toy shop. By the time he left it, Emmie had become simply his dear, sick child who had to be amused. The uneasiness in his mind had disappeared altogether.

*

The morning's post brought an astonishing letter. Martin spent the next few hours in a state of bewilderment and pride mingled with a strange embarrassment. It was not until after lunch with the Sargents, with half a bottle of claret and a second brandy inside him, that he was sufficiently uninhibited to tell them about it.

'I was bowled over,' he said, 'you can imagine. I can't think what put it into her head. Sending it off in her mother's name. Dishonest little chit!' He stubbed out his cigar and smiled with tender disapproval. 'Of course they knew it was a hoax but the address was the same so they wired Clemence. Apparently she was hugely amused. She wired back saying it was Emmie's notebook – she'd encouraged her to start it, as a sort of Nature Diary – and that she was sure her agent would be delighted to draw up a contract.'

'They're actually going to publish?' Nick said incredulously.

'So they say.' He blew through his moustache, rather pink in the face. What a fool he felt! The thing sounded so damned unlikely. 'I'm as surprised as you are. Of course they'll have to do a lot – it's a bit of a stunt I suppose, really – but that won't affect Emmie.'

'She must be enormously excited,' Nick said.

The affectionate pleasure in his voice reassured Martin. He wasn't sure what he was embarrassed about, exactly. Chiefly he had been nervous in case they should laugh at her – at her extraordinary presumption. He felt she was very tender and vulnerable.

He said, 'She didn't seem to be excited. Maybe she didn't really take it in or something. All she said was, "How much money will I get?" Just like that!'

'How very practical!'

Their laughter was entirely kind.

Martin said, 'D'you think so? I must admit, I thought it a bit unnatural, myself. Though she probably wasn't really thinking . . . I've – I've had a telegram from Clemence. She's flying back. It probably crowded out everything else. At Emmie's age, I imagine your mother coming home is more important than suddenly finding yourself a celebrity even . . .'

There was a brief silence. Then Marjorie said, 'I'm so glad. So glad she's coming back.' She smiled at Nick, rather tremulously and he stretched across the table and took her hand. Holding on to it, as to an anchor, she said, 'Have you made plans? What you are going to do and so forth? I mean – I don't suppose you'll want to stay here?'

Martin grinned. 'No. Especially not after what's happened.'

He glanced at the window and Nick said quickly, 'It's all right. They took William off for a walk. Though I don't suppose the poor old dog'll get far in this heat.' All the same, he lowered his voice. 'They don't know about the man, I take it?'

Martin shook his head. 'Apparently not. Seems odd,

but coincidences do happen. Police seem to think so, anyway. Hellyer had a longish record—petty thieving. They think he got into the house when it was empty, heard the children downstairs and lay low. Smoke choked him before he could get out.'

'Poor devil,' Nick said. 'Still – I suppose it's a good thing the children don't know.'

'I thank God they don't,' Martin said piously. The expression on Nick's face conveyed a new idea to him. His voice rang with horror. 'Why – when you think about it, they're responsible in a sense.'

'If they knew, it might scar them for life,' Marjorie said in the same awestruck tone.

'It's another reason for getting them away as soon as possible. People are such idiots – anyone might tell them. They've suffered enough, without that.'

'Oliver seems cheerful enough ,' Nick said.

Marjorie shook her head reproachfully. 'Darling, you can't tell. It's the inward shock . . .'

'You're right,' Martin said. 'Kids hide things. For example, he had a nightmare last night. Yelled out something – he said, "Don't let them cut off my hands." '

'Oh Martin . . .'

Nick said. 'I expect it was because Emmie's hands were burned. It got mixed up in his mind.'

Martin gave a gentle sigh. 'That's bright of you, Nick. I hadn't thought of that.'

'There's usually some obvious answer if you look for it,' Nick said modestly.

The back door suddenly slammed. Then there was silence.

'Who's that?' Nick called.

Oliver appeared in the doorway. His face was flushed, his eyes brightly shining.

'I want to go home, Dad,' he said.

'Already?' The three adults smiled at him kindly.

'I want to go to the bathroom.'

'There's one upstairs, old chap,' Nick said.

Oliver frowned. 'I want to go to the bathroom *in the hotel*,' he said.

Martin glanced at Marjorie. He said indulgently, 'It's rather a splendid piece of mechanism. A terrific flush.'

'It's called Niagara,' Oliver said. 'After Niagara Falls.'

*

Emmie lay still in the hospital bed. The new books her father had brought her lay neatly stacked on her locker with a bowl of fruit and an unopened bottle of lemonade. The Sargents had sent the fruit. The lemonade had belonged to a patient who had died a couple of nights before; it had been given to Emmie by the Staff Nurse who had made a pet of her.

Emmie did not want to eat or drink or read. She had too much to think about. She had to decide what she would do with the money she got for her book. She wondered how much it would be and decided on five hundred pounds as a suitable amount. It was a nice, round sum. She set about spending it. She would let Dad have two hundred and fifty pounds to help buy a house. Then she would buy Alice a bicycle so it would be easy for her to get to the hospital when she started her training. The rest she would put in her savings bank so it would always be there if they couldn't pay their bills. Or perhaps she would give it to Mother. She was better at handling money than Dad.

Thinking about her mother made her uneasy. And a little angry with Dad. Why hadn't he said something before? Though, to be fair, what could he have said? Her mind became filled with a terrible shame as she remembered her silly, half-formed fears. Her face went bright red and she kicked her legs up and down to distract herself. Oh God – she could easily have mentioned it to someone – even put it in her Diary. She groaned aloud and pulled the pillow over her face, biting into its starchy softness. Of course she hadn't ever really believed it . . . Slowly her spasmodic kicking grew less, she pushed the pillow away and lay quiet and still.

About what happened on the night of the fire, she barely thought at all. She had walked a frail, swinging bridge across a chasm, refusing to look down. Now that she was safe, on firm ground, it would be madness to look back. Even to think about thinking about it made her feel dreadfully tired; her eyes filled with tears and she yawned until it felt as if her face would crack.

It was difficult to believe that the house had gone. It was going to be demolished, Dad said, because it was unsafe. But they had been going to pull it down soon anyway. In the end, the gravel pits would move in and dig up the place where the house had stood and the house next door and the gardens. They would dig up everything and no one would know anyone had ever lived there. Years later, she would come back and wouldn't be able to tell where the house had been.

They would dig up Mo's grave. Poor Mo, poor darling Mo. When she thought about him the tears came, scalding and hot and queerly comforting.

*

Staff Nurse clicked her tongue against her front teeth – her stock reaction to distress.

'Good heavens above. What are you crying for? What a silly girl – here's a handkerchief, love. Fancy crying, just when I've got a nice surprise for you. *Someone's* coming to tea.'

Sleek, fatly smiling, perfectly poised, Oliver advanced through the door.

'Now you must eat everything up, every *crumb*. I've given you a big glass of milk. You like milk, don't you?'

'Yes thank you,' Oliver said politely. He watched her closely while she set the tray down on the bedside table. His expression was wary as if she were a strange animal of whose habits he was doubtful. When she was gone, he gave a little sigh, looked appraisingly round the room and said, 'Is it nice here?'

'Quite nice.'

'Is *she* nice?'

'Quite nice.'

'She's fat in the chest.' He looked at Emmie. 'Were you crying about Mo?'

Emmie nodded.

'I'm never going to cry about Henry,' he said. 'Henry's gone to be with Jesus.'

They ate their tea without speaking. Peeping in, Staff Nurse thought they made a pretty pair, the dark child in the bed and the little, blond beauty sitting beside her, steadily munching bread and jam.

When he had finished, Oliver wiped his hands on his blouse.

'Shall we play Nim? I've got some matches in my pocket.'

He set them out on the table in groups. They played three games and he won each time.

'Dad says I'm going to be good at it because I've got a mathematical mind,' he said.

'It's just that I'm not thinking.'

'It isn't. Do you know what binary notation is?'

'No. Nor do you. Oh – don't show off.' She sulked for a minute and then said, 'If I make enough money out of my book, I'm going to send Mrs Hellyer some of it as a leaving present.'

Oliver said nothing. There was nothing to say. He swept the matches off the table and put them carefully back into his pocket.

He said, 'We went to see Marjorie today. Alice went to sleep on the grass and I had a look in the boathouse.'

He paused and kicked thoughtfully at the chair leg.

'D'you know what I found? I found some of the money. It must have fallen out of the suitcase.'

Emmie drew in her breath sharply.

He said, 'D'you know what I did? I took it back to the hotel in my pocket and tore it all up and sent it down the lav. It was *easy*.' He hugged his knees, cock-a-hoop at his own cleverness.

Emmie whispered, 'You didn't keep any of it?'

'Of course not. It would've been wrong,' he said smugly.

Emmie sighed gently, with relief. She felt very content and happy, suddenly. Everything had gone right at last. She had been so afraid that Oliver would never be able to stop. That he would grow up, being a thief. Now she saw that it had only been a phase, like Alice wanting to marry Dickie. And like all phases, it was wearing off.